SAINT & SINNER

GEORGIA LE CARRE

Saint & Sinner

ISBN: 978-1-910575-99-4

ACKNOWLEDGMENTS

Many, many thanks to:

Caryl Milton
Elizabeth Burns
Nichola Rhead
Kirstine Moran
Tracy Gray

PROLOGUE

Willow

(10 years previously)

"People will understand one day, but not yet. Not yet."
https://www.youtube.com/watch?v=SjwVrEMjyxY
-Honor Him-

The fire filled the windows of the house. It was yellow, orange, and bright red and it was spreading quickly, eating through the house, like a fiery, revengeful monster. Soon the whole house would be up in flames. It was terrible and awesomely beautiful at the same time. Like a saint who turned into a sinner right before your eyes.

I wished I could stay and stare at the beautiful destruction, but I couldn't. I had to run and pretend to call for help. Pretend I was asleep in my room. Pretend I didn't hear anything.

"Willow," Caleb called over the crackling, angry noises coming from the suffering house.

I turned my head and looked into his mesmerizing eyes. Caleb had the most amazing eyes you ever saw. Piercing blue, with long, thick eyelashes that should have belonged to a girl. Staring into their beauty you could never imagine how much he had endured. I let myself drown in those magnificent blue starbursts for a few precious seconds.

I wished I could stay a bit longer. I wished we were somewhere else. I wished we had been born elsewhere, in different circumstances. But more than anything else in the world I wished I was not seeing the reflection of fire in his eyes.

"So, it's done," I whispered. I could feel the shock and wonder in my eyes. We did it. We actually did it.

He nodded slowly, his eyes never leaving mine.

"What do we do now?"

He reached out and took my hand in his. His flesh felt hot and damp. "We stick to the plan."

"Are you afraid?" I whispered.

He shook his head calmly. "No. Are you?"

"I'm afraid for you," I confessed.

"Don't be. I will be fine. Even if they come for me they can't do anything other than send me to a juvenile detention center. I'm tough, I can survive that no problem. Just stick to the plan. They will try to trick you. They will try to say I have confessed, but it will all be lies. I will never admit to anything and neither should you, and no matter what they say or threaten to do. Loyalty forever, Willow. This is our secret. Never trust anyone enough to tell them no matter how close you get to them."

"I will take this secret to my grave," I promised solemnly.

His chin jutted out with determination. "So will I."

"If they don't catch you, can I contact you then?"

"No," he said immediately. "It could be a trick. There should never be a connection between us. After your eighteenth birthday if I'm not caught then we will meet at the bridge, but if I'm behind bars, then you can start to write to me wherever they're holding me."

I nodded. All the adrenaline rushing through my blood was making me feel jittery and almost high. As if I'd had a hit of Caleb's pot. My fingers tingled. "Caleb, you won't forget me, will you?"

His eyes flashed. "What kind of stupid question is that? Forget you? I would die for you, Willow. Are *you* planning to forget me?"

I shook my head vigorously. "Never. I love you, Caleb. More than I love myself."

His face softened. "Then let's swear it in blood."

"Alright," I agreed.

He took the knife, red with the other's blood out of his belt, and wiped it on the grass first, then against his pants. When it was clean he used the sharp point to slice his finger open. Blood seeped out quickly. I held out my hand and he moved the knife towards my flesh, but as the knife touched my skin, he froze.

I raised my head to look at him. "What is it?"

The light from the fire licked the side of his face. "I can't. I can't cut you, Willow."

"Why not?" I whispered.

"I can't hurt you."

I took the knife from his hand and pricked my finger. Then we touched our bleeding fingers together. "I love you, forever," he said, his voice hoarse.

"I love you, forever," I echoed.

Then he leaned forward and kissed me. It was a hard, desperate kiss. The wind blew against us. And I smelled the smoke and fire in the wind. Then he tore his mouth away, looked at me one last time with desperate eyes, as if he was memorizing me in his mind, and loped away towards the woods. I stood there alone with the burning house and the night stars watching me.

Tears started to well up my eyes. I had lost so much and now I was being asked to lose him as well. My heart felt as if it was breaking. "I will never forget you, Caleb. Never," I promised. I hoped the wind would carry my promise to his ears.

Then I started to run.

I ran as fast as I could, until my foot caught on something, maybe a root, and I fell backwards. My head hit something so hard, maybe a stone, it made a cracking sound.

Pain exploded through my skull, then blackness enveloped me as if it was a soft, thick blanket.

There was no pain.

There was nothing. Not even Caleb.

Caleb

https://www.youtube.com/watch?v=0Fy7opKu46c

"You might as well admit it. I know you did it," the Sheriff of Redburn, said in an almost kind tone.

We were in the interrogation room that was not much bigger than a broom closet. They had taken away my shoes and clothes as evidence ten hours ago, and I was barefoot and wearing some badly fitting clothes they had given me. I stared at the scarred surface of the wooden table and said nothing. I planned to say nothing at all.

"You've been a trouble-maker all your life, and I've always turned the other way, because of your background and because I thought you were a good kid underneath it all, but now you've gone and killed a man in cold-blood, and not just any man, a man of God."

Calling that monster a man of God was an abomination, but I didn't raise my head. I didn't speak. I didn't even ask for a lawyer. I was sticking to the script. I wouldn't react. No matter what they said.

"Why, Caleb? What has he ever done to you? Why did you stab Father Jackson to death and burn down his house?"

Under the table my fists clenched and slowly unclenched. No reaction. No matter the provocation. They would not trick me.

Sheriff Winters suddenly slammed his palms on the table. So hard I felt the vibrations run through me. "You killed him because you wanted his niece, didn't you?"

I looked up slowly and met his gaze scornfully. Was that the best he could do?

Instantly, his eyes flashed with triumph and I realized my mistake. I had reacted. Furious with myself, I looked away.

Like a terrier with a bone he changed his questioning tack. "She's a pretty girl, that Willow," he said slyly.

I said nothing. He would not trick me into responding again.

"I get why any boy would want her. If I was thirty years younger I would too. But if I was your age and I wanted a fine girl like that, I'd save up to buy her one of them big boxes of chocolates wrapped up with pink bows, turn up on her doorstep, and invite her to Berry Bear for an ice-cream sundae."

He stopped suddenly and stared hard at me. I stared back

expressionlessly. As if I would ever have taken Willow to Berry Bear. Willow hated crowds.

He continued. "I certainly wouldn't have killed her only living relative, the man who was good enough to take her in when she lost her parents in a horrendous car crash, then burn his home and the house she lived in down to the ground. Do you know what's going to happen to her now, Caleb? They are going to come and take her away. She will have to go and live with total strangers, who might not be very nice to her. Well, that is, after she leaves the hospital."

I didn't even try not to react. "Hospital?" I barked, a cold claw gripping my insides.

His eyes glittered with the first taste of victory. He knew he got me. "Yes, hospital. While she was running away from the fire you started, she fell and hit her head so badly, she was out cold for hours. My officers tried to question her when she came around, but she drew a blank about the fire ... and everything that has happened to her. As a matter of fact, she remembers nothing of the last two years."

He paused to let that sink in.

"Apparently, her last memory is from a couple of days before her parents died. She started crying and asking for her parents. She became hysterical when she was told they died two years ago."

Even though I stared at him in disbelief, I could tell, this was no trick. He was telling the truth. Part of me was glad she wouldn't have to tell a pack of lies to protect me, the other part of me felt horror that she would have to go through all the pain of losing her parents all over again. Only I knew how much she suffered when she first came to this town. She was so inconsolable she was mute. For a long time, nearly a year, we never exchanged a word. Just sat together in silence on the bridge, and watched the water rushing below us.

Until one day, she turned her pain-filled, big brown eyes in my direction and whispered, "I was in the car. I saw them dying. Papa went first. He tried to speak, but blood came out of his mouth. I was screaming. Mama held my hand and said, 'don't cry. I'll be watching over you. Nothing bad will happen to you'. She lied." That was the first day she cried. Horrible, racking sobs, that made her whole body shake. The water rushed underneath us as I had held her and told her, her mama had sent me to protect her.

The Sheriff made a sound, it shook me out of my recollections and brought me back to the bare interrogation room. Suddenly, another thought even more horrifying than that old memory hit me. If she only remembered up to two days before her parents died, then what had happened to her memories of me? Of us? Had her mind erased me too? It seemed too incredible to believe.

"Where is she now?" I asked.

"In the hospital, sedated. They will keep her under observation for a few days more." He shrugged. "Thanks to you she has nowhere to go, anyway."

I blinked. We had a plan. It was a good plan, but we didn't foresee this part.

"Why don't you just confess. The law will be much kinder to you if you do."

I squared my shoulders. I had to stick to the plan.

"Look, Einstein, you even left your footprints around the house. And there is a trace of blood on your pants. We'll DNA the hell out of that and I'll bet that the results we get back are a positive match so you might as well co-operate now, and the judge will go easier on you."

My whole world had just fallen apart, but I looked at him expressionlessly. In my head a little voice was saying again, and again.

"He doesn't know. No one will ever know, but you did good, Caleb. You did good."

That same voice spoke to me as my mother, who was already drunk at ten in the morning, came to see me.

"How could you? How could you?" she cried furiously. "Everybody in town is going to hate us now."

I let her carry on in that vein. All her ranting and raving mattered not one bit to me. All I wanted was more information about Willow. As if to punish me, Sheriff Winters refused to speak about her anymore.

"How is Willow?" I asked, when it appeared she had blown off some of that steam.

She jerked her head violently with surprise that I had spoken. Then her eyes filled with rage again. "She's in hospital. Why are you asking?"

I shrugged. "Would you be able to go and see her?"

Her eyes bulged so hard they almost fell out of her face. "Me? Go and see her in hospital? Are you mad? Have you heard a word I've said? We are pariahs in this town now. I can't go anywhere without people spitting and snarling in my face."

"They did that before this," I reminded dryly.

She got so mad, her whole face became an ugly red. She forgot the camera in the ceiling, and swung her hand out. Her blows were always easy to avoid, unlike my stepfather's, and I could have ducked, if I'd wanted to, but I didn't. I let her hit me. That would be good evidence in court.

I shouldn't have bothered.

Despite my age, and in spite of the five people who testified about the horrible abuse I'd endured at my stepfather's hands from the time I was a kid, the jury threw the book at me. The people of Redburn were God-fearing folk, and I had done something unforgivable. I'd killed a representative of God. If they didn't punish me suitably they would burn in hell.

So, in good conscience, they handed me the maximum they could give to a minor. Twenty fucking years.

"You'll be out sooner with good behavior," my court

appointed lawyer mumbled carelessly, before he hurried off to lunch.

Not that I cared. That voice in my head had just grown stronger.

"You did good, Caleb. You did good."

2

Caleb

Twelve years later
https://www.youtube.com/watch?v=6GYt6mzQ3Xo

I pulled her watch out of the box and nostalgia hit me like a physical punch in the gut.

The years had done nothing to dull or sully the girlish, bright pink accessory. Across the strap was printed, 'the power puff girls' and on the face were the three superhero characters.

My hand closed around it, as heavy waves of emotions washed over me. Longing burned in the pit of my stomach, and fear filled my chest.

"Is it all there?" the correctional officer asked.

I tucked the dead watch into my pocket, but didn't even bother to look into the other bag. It held the possessions I'd brought with me into the prison twelve years earlier. A pair of jeans and a faded grey t-shirt, the edge of its collar stained with ink.

"Yeah," I replied.

"Sign here, Wolfe," he said, pushing a clipboard with a form attached to it towards me.

I did as I was told, but in my heart, I swore it would be the last time anyone told me what to do. I was never coming back here or being at the mercy of such brutes again.

"So," he said with a smirk. "You came in with nothing. Fifteen-years old and wet behind the ears, but word is ya fell in with the in-crowd and became quite the mogul in there. You're one lucky bastard, aren't ya?"

I placed the cheap plastic pen down and straightened to look at the officer. Ginger hair, mid-thirties, bad teeth and thought he knew everything because he watched the news on TV. He had no idea. Luck had nothing to do with it. I had a plan and I stuck to it religiously. Not for one moment did I deviate from it. Not even when I was sleeping.

He wagged his finger at me. "Don't go blow it all on greedy hookers and fast cars, cause, once the money's gone you'll be back on the hamster wheel until you run right back into this place. If ya don't have money in the big bad world you're about to head out into, ya might as well still be behind bars, only now the world gets to mock you for it ... to your face ... every goddamn day."

Even when I was dirt poor no one dared mock me, but he was entitled to his opinion. I grabbed my things.

"How d'ya do it, anyhow?" he asked. "Word is you got some sort of financial education. Met the right crook, did ya?"

"Ask around," I said, and turned away.

"Arrogant bastard," I heard him swear in a low tone. Then he called after me. "Hope you don't get sent back in here too soon. I need a bit more time to work my way up to captain, or one of his bitches. There's no way you're getting out of here again without me benefitting from that wizard brain of yours."

His dark chuckle serenaded my exit, as the iron gate unlocked, and I was escorted out by another guard. The metal doors clanged behind me.

When I was let out of the gates of the prison, I stopped and took a deep lungful of air. Freedom. Obviously, it was my state of mind, but the hot, desert air smelt sweet. I'm coming, little Willow. I'm coming for you.

Just as had been arranged, there was a dark Mercedes with tinted glass awaiting me a little distance away. It made its way toward me. The driver immediately jumped out of the front seat, and headed over to me.

"Caleb Wolfe?" he called.

"Yeah."

"I'm Bernado Barros. Marie Spencer sent me to pick you up and take you to your home."

"Good," I said, and started walking towards the back of the black Mercedes.

Bernado leaped into action and pulled the door open for me. I got into the wonderfully air-conditioned space and he closed the door. After he slid into the driver's seat, he turned around to hand me an envelope. "That's from Ms. Spencer."

The car pulled away smoothly.

I didn't look back. I leaned into the plush seat and opened the envelope from my lawyer's understudy. Inside was the property deed of my new house, along with the keys, credit cards, a note telling me someone had fully stocked my fridge and wardrobe, and a cell phone.

I switched the phone on, and found Marie had already set her phone number on speed dial. I cracked my first smile in a long time. She was definitely efficient. I placed a call to her.

"Welcome back, Mr. Wolfe," she said crisply.

"Thank you, Marie. When's the meeting with the psychiatrist?"

"Just a second." I hear the sound of her typing on her keyboard. "Your appointment with Dr. Gregory Aggarwal is tomorrow morning at 190 Blue Ravine Road. It's a forty-five-minute drive from your house. I've arranged for Bernardo to pick you up."

"No need," I said. "I'll drive myself."

"Well, um ... you can't, yet. Legally speaking. You'll need to take your test first. The license you had at fifteen would have been a restricted permit." She paused. "Might be a good idea to stay on the straight and narrow path from now on."

"Send Bernardo," I muttered.

"Thank you. You'll be glad to know your driving license test has been scheduled for after your meeting with Dr. Aggarwal. And right after that you'll be able to pay a visit to our offices … if you wish, of course."

I said nothing, my thoughts filled with what Dr. Aggarwal would say.

"Shall I pencil you into Mr. Albright's diary for tomorrow, then?"

"Maybe, let's see how things go."

"Oh," she exclaimed, surprised. "I thought you might want to. We've been in contact for a couple of years now, and only met twice in person. Plus, it'd be good for you to see the firm and meet the team that have been managing most of your affairs so diligently, would it not?" She cleared her throat. "It's Valentine's Day the day after tomorrow, and it will be a great opportunity for us to express our gratitude to you for the relationship we've forged over the years."

"Marie," I said quietly. "I'll do my best, but since you've been managing most of my affairs you must be well aware of what my priority is."

"I am," she said. "Of course, I am. Willow Rayne is one lucky woman."

I didn't respond to that. Willow was a lot of things, but lucky, I was certain, was not one of them.

I ended the call quickly after that and pulled the watch out of my pocket. The pad of my thumb brushed over the strap, the memory coming to mind of why it was in my possession.

It seemed as if a lifetime had gone by since those days, but in my head and in my heart, it felt like it was just yesterday, we had stood next to the burning house and mixed our blood. Even now, if I closed my eyes, I could see her. Her lips trembling, her hands cold. So cold. But her enormous eyes filled with love. So much love it kept me alive for twelve years.

"Bernardo," I called.

"Yes, Sir?"

"Do you know a good florist in Folsom?"

"A good flower shop, Sir?"

"Yes."

"Not really, Sir," he replied, looking at me in the rearview mirror.

"Alright. Then take me to Natoma Street. There's one there, if I remember correctly."

"Uh, we're no longer heading to your house, Sir?"

"It's just a detour," I replied.

"Yes, Sir," he said sharply, as he changed his route.

3

Willow

https://www.youtube.com/watch?v=Gonp-5xbkus

-if it takes a thousand tears-

I snipped off the stem of a Red Magic Daylily, and brought it to my nose. Its scent was not the most fragrant, but it filled my body with a strange sense of wistfulness. It was the same as being transported to one's childhood by the smell of apple pie baking or incense smoke. Although in my case, bizarrely, I had no memories attached to the flower, so couldn't understand why it had such an effect on me.

Perhaps it belonged in that black hole of my life. Those two years that are lost to me. In the beginning I used to try to remember, but every time I did, I would end up with a pounding headache. The doctor advised me not to force the memories. If they were going to come back they would come back on their own, one by one, or all at once.

After all these years I knew they were not coming back. I didn't mourn for them, but I couldn't help the niggling feeling that I was missing something important. My friends tell me I was just a kid. Nothing that important could have happened to me in those years. I had just moved into Redburn and probably just went to school and hung around with the other school kids. Although it did bother me that none of my friends came to see me in hospital or afterwards. Not that I would have remembered them, but still. Did I have no friends at all?

Rising to my feet, my full basket dangling from the crook of my arm, I headed for the back door of the shop. A gloved Sandra was repotting a rubber tree.

Her nose wrinkled at the sight of the flowers I carried. She waved the trowel in her hand at me. "Ugh, you're not including those again, are you?"

"I have some ideas," I said. "Roses are pleasant, but this should add a new twist to the bouquets."

"Well good luck keeping them fresh," she remarked, as I continued on my way.

I set the basket down on my work surface, and was about to begin when the hum of a car engine arriving at our front door made me turn my head.

"I think the roses are here," Sandra said, pulling off her gloves. She headed out of the store and the sound of low laughter as well as some friendly banter filtered over. Ah, Bradley was here. They would make a good pair. I wished Bradley would ask her out. It was obvious by how much time Bradley spent in the shop that he liked Sandra, but was too chicken to make the first move.

Soon enough both of them came in carrying three buckets of flowers.

"Hey, Bradley," I greeted with a smile.

"Willow," he responded, with a big grin. "How's it going?"

"Well, as of last night, I will officially make a healthy profit for the first time since I started this business three months ago," I said quietly, but the words made my heart swell with happiness and pride.

"That's grand news," he said sincerely. "Don't forget. You'll have an insane patronage today and tomorrow too."

"Yeah, the online orders have been pouring in too," Sandra said on her way out of the shop to bring me the rest of the roses.

"Wait for me," Bradley said, and hurried after her.

"Wow," Sandra exclaimed, pushing open the door. "I didn't know luxurious cars came to our street."

I looked up from my arrangement and saw the shiny black Mercedes parked in front of the Caribbean grocery store a few shops down from us. Its windows were tinted, and there was very little that I could see so I lost interest very quickly.

"I'd love to see who it belongs to," Sandra said dreamily. "Maybe it's a handsome, cocky, twenty-something that was sent over here to sweep me off my feet."

"Hey!" Bradley protested. "I'm a handsome, cocky, twenty something."

"Aren't you thirty? Plus, you're not loaded. That person over there has a life that I very much want to have a taste of."

"Well, I'm afraid he's not coming over," I said, nudging her arm with my elbow as I returned to the store. "Back to work you. We only have three hours before we have to send the flowers to the restaurant."

"Fine," she groaned, "but you all keep an eye on the car. I want to at least see what the owner looks like. I bet it's some celeb from LA."

"Or it's some older man with an erectile dysfunction and an estranged wife," Bradley muttered.

We both turned to Bradley at his bitter comment, but he shrugged and winked. "You never know," he said. "The wildest things happen these days."

"You mean in your mind," Sandra said. "The wildest thing to happen in this town since Johnny Cash was that Whitney Gallow starred in *Hoarders*, so I don't know where you're getting your news from."

"He's leaving," I announced, another carton in hand. Bradley and Sandra both paused to watch as the vehicle pulled out of the curb and began to slowly head our way.

"He's coming over," Sandra squealed and spun around to face me, her hands quickly smoothing her hair. "I bet he wants to buy flowers for someone. For Valentine's Day. Oh my God, he's probably a Hollywood director or something. We should take a picture and put it on our Instagram page. Just think, this shop could become famous," she babbled excitedly.

I was amused, but I couldn't help the flare of hope in my heart. What if he truly was rich with an Elton John personality who needed his home to be filled with flowers? That's exactly what the shop needed. Regular income.

Just as the car reached our shop, we all stared at it, trying to see beyond the tint. However, it did not slow down, but sped up. We watched as it zoomed past.

"I guess he really came just to buy groceries," Bradley mocked.

"What a bummer," Sandra said. "The one time we have an interesting visitor on our street and he speeds off without dropping in here."

I agreed with her. There goes my fantasy of an Elton John type customer who spends an insane fortune on flowers every month.

"At this rate, Willow, we're going to end up alone with fifteen cats and fifteen cat litter boxes to clean out."

"Fifteen?" Bradley asked. "That's quite a specific number.

"I have a thing for the number."

I smiled because I knew all about her attachment to that

number. It was a bit crazy, but who was I to judge? I was more than a little crazy too. She had a thing for the number fifteen and I had a thing about lollipops. I couldn't bear to see anyone eating a lollipop. It actually made me feel physically sick. If I accidentally, come across a child sucking a lollipop, I have to immediately turn away, otherwise, I would have to snatch the thing out of that child's mouth. That was how weird I was.

"Are you going to tell us about this fifteen thing you've got going?" Bradley asked, his voice teasing.

"It's my birth date, my mom's birth date, the day I first got my period, my first job at Target, the day I got accepted into college, the day my brother got married, the day—"

"It is now clear that the fifteenth of all months should be renamed Sandra's Day," Bradley said, handing the delivery receipt to me.

"No arguments there," she agreed heartily. Then she turned towards me. "Anyway, Willow, tomorrow evening we're painting the town red. We're going to close the shop early. No, don't you dare give me that look. We are closing early. Anyone who hasn't bought their flowers by 7pm on Valentine's Day is a piece of shit that we don't want as a customer."

I was shaking my head so she changed tack.

"Fine, we'll bring our cute clothes here, close up by eight, and go man-hunting then. I am ready to be devoured."

I wasn't, but I kept my opinions to myself.

"Okay, I'm leaving," Bradley said, and quickly exited the shop.

I returned to my flowers without a word. "I haven't gotten your response, Willow," she said in a cautionary voice, and I turned a sheepish smile on her.

"Let's see how tomorrow goes."

"You're not getting out of this," she warned sternly. "I've already seen how it'll go. You, in that gorgeous red dress of yours with those sexy strings at the back, and my red stilettos. I'll be in my black halter-neck and my brand-new pumps."

"Ah, I get it," I said as I reached for a packet of flower food. "We're going as sin and death."

"Exactly," she agreed roundly. "The men will flock to us like greedy little bees around a honey pot."

I swallowed a lump in my throat. Men flocking around us was the last thing I wanted. That was the other bizarre thing about me. I had a vague, explainable fear of men. Which was, quite frankly, weird, because no man had ever been anything except gentle and respectful toward me. And what was even more crazy, was a deep, unshakeable impression I had that I was waiting. Waiting for someone. Like the bride of a soldier that was waiting for her sweetheart to return from a war in a far-flung country. Sometimes I even felt a pang of longing. As if I was calling for my other half to come back to me.

Totally bizarre.

Once I went out on a date, and I had to pretend I had a

headache and leave halfway through, because I felt guilty the whole time. As if I was cheating on this invisible, unknown man I was waiting for.

It was strange, very strange, but there was nothing I could do about it. My skin actually crawled when my date touched me. And that reaction was the same for any man who came on to me.

4

Caleb

https://www.youtube.com/watch?v=yeBlɪqcWjSg
-You will remember me for centuries-

"**N**o, I wouldn't recommend bringing up any recollections of the past you shared with her. Her mind has obviously shut out the entire period because it is too painful to bear. Telling her what happened between the two of you might even mean planting memories. That could cause her to get confused and start to distrust which memories are real and which are imagined. I cannot express enough what harm that could do."

I stared at Dr. Aggarwal's sallow-skinned, gaunt face. Behind his spectacles, his eyes looked watery and full of sorrow or exhaustion. It was as if he had absorbed all the troubles of his patients into his own body.

I glanced down at my hands, the complicated blue tats

snaking up my arms. I was a kid when I had them done. They looked childish and cliché now. HATE on the four fingers of one hand and LOVE on the other. First came hate, then after I met Willow came love. I asked my next question. "It's been more than twelve years since her accident. Isn't that way past the norm for her to recover her lost memories? Isn't there something we can do to help her regain her memories?"

He nodded. "You told me she was undergoing dialectical behavioral therapy to help process her trauma, but gave up on it due to its ineffectiveness?"

That was what the private investigator I hired found out. "Yes."

"That's the thing about dissociative amnesia," he said. "Lost memories will return when they want to, and there's little that any one of us can do to force it. It is an extremely frustrating thing not to be able to remember vast chunks of your life, but it looks like she's accepted her own limitations in forcing them to come back and is allowing nature to take its course instead."

"I don't want to cause her any pain or discomfort whatsoever," I muttered.

"No, of course you don't. I can see you care very much for the young lady."

I looked down at my hands curiously. They were trembling. All the fights, all the danger, all the pain I endured in prison and I'd never seen them tremble. "Is it possible then, she might never regain her memories?"

"Yes, I'm afraid you'll have to accept that possibility. You were present during this traumatic time, weren't you?"

I nodded.

"Then maybe your future interactions with her will trigger some old memories that will in turn help in her recollection. But it would be wise not to rush her, or force her. Don't be the one to bring it up." He paused. "Perhaps just seeing you might trigger something."

"She was just twelve when we parted," I explained. "I was fifteen, and now I'm almost twenty-eight. My appearance has changed a lot. It's very likely that she wouldn't be able to place my face at all."

He was silent as he stared at me. "I thought you were very close back then?"

"We were, but like I said I was just a boy then. Even without the accident it would be hard for her to recognize me. Even I can hardly see any trace of that kid in the mirror anymore."

"If you were as close as you've mentioned, then her recognition of you should go beyond just your physical attributes, unless you've done a complete 180° change in every single aspect of who you were. Mr. Wolfe, if she can't recognize you through your face, perhaps she'll be able to with her heart."

Another thought occurred to me. "What about my name? Do I give her my real name? Will that cause any problems?"

"Isn't her recollection of you what you want?" he asked gently, and I could clearly hear the exhaustion in his tone now. I'd been sitting in front of him asking him a plethora of questions over the last hour and a half. In the beginning, he'd been quite glad to answer all my questions, but as I kept on repeating them to be sure of every instruction he was giving to me, he seemed to fade before my eyes.

But I was terrified of making a mistake with her. I couldn't make any mistakes with her. This was my only chance, and I would rather kill myself than screw it all up by being careless.

I gave him my response. "It is, but ... if there is even the slightest chance I will damage her."

He leaned forward. "Let's do things this way. Let's play it by ear. When do you intend on paying her a visit?"

"Tomorrow."

"Well then, go up to her, and watch her face for any recognition of you whatsoever. If there is none, then you can go ahead and introduce yourself."

I frowned. "By a different name?"

He sighed heavily. "If that's what you want."

"Won't that complicate things? It won't be in my best interest if she eventually regains her memory, and finds out that I lied to her."

"Caleb," the man said, completely fed up. "We spoke about this exact thing thirty minutes ago. I cannot tell you what to do. You can bounce ideas off me, but in the end, you must decide yourself. Let's break it down. You definitely don't want her to remember the details of her terrible past."

I nodded. "That's right."

"But you want her to remember you?"

"Only if it doesn't bring the other stuff back," I replied.

"Caleb," he said gently. "It will not be your fault if she remembers the darkness again. No matter how bad they are, they still belong to her. Don't keep obsessing over what she will or will not remember. Be honest with her, and allow things to take its natural course. One thing I can tell you is people who lose parts of their memories often feel vulnerable and exposed. They have to live with the fact that there is a crucial part of their history that is missing and the unsettling feeling that out there someone knows something about them that they themselves don't."

He paused.

"In fact, the patients I've treated, who have suffered from memory blanks caused by trauma, ended up being incredibly guarded and careful around people. They had little habits, fears, and instinctive bodily reactions that they couldn't understand. One woman I was seeing was afraid of only one breed of dog. For many years, she couldn't understand it and it bothered her immensely. Then one day she found out from an old school friend that breed of dog had almost bitten them and chased them up a tree. It was a great relief for her to find out and after that she could put that irrational fear aside. With such a dark and horrifying past hidden away from your friend, she must be a bundle of nerves and paranoia. My advice to you is this. Go slowly. Don't push or try to force her memories. You'll make mistakes along the way as you try to find a way back into her life, but the one thing she should never fault you on is that you were dishonest with her. Or you used the vulnerability of her missing memories against her. That is the last thing that you want to do."

He then rose to indicate the meeting was over.

"Thank you, doc," I said slowly, and finally forced myself to leave his office.

5

Willow

The store's front door tinkled as it was pushed open.

I was going through our surprisingly impressive sales report for the day, and although I wasn't really expecting any more customers, I wasn't averse to more.

When I lifted my head and saw the three girls who had come into the store though, my heart fell into my stomach. Sandra, Victoria, and Helen were dressed to the nines in scanty dresses and ankle-breaker heels. If they had intended to look as if they were man-hunting, they had succeeded. I gazed at them blankly, at the cans of beer they already had in their hands.

"It's almost nine, Mother Teresa," Sandra called out, almost giddy with excitement. "Get away from that counter and come change. I brought gorgeous things with me."

"C'mon, Willow. Don't be a stick in the mud," Helen screamed. "It's going to be an awesome night."

I dragged Sandra in the back of the shop and whispered fiercely, "Why are they here?"

"Victoria called," she said with an unconcerned shrug. "She said they were heading over to Bacchus House. Apparently, there's a speed dating event for singles there, and of course, a whole hour of free sangrias on the house, so I thought we could all get drunk and loosen up a little there before we hit the town. What response did you expect me to give them?"

"Uh ... 'a no, thank you I already have plans with Willow' doesn't sound reasonable enough to you?"

"Oh c'mon. We all went to high school together. Sure, they were occasionally mean to you then, but we've all moved on in life. Helen is in community college, and Victoria, well, she got knocked up, didn't she? Wait a second," she paused, her eyes suddenly widening, "Why does she even have a drink in her hands?"

"Whohoooo." The subject in question released a shout, and then came crashing into the back, her eyes sparkling with excitement. "What are you guys doing? Let's get going! It's gonna be a fucking awesome night. I'm so going to get laid tonight."

"Victoria, aren't you pregnant ... and engaged?"

"Oh, calm down," she waved her hand in dismissal. "Arthur and me are testing out this open relationship thing since he's going to be out of town almost all the time for his sales gigs. I don't want to restrict or frustrate him, and he doesn't want to do the same to me either so we're trying to work things out."

My eyebrows shot to my hairline, while Sandra headed over to her, her face filled with concern. "I'm not talking about Arthur. I'm talking about your baby. You're not supposed to be drinking."

She wobbled and even I felt alarm. I moved to catch her, but she straightened herself.

"Oh relax, both of you. There's no alcohol in this."

"Then why are you wobbling?" I asked.

"Force of habit," she replied with a grin.

Just then, Helen joined us, actually she staggered over, but Sandra caught her before she could crash into the table of freshly potted plants that Sandra had spent the last few days slaving over. That would have brought an immediate end to any fun that the girls planned on having for the night.

"I tripped," Helen giggled, the beer from her can spilling everywhere, much to my irritation. "But I'm not drunk. Not yet"

Both of the girls burst out in laughter and I turned an unimpressed face to Sandra. At that rate we would have flies not bees flocking around us.

But Sandra was not to be put off. "The more the merrier," she said, pushing me towards my tiny office. "It's going to be a fantastic night. Now go get changed before the free bar closes."

. . .

To be perfectly honest, I didn't want to go. It looked like it was going to be a disaster of a night, but I felt almost obliged to go now, because I could see the state of the girls. Someone had to watch over Sandra. I quickly slipped out of my comfortable jeans and T-shirt. Then I shimmied into the red dress with the two tiny strings connecting the back together, and stared at the stilettos that Sandra wanted me to switch my dark Converses for.

My heart bled at the thought.

But I couldn't very well wear my Converses with the red dress so I slipped into them and returned to the front of the shop.

It was empty. I saw Helen and Victoria standing outside smoking and Sandra was not amongst them."

I pulled the door open. "Where did Sandra go?"

"To the store," Victoria answered. "She wants to get some water and snacks for later, in case she gets hungry."

"Oh, okay." I returned inside and decided to finish the sales report for the day. I immediately got sucked into it, until the doorbell tinkled again.

I didn't even bother looking up. "Sandra, I just need five minutes to round this up or else I'm going to be thinking about it all night."

There was no response.

Suddenly, my skin started to prickle. I lifted my gaze and the words I had planned in my head died in my throat.

The person standing before me was definitely not Sandra.

6

Caleb

https://www.youtube.com/watch?v=aY2sBDPgOXU

I forgot how to breathe.

The photos I had seen of her gave her no justice. The woman in front of me was even more beautiful in person. Not just beautiful. She was why the term breathtaking was coined.

The enormous, soft brown eyes full of innocence were exactly as I remembered them, but the adorable gap in her teeth was gone. Deep inside me, I mourned for its loss. Back then, her chestnut brown hair had been wavy and barely brushed her shoulders, but now it was bone straight, side-parted, and flowed all the way down to the arch of her back in a silky curtain.

And that dress! Jesus!

The blood red material clung to every inch of her woman's body, hugging the curves of her hips and stretching across her full chest. One of the red straps holding the whole ensemble together, had dropped off her shoulders and it didn't just show the creamy perfection of the exposed skin, it made her appear half-undressed. As if ...

I couldn't tear my eyes off her body.

Of course, I'd expected to feel something when I showed up in front of her again, but searing lust that cut me to the bone had not been one of them. There had been no lust when I was fifteen. All I wanted to do then was protect her from the world.

I released a shuddering breath, and tried to wipe from my expression any trace of emotions that could betray the craving I felt. As far as she was concerned, I was a complete stranger ... a customer just stopping by. To me she was my life, the girl who kept me going in prison, who had been in my every waking moment for the past twelve years.

"Hi," I greeted softly.

She seemed to have gone completely still from the sight of me, but it didn't appear to be out of recognition. At least I didn't think it was. Most probably because I had startled her.

She stared at me as if she couldn't believe her eyes. "You're here to buy flowers?"

My heart thudded in my chest. "I am."

She pushed the red strap back onto her shoulder and straightened her spine. "Then you're in luck. I was just about to close up for the night. Do you know what you want?"

For a second it felt as if there was another, underlying conversation going on. As if we were not actually talking about flowers and bouquets, but were connecting on a deeper level.

Then she frowned and shook her head as if to clear it. "I meant ... your preference. The type of flowers you want."

"Yes, I do."

She brought her palms up and pressed them against her pale cheeks. "I'm sorry. It's been a long day. I guess I'm a little out of it."

"That's alright," I said quickly. "I know exactly what I want."

"Roses. I suppose you'll want roses."

She had sounded quite stressed and I didn't want to overwhelm her so I dragged my gaze away from her and pretended to glance at the silver buckets filled with flowers. It gave her time to go to the small counter. She stood stiffly behind it and waited for me.

"Not roses, I want Red Magic Daylilies," I said, and turned to watch her reaction.

Her eyes widened. "What?"

"I'd like a dozen Red Magic Daylilies," I repeated softly.

"I ... I ... uh ... I'm afraid we focused mainly on rose bouquets today since it's Valentine's Day." Her teeth sank into her bottom lip. I watched her chew at the juicy plump flesh. "We do have some Red Magic Daylilies, but I doubt that it'll suffice."

"That's alright. I'll take what you have."

"Perhaps I can mix it up with some other flowers so it should make for a splendid bouquet."

"I'll leave you to decide," I murmured.

Just then, the bell attached to the door rang. Already the outside world had come to intrude. We both turned to see three women enter the store. They were speaking in loud excited tones, which quickly died down when they noticed my presence.

"Oh, hello," one of them greeted, while the other two stared at me with slack-jaws.

I gave them a curt nod, and turned back towards Willow. "I'm in a hurry. Do you deliver?"

"Yes, yes, we do."

"Good. Sometime tomorrow afternoon?"

"Yes, we can do tomorrow afternoon."

I stepped closer to the counter so that she could take down my information.

As she typed my address into her computer, I couldn't help gazing at her, greedily taking in every detail. She still had the same impossibly long eyelashes that made her huge liquid-chocolate eyes even more mesmerizing. It was easy to drown in them. The softness of adolescence still clung to her cheeks and her eyebrows were gently arched. Her nose was straight and narrow, and her lips, were as plump as they had always been. There was not a trace of makeup on her face, but I couldn't imagine makeup could improve her. It was no wonder she did not use it.

She was still small though. Back then I used to tease her and she had sworn to me that she would eventually become as tall as me, or perhaps even taller. How I wished that I was able to bring it up, to tease her about it.

I could still remember her laughing. She didn't laugh often. She didn't have reason to, but when she did... She would throw her head back and laugh out with wild abandon... the soft belly sounds deep, and rumbling up her chest. I had fallen in love with that sound, and at that moment I longed to hear it once again.

She raised her eyes up to me. When our gazes met, it was like touching live electricity. Her eyes widened with shock. We stared at each other. I could smell her scent. It had changed. It was no longer almost milky, but stronger, sweeter.

The rest of the world fell away.

Until one of the girls behind us cleared her throat loudly. The sound startled her out of her trance-like state and she flushed a deep red. Hurriedly, she yanked my credit card out of her machine and held it out to me. "Here's your card, Sir."

"Thank you," I said, and taking the card, walked past the three utterly astonished girls.

7
Willow

All of us turned around to watch him leave.

"Who the hell, was that?" Sandra asked in a dazed voice.

Someone released a breath while I quickly began to shut down my computer for the night. To be honest I felt pretty dazed myself. Who the hell was he? And what was he doing in a small town like Folsom? The address he had given was from the most exclusive part of town though.

"Did you guys hear his voice?" Victoria asked. "How could anyone's voice be that low ... and deep?"

"And smooth," Helen added. "Hell, when he spoke it felt like someone was pouring warm honey down my back."

I couldn't have agreed more. There was a lot of honey still running down my own back.

Sandra came to her senses suddenly, because she dropped her plastic bag, and ran to the door for a glimpse of him.

I slipped my heels off my feet. They were already killing me and I'd had them on for less than half an hour. No way was I wearing them.

"Damn!" Sandra turned around, disappointed. "He's already disappeared."

I lifted the shoes up. "I want to talk about these."

"What was his name?" Sandra demanded, completely ignoring the issue of my shoes.

"Caleb Wolfe," I replied with a little sigh.

"Whoa! Even his name is sexy," Helen breathed.

"Who was he buying the flowers for?" Sandra asked.

"How would I know that?" I replied.

"He didn't mention it?" she prodded.

"Nope."

"Why on earth didn't you ask? You usually do."

"Well, since it's Valentine's Day I thought it would be a given he'd be buying it for a girlfriend, or sweetheart?"

"No!" She shook her head decisively. "It could be for his mom, or aunt, or sister, and that would make me very happy."

"What are you planning to do, make a move?" Helen asked.

"Of course. Have you ever seen a man that hot? I could lick him for days"

"I have," Victoria piped up. "My Arthur. All that construction has built him into a beast."

Oh great. We were in for another night listening to how great Victoria and Arthur's sex life was. I raised the shoes up again. "I'm not wearing these. They're going to hurt. I'm going in my Converses."

That immediately grabbed Sandra's attention. "Are you joking? How the hell are you going to go to a bar on Valentine's Day wearing those?"

"If I have to put these on then I'm not going," I said, and from my expression she knew that I was serious.

With a sigh, she yielded. I locked the shop and we bundled into a cab and we were on our way to the bubbling town center.

A little while later, with a cocktail in hand, I was perched on a stool at the bar.

Victoria and Helen had from the moment we arrived, headed over to a couple of guys seated in a booth, and asked to join their party. Thank God Sandra was not ready to get that friendly yet.

"What happens now?" I asked.

"We wait," she said, and took another long drink of her sangria before setting it down on the counter.

"For what?"

"For someone hot to come up to us."

I was amused. "And what if they're not hot?"

"We ignore them," she replied with a bright smile, but then the smile faltered when her gaze once again fell to my shoes and her expression turned to one of distaste. "Or you can take them. I'm sure that they'll mostly be coming up to you,"

With a little laugh, I lifted my glass once again for another sip and let my eyes wander around the bar. But I was not really seeing anything. In my mind I could still see Caleb Wolfe's breathtakingly translucent-blue eyes ... so light I, at first, thought that it was a trick of the light. But then he moved and I could see it wasn't. His eyes were truly that beautiful. Every time I'd raised my head, I would see him watching me intently, so more than once I had stared straight into those unnerving depths.

It was weird but something about him made me feel... safe. I never felt that with other men. And he had ordered my favorite flower. Most men have never even heard of a flower called Red Magic Daylily.

"What if he's the one?" I realized with a start that I'd spoken the words aloud. Given the lively chatter in the bar, and the music playing through the speakers, I hoped Sandra wouldn't have heard me, but it was not the case.

She immediately whirled her head around. "Who? What are you talking about?"

"You know how I've always said that deep inside, something feels missing? As though I lost someone or something, and I've been waiting for him/it to come back?"

"'Yeah?'"

"'Well I was just thinking. Wouldn't it be awesome if that Caleb Wolfe was the one? That missing person ... the one I've been waiting for.'"

Sandra stared at me like I lost it. "Well firstly, it's definitely not him. I have dibs."

I almost choked on the sip I had just taken. "What?"

"I'm serious. And secondly, what you're missing are your memories not 'the one'. You were just ten at the time—"

"Eleven," I corrected automatically.

"Well, even if you were eleven, no one and I mean no one finds 'the one' when they're eleven," she finished aggressively.

"Calm down, Sandra," I said. "I was just playing around."

She looked at me seriously. "No, you weren't. You've been this way ever since I met you in high school. Losing such a chunk of your memories is a massive deal, and it's bound to always leave you feeling like something's missing because you don't have the whole story. I understand that, but you can't let it hold you back from the present."

"What do you mean?"

"You're incredibly guarded, Willow. It's near impossible for you to trust anyone or anything, especially men, as though you're afraid that if you live a little, something terrible will happen. It's like you're tip-toeing around as if you're scared you'll fall into some hole that you weren't aware of."

"People do fall in holes," I mumbled.

Her voice softened. "'Stop that, babe. Those years, although important, shouldn't be more important than your present and the memories that you can make with it. You're here and you're alive, and I want you to start acting like it. For instance, tonight, you're going to kiss someone. And I'm going to make sure of it."

I jerked back in horror. "No way!"

"Yes, way," she said firmly. "And if he's hot enough I'm going to make him take you somewhere and screw your brains out. It's Valentine's Day, and you're twenty-three years old and as uptight as a nun in a brothel. What you need is to start making some new stories and a good drill in one of the toilets of this bar is a good place to start."

I was astounded. Quietly, I took my drink and moved away from her to the next stool. "You're insane," I told her.

She burst out laughing.

Someone soon came up to her for a little chat, and soon they were lost in each other's mouths. I rejected the few advances that came for me and was content to just relax alone with my thoughts. My chest began to warm up as a very familiar memory came to mind.

The memory of a kiss being pressed against my forehead … and then my cheeks. Maybe even softly on my lips. Of strong warm arms, completely embracing me. Feeling so safe. Nothing could ever hurt me while I was in those arms.

For the longest time, I'd assumed that it was my father's arms before he had been snatched away, but in my memory, my heart was always pounding so hard it felt like I would pass out. That couldn't have been because of a hug I'd received from a parent. It had always made me wonder. For years and years, I had chased the memory, but it had always remained so near, but just outside my grasp. Until finally, I had given up. It was alive in that dark blank space inside my head that I could never access no matter how much I tried.

Sandra decided to go home with the man, and the other two girls had somehow disappeared too, so I took a taxi home. It was a relief to fall into my own bed ... and dream of Caleb Wolfe.

Caleb

The flowers arrived just after the clock struck noon. I stared at the blood red flower for the longest time. She had twined it with some other red flowers and the effect was quite spectacular. I felt oddly proud of her. She had made something of herself. In spite of it all, she had made it. It made every long second I spent in prison worth it. I hadn't wasted my life there if this was what she had achieved.

I reached out and touched a soft petal. I let my finger gently stroke it. She had touched this. I bent my head and breathed deeply, but only the faint smell of the flowers and the plastic wrapping it had come in filled my nostrils.

God, how I wanted her. I longed to rush over to her shop and blurt everything out. Tell her what we were to each other. Tell her about the promise we had made, take her in my arms and kiss her until she remembered me again, but I filled my lungs with a deep breath instead.

Patience, Caleb. Patience. You have waited this long. You can wait a little longer.

I turned away from the flowers and went back to my computer screens. Work had been the only thing that could take my mind away from her. It had been much harder in prison to run my stock brokerage business without the latest software or even these real-time screens, but I had found a way. It was instinctive with me. I was good at this. As soon as Frank the fraudster taught me something, I instinctively knew exactly how to implement it. Now, with the help of the latest AI software and screens, trading had become a doddle. I almost couldn't believe how easy it was.

An hour passed in front of my computer before I stopped. I had arranged a meeting with Marie's boss, Stanley, at their law offices.

I drove over and we got straight to business, reviewing the financial operations and assets I had generated in prison and the tax implication of me bringing the money back from the safe havens they were currently parked in.

During the meeting, Stanley had a domestic emergency. It sounded like his wife had found out about his mistress. Flustered, he asked to be excused for ten minutes.

"Sure, man," I said with a shrug. I didn't want to judge, but what a dick.

After he rushed out, Marie cleared her throat and spoke. "Would you like more coffee?"

She looked embarrassed. "Nope." I was wondering if I should

leave and finish this meeting another time when she filled the silence again.

"How did your visit to Willow's shop go yesterday?"

I stared at her in surprise. Gone was the super-efficient, Marie. She was looking at me with an expression that was softer, more caring.

"I know it's a very personal matter to you, and asking is intrusive, but I can't help it. It is the most romantic thing I have ever seen. When I came to see you in prison, the first thing you asked me, before even your own freedom, was for me to find her. Your reunion with her makes me incredibly happy. Did she recognize you?"

I shook my head slowly. "She didn't."

"Is that a good thing or a bad thing?"

"I'm not sure yet."

"What now?"

"I have no idea," I said truthfully.

"What do you want to happen?"

"I want to get close to her again … to become a part of her life." Actually, I wanted to become her whole life, the way she was to me. The way we both once were.

"Date her. Go back to the store and ask her out to dinner."

I nodded in agreement. That indeed was the logical step, even though my chest tightened at the thought. At this stage in my life very little had the ability to crush my spirit, except the possibility of Willow rejecting me.

"I do have another idea," she said with a smile, "one that will make a meeting between you two a bit more natural."

"What do you have in mind?" I asked curiously.

Her smile widened, then she headed over to her windowsill towards the small cactus plant there.

She brought it over to me, her face beaming with pride. "Do you know, I've killed everything I've ever grown, except this cactus plant. It has been with me for two years and it has been thriving. So I'm very proud of it and it means a lot to me, but it's sort of outgrown its home and I've been meaning to get it repotted, but I just haven't found the time so this is the perfect opportunity to have it properly repotted by a professional."

She passed the plant over to me, and I received it gingerly. She seemed to be very proud of it, but it actually seemed to be a sorely neglected thing. If I was being honest, almost half-dead.

"What should I tell her I want done to it?"

Her smile was kind. "Just tell her that you want it repotted. If she asks you if you want to do it yourself, say no. Ask if she can help you with it, so that way, you both get to spend a little time together even if it's for a few minutes. I'm sure you'll be able to find your opening line from there."

There had not been too many people who were kind to me in

my life so I appreciated it wherever and whenever I found it. "Thank you, Marie. I've got to go. Tell Stanley to call me later when he's not so distracted. We can finish our discussion over the phone."

"Sure, I'll do that."

I rose to leave.

"If she offers you some pebbles, please accept them, and if you see cactus pompoms then please get a few for me. I love them in bright colors ... so blue, green, red, all of that will be great."

I frowned. "Cactus pompoms?"

She grinned. "I'll send a photo to your phone."

9

Willow

https://www.youtube.com/watch?v=bjrOcrisGyI

I was reviewing flower arrangements with Sandra late that afternoon, when the doorbell tinkled.

We both looked up and there he was, the man who made my heart flutter. I heard Sandra's breathing hitch, and I didn't blame her one bit. It was almost as though in the space of just a few hours he had gotten even more handsome. The previous evening, he wore a close-fitting, navy blue suit, with a white, open collared shirt.

But today he had gone all black, with a banded collar dress shirt tucked into tailored slacks, and highly polished black shoes. His jet-black hair was combed away from his chiseled face. He looked as though he had jumped off the pages of a glossy men's magazine.

"Remember, I have first dibs?" Sandra muttered under her breath.

I softly shoved her.

"I'm serious," she hissed under her breath.

"You came back," I said, as he neared us. My heart was pounding in my chest. My intention was to ask him if there was a problem with the delivery, but just as he had yesterday, he caught my gaze and held it.

And I became completely enthralled. Every rational thought flew out of my head. Speechlessly, I stared into those mesmerizing eyes.

He watched me without blinking, as though he couldn't look away either. I felt my skin begin to burn. I stood there totally lost, staring at him like an idiot, until Sandra stepped forward with her hand held out.

"I'm Sandra," she introduced herself. "I run the shop with Willow."

It took him about two seconds before he was able to drag his gaze away to respond to her, and something extremely warm began to pool at the pit of my stomach.

"I'm Caleb," he said.

She gave him her best smile. "It's a pleasure to meet you, Caleb. How may I help you today?"

He returned his gaze to me as he held up a brown bag that he'd walked into the shop with. Incredible that I had not noticed it until now. "I have a cactus plant that needs repotting."

"Ah," she cooed. "Come with me, I'll take care of you ... I mean the cactus."

By this point, I was wisely staring at the area behind him, rather than risk looking at him and losing myself in the vortex of his eyes. I recovered slowly. However, after Sandra's offer of help, the room went strangely silent and tense and I dragged my gaze back to his.

"Could you help me?" he asked.

I frowned. Why was he asking me when Sandra had just offered her assistance? My gaze moved between his intensely beautiful eyes and Sandra's startled ones.

"Um ... uh," I began. "Sandra would actually be the better person for this job ... around here, she does the repotting and I stick to flower arrangements."

"I forgot to mention I also need a custom bouquet. Could you help me with that?"

I chewed my bottom lip and glanced at Sandra. Her mouth was agape with surprise.

"Of course," I said. My voice sounded hoarse and strange even to my own ears.

He turned around and handed the bag with the cactus to Sandra.

"Thank you," he said to her.

Her reply was through gritted teeth. "No problem."

As she stalked off to the back of the shop where repotting was done, I swallowed hard and, turning away from him, began to walk towards the small rows of wooden shelves where our flowers were displayed. "What do you have in mind?"

"I'm not sure," he replied from behind me. His voice was quiet, almost thoughtful, and perhaps too near to me.

I took a deep breath, steeled my spine, and turned around to face him.

I was startled by how close to me he was. There was hardly a foot between us. He had thoroughly invaded my space, but the strange thing was I didn't want to move away. As my gaze collided with his, my breath caught in my chest, and I felt as if I'd turned into stone.

To my surprise, I suddenly felt that total and complete sense of safety that I'd only ever known in my dreams envelop me. My mouth dropped open with astonishment and I just stared at him. God knows how long I stood there like some mind-less goldfish gaping at him. It was only the sound of Sandra banging something so hard it reverberated all the way to the front of the shop that I was jolted out of my awkward trance and found my voice again.

"What's the occasion?" I croaked.

"It's just a present, of appreciation for my solicitor's assistant."

"More Red Magic Daylilies?" I asked, and I could feel an intense jealousy creep into my heart. I didn't even want to admit it to myself, but I already *hated* the woman he had given the flowers to, unless, Sandra was right and that bouquet was for a female relative. I found myself holding my breath as I waited for his answer.

"No. That was not for her. That was for me," he said softly.

I just about stopped myself from grinning from ear to ear with pure happiness. "Oh, okay. So what do you think she would like?"

He looked away towards the flowers to consider my question. I noticed then just how calm he appeared, and it made me feel like a fool. Here I was, unable to breathe, while he moved and acted as though haste or anxiety didn't even exist in his dictionary. He slipped his hands into the pockets of his pants as his gaze moved across the floral displays in the small store.

I took my time too, and noticed the build of his body.

He was so tall, I barely reached his shoulders. I had to bend my neck back to look up at him. Maybe that was why I felt so unsettled, because at that angle, it felt like he was staring into the depths of my soul.

When he stood further away he appeared fit and lean, but from up this close his broad shoulders seemed to completely block out my view of everything behind him.

A blue tattoo of an owl on a branch snaked up his neck and my hands itched with the need to touch it and gently run my fingers down the branch. I wondered where it would lead me.

What else would I find on his chest? How I wanted to feel his heartbeat underneath his inked skin. As the thought swirled in my head, I had a strange sensation that if I actually reached out and made the move he wouldn't mind

It stunned me.

He was a complete stranger, but there was something about him that made my soul soar. It was not because he was so good looking, because I once took a trip to Hollywood and stood next to dazzlingly good-looking men and felt nothing. But when I was with him, I felt refreshed as if I'd been wandering in a desert for a long time drinking only the tepid, foul-smelling water from a goat-skin bag that I'd forgotten the taste of cool, fresh spring water.

He returned his gaze to mine, and it made me retreat a step backwards. I felt my cheeks flame when I remembered how inappropriately I'd touched him in my mind.

"Make something that you'd like," he murmured. "And that will be just fine."

Caleb

https://www.youtube.com/watch?v=y2zeudxXjuU

All my life, I'd never considered myself a coward, but right then, I felt like the worst coward who ever walked this earth. For whatever reason the words I had practiced all night long, the words I wanted to ask her like forever, were smooth stones lodged in my throat, and no matter how hard I tried to get them out I couldn't expel them.

Furious with myself, I kept my trembling hands in the pockets of my trousers, and watched as she opened her arms and released the stalks of flowers she had gathered from around the store onto the surface of her worktable. With a pair of shears in hand, she began to cut the stems and trim away the excess leaves on them.

We were both silent, the only sounds between us was the

faint sound of our breathing and the sharp sound of her shears. I'd never been much of a talker, not even when we were kids. Whenever we would meet, all I wanted to do was to simply look at her or listen to her sweet voice. Back then she talked enough for both of us.

Now I needed to stop being such a yellow wuzz and ask her out.

I searched my head for something to say as I watched her add orange flowers to the bouquet she was building, then small yellow ones, before pausing to peruse the arrangement she had put together so far.

Obviously, she was not the hot mess I was, because she spoke ... and sounded sickeningly normal too. "Did the flowers you ordered yesterday arrive safely?"

I cleared my throat and swallowed the smooth stones in my throat. "They did."

"Was everything to your liking?"

"Yes." Even as the empty word left my lips, I knew my brief sentences would make her uncomfortable, but I couldn't help myself. My mind had gone blank. She had reduced a big, grown man like me into a dome of shaking jelly.

"How's it looking?" she asked, lifting those pools of warm chocolate towards me.

God. I wanted to touch her. How I wanted to. At that moment, it felt as though I would lose my mind if I couldn't at least place my hand on hers.

"Good," I replied, awkward as hell. I kicked myself hard mentally. Fuck it, Caleb. You're going to blow it. I took my hand out of my pocket and pointed at one of the flowers in the bouquet. "What flower is that?"

"This one?" she pointed at one of the orange flowers.

It wasn't the one I had referred to, but I nodded mutely.

"It's a Marigold."

"Can I take a look?" I asked, even my voice sounded shaky.

Immediately, she picked it out of the bouquet and held it out to me. All I wanted to do was accidentally touch her hand, but the moment my hand came near the stem, she let it go as though even the possibility of contact with me would harm her.

I pretended not to be fast enough to catch the stem. It fell through my fingers and landed soundlessly on the wooden table.

She went to pick it up, so did I.

I was a whole lot quicker this time. My hand touched hers, lingered. The contact instantly froze her to the spot. She raised her head, our faces were mere inches apart. Her warm breath tickled my face, and my eyes roved greedily around her beautiful face. The words came out then, in a rush and straight from the heart.

"Will you have dinner with me?"

Her eyes slightly widened.

The fear that she would reject me gripped me so hard, I couldn't move. The moments began to tick by. It seemed as if an eternity passed, but surely it couldn't have been more than a few seconds. Before she could answer, the other girl working at the store returned. Willow jerked away.

"I'm done repotting your cactus," the girl announced, a bite in her voice.

"Thank you," I replied, turning towards her, trying to keep my attention on the white ceramic pot she'd transferred the plant into. I remembered Marie's other requests. "I'll need pebbles and pompoms to go with those." Hopefully, searching out those things would take her away for a little while more.

"Come over here to the counter and you can choose your own," she said instead.

Before I could even respond, Willow spoke up. "Please ... go ahead. I'm nearly done here. I'll finish it and bring your arrangement over to the counter."

Foiled again.

Frustrated, but unable to do anything else, I followed the girl. I glanced back at Willow and she had her head bent towards her work. Another man would have thought her preference was to remain as acquaintances and walked away.

Not me. I could never accept that. It only meant my next round of effort would be aggressive enough to convince her to see me as something more.

I chose the pebbles and pompoms without too much

thought, and by the time I was done, Willow was walking over with the finished bouquet.

"It's beautiful," I said with genuine appreciation.

She placed it on the counter, and for a heart-stopping moment she tilted her head and looked at me ... as if she recognized me, but then she shook her head, gave me a polite nod, and went on her way. I watched with longing as she walked towards the back of the shop.

The other girl's voice brought me back to the reality. I dragged my eyes away from Willow, and refocused on the transaction at hand.

Willow

The pot slid out of my hand and dropped to the floor. I stared at the mess on the tiles.

I had taken over repotting plants for the afternoon, because I needed to have my hands and mind completely occupied, but thus far it had been disastrous.

Sandra looked up from the packets of flower food that she had been taping onto a bouquet, and yelled at me. "Another one? What's going on with you?"

"I was trying to put it on the table," I said, wrinkling my nose at the broken pieces on the floor.

"And you missed? Ten minutes ago you tripped over that massive fertilizer bag and almost broke your neck. Where is your mind?"

"I'll clean it up," I muttered.

I had just bent down to pick up the shards of broken ceramic when a pair of feet encased in leather flats stopped in front of me. I looked up to see Sandra standing in front of me.

"Where's your phone?" she asked.

"Why?"

"Just give it to me," she groaned, and bending down proceeded to search in the pockets of my apron.

"Hey!" I protested.

But she took no notice. She pulled it out with a triumphant smile. Moments later however, she had gained access and was punching in something that was written on a small piece of paper.

My forehead furrowed. "How do you know my password?"

"Oh, please," she mocked. "How long have we been friends?"

She handed the phone back to me, and I looked at what she had done. She had added a contact, and when I saw the name I felt my heart start to pound.

"Caleb?"

I jumped to my feet. "You asked him for his number?"

"You left him hanging, Willow."

I was perplexed. "Wait, did you ask him for it or he gave it to you?"

"I asked him for it," she answered.

I was horrified. "Why would you do that?"

"It's a small store, Willow, and I could see the both of you clearly. It was almost uncomfortable to watch."

"What do you mean?"

Her chin jutted forward. "Are you trying to play dumb? I'll be offended if you are."

"Why?"

"I told you I was attracted to him from the beginning, but you acted as though you weren't."

"Well I wasn't. I mean I'm not. I mean, I don't know."

"Okay. If that's true then contact him, and go on a date. You'll get a great meal out of it, perhaps some good conversation, and then you can decide never to see him again. I don't know what's holding you back, but I feel like I have to remind you of this; a date is not a marriage proposal. You can still come right back and forget it ever happened."

I sighed, because with him it felt like it would be a marriage proposal. There was something so absolute and life-and-death about him in my mind, but I just couldn't place my finger on what it was.

"Did you really want him, Sandra?"

She shrugged. "Who wouldn't? But he's very clearly not into me. He's into you. In a big way."

I frowned. "What makes you say that? We were just talking normally. Actually, we didn't even speak to each other that much. I was busy with the arrangement and he just watched me."

"Watched?" she scoffed. "Are you kidding me? He devoured you with his eyes."

"He did not," I breathed.

"Hell, the way he looked at you, I thought he was going to pounce on you and do the deed right there on the table. And you, you couldn't even look him in the eye. I've never seen you like that. You always look everyone in the eye. Plus, the proximity? It was like you were old lovers or something." She paused. "There was so much sexual tension between you two that I could have sliced through it with a knife."

"Now, you're just being dramatic. If he was that interested, why didn't he give me his number? A guy like that, living at the address he lives at, is definitely not shy." I took a deep breath and exhaled it slowly. My assessment of him was correct and what Sandra must have picked up on was the sexual tension I was putting out, not him.

"So," I carried on, "there's no way I'm calling him. In fact, I'm going to delete his number."

"He knows you have it," she said, folding her arms. "So not contacting him will just be rude. The message he's going to receive is you can't even be bothered to be civil. He'll never be able to come back here with his head held high, and we will lose an obviously wealthy customer. That's not very smart, is it? And if my aunt asks how the shop is going after she approved your bank loan, I'm not lying for you. I'll let her know, and that's not a threat, it is a fucking promise."

I tried to laugh at the Mafia talk, but the laughter died in my throat at the expression in her eyes. She turned around haughtily and returned to her desk. The phone in my hand suddenly seemed to weigh a ton. I put it down and began to clear the table. It was a slow day and I let Sandra leave early.

I stayed alone in the shop with my flowers. They had always given me great joy. Just being around them made my heart glad. I went over to the bucket of daylilies. "What do you think? Should I call him?" The flowers remained silent. "Easy for you," I muttered and continued to pace the shop floor. By the end of the work day, I was exhausted with thinking about the new number stored in my phone.

I'd thought to call, but my throat had tightened with so much anxiety that I was scared that when the time came to speak, my mouth would stop working. When I got home, I made myself a quick pasta, but had no appetite to eat it. I switched on the TV and stared at it blankly. I scolded myself for being such a little coward.

Finally, I picked up my phone and typed out a message to him. Deleted it, and retyped it again. Took a deep breath and deleted that. Thought about it. Wrote another couple of lines. Nope, that would be forward. Tried again, from another angle. Nope, too pathetic. Went for something simple. Delete. Too simple. After countless efforts, I went back to the original message. And before I could think anymore about it, I hit send.

Then I buried my face in my pillow. My heart was beating so fast I could hear it.

12

Caleb

I was going through the Annual Reports of the company I was interested in acquiring, when the message arrived on my phone. I knew instantly it was her. I snatched up my phone and stared at the words half in shock, half in disbelief.

Hello. This is Willow ... from the flower shop.

My heart slammed against my chest with the surge of intense joy. I had made contact. I had finally cut a direct path through a forest of thorns to her. I read the message over and over again. As I stared at the sweet words, another text came in from her.

I'm sorry I didn't give you a response to your question back at the shop. I was a bit taken aback. If the offer is still valid, I would like to take you up on it. Dinner sounds awesome. Again, I apologize for not responding immediately. I tend to be shy sometimes. Have a great night.

I launched myself into the air. It felt as though my chest was on fire and fiery currents of wild excitement were buzzing through my veins. I gave a whoop of joy and punched the air.

"Yes, yes, yes," I shouted into my silent house.

All the pain, all the disappointment, all the frustration, the endless waiting fell away. I'd been so worried I'd come and find she'd given her heart to another man. That I would be too late. That the magic would not be there for her.

But the world had spun around once again and this time it seemed to be working in my favor.

I felt as if I had grown wings. I laughed like a mad man as I paced the floor. If my prison mates could see me now. They would never believe it. Back there, I never cracked a smile. I hardly spoke. Not even in the Chow Hall. My look was one of cool intimidation. Grown men trembled when I looked at them. I was utterly, totally and completely left alone.

I took a couple of deep breaths, then seated myself back on my chair. *Don't fuck this up, Caleb.* I cradled the phone and brought my thumbs to the keypad to begin typing out my response.

But just as I did, my phone vibrated at an incoming call. At first, I thought she was calling. Then I saw the number and my eyes narrowed. This was a relationship I'd thought had been completely severed in prison, but it seemed that it wasn't going to be the case. It felt like a cold claw from the past had come to take back my joy, my excitement.

Yet, I couldn't reject the call. I was never one to run away from my enemies. I always took them on head-on. I hit the accept button and lifted the phone to my ear.

"Caleb?" the familiar voice came through the receiver.

"Frank," I answered, and the other Caleb, the cold, hard man came back.

"Hey! Wow. This is truly your phone number. I was wondering when you left how and if I was ever going to be in contact with you again."

"How did you get this number?"

"Yikes," he said. "Look, I know I'm reneging on our agreement. No contact beyond the wall, but we're old friends, right?"

I walked over to the massive windows that overlooked the outdoor pool and garden beyond. "We're not friends," I corrected. "I protected you and in exchange you taught me, but even that was over a long time ago. We haven't spoken in two years, or have you forgotten?"

Fraudster Frank's laugh was forced and fake. "Man, I will never understand how you could hold a grudge for that long. Our cells were just across the corridor and yet you acted like I was dead to you."

Frank was a textbook psychopath. A man devoid of morals. You couldn't trust him as far as you could spit. "You sent someone to shank me in the boiler room, Frank."

"I was jealous, man. C'mon, you're human too... aren't you?"

I almost laughed. See what I meant about him being a psychopath. They always accuse you of being or doing the things they are guilty of. It was him who needed some lessons on how to be a human being.

"C'mon man, how would you feel if you were in my shoes? I taught you everything about trading and you go and outperform me a hundred times over. Jenkins was going to completely shut me out... take away my privileges and crown you king. I didn't even mind that... all I wanted was the crumbs from your table, but he wouldn't even agree to it, the selfish bastard."

I didn't care to listen to his whiny bullshit any longer. "How the hell did you get this number?"

"Caleb, it doesn't matter how I got it," he said, his voice low and urgent. "What matters is I did."

My brows furrowed. "What the fuck are you talking about?"

There was the sound of a man's voice in the background and Frank saying, "Yeah, yeah, yeah," before he returned his attention back to me. "Fucking assholes. I just got on the call and already they're telling me that I've got to finish up so I'll have to make this quick. Remember Trilium?"

"Sure. You scammed them."

"Whoa, that's harsh. It was a misdemeanor. I just exaggerated the percentage of returns."

"And they lost a hundred million."

"Yeah, I paid for it. I'm here, incarcerated, locked up like a fucking animal, ain't I?"

"Your time is running out, Frank," I reminded.

"Okay, okay. Anyway, as you know, it was Mafia money, so I've been paying back over the years, but Jenkins shut down the trading hole here the moment you were released, so there's no way I can try to pay them back from in here anymore. I need some help, man. I got some information. I can get it out to you."

"I'm not front running, Frank," I said through gritted teeth.

"I know," he said. "I fucking know."

"I just got out of prison, I have no intention of ever going back."

He moved away from the receiver then, and roared at someone who was speaking to him. "For fuck's sake. I'm almost done! Fuck."

Then he returned to me. "Caleb, listen to me. I'm running out of time. They don't want you to front run. They want a product. They're not looking for unrealistic numbers, but just one with low volatility. Something that will earn unspectacular returns regularly. They want to market this to a couple of big shots and create a fund for it. And they want you to create it."

"Me?"

"Yeah, I mentioned you and your... idea. Remember the one you talked about four years ago."

The moment the words came out of his mouth, anger flooded through my entire system. "You told them about that?" I couldn't believe it. "You fucking bastard!"

"I had no choice. They threatened my family!" he yelled desperately. "Caleb, they fucking threatened my family. I told you about Laura, and Carlie, and Tristan. Carlie finally opened her boutique last month, and Tristan is going to college this fall. He got into Yale, Caleb. Fucking Yale. He's going to be a lawyer so he can get my sorry ass out of here."

I took a deep breath. "Frank, I owe you nothing. I've paid you back and then some more for teaching me the ropes. That boutique you're so proud your daughter opened, Tristan's tuition? I helped you earn all that to send to them. I don't owe you anything."

"I know," he said. "I fucking know but... Caleb. This is just one product. You're the smartest motherfucker I've ever met in my life, so I know you can do it. I've already sold it to them. Please let them have it."

"Are you out of your bloody mind? This was something I mentioned in passing to you four fucking years ago. I don't need to play with fire anymore."

"C'mon man. It will be one last hurrah. It was a great idea then, and it still is. I hear you're opening a new firm."

I scowled, the first strings of disquiet rattling through my consciousness. Frank knew too much about my life.

"Which is a good thing," he was saying. "You'll want to make it all official and legal. There's something in it for you too.

You'll make a shitload of money too. For me I just want them to leave my family alone."

"Fuck you, Frank!" I snarled, and pulled the phone away from my ear to end the call. At that moment he screamed out a name that drove a punch into my gut.

"Willow! Willow Rayne!"

I froze. My hand trembled with fury as I returned the phone back to my ear. "You told them about her?" My voice was ice, pure ice.

"I didn't mean to, but it might have slipped out," he replied evasively. "But even if I hadn't told them they would have found out. If you refuse to comply, she's going to become their target. That's how they run, man. They catch you by the balls and squeeze. For God's sake man, just make this product and get us out of this mess."

The call was abruptly cut off by one of the screws and I was so damn furious, I wanted to smash my fist into a wall. I was so livid, my whole body vibrated with it. I clenched my fists and tried hard to control my ragged breathing.

I'd thought I'd tied up all the loose strings that belonged inside the four walls of Folsom, but they were coming loose once again. Willow! A chill went down my spine. I hadn't yet responded to her message yet. I pulled it up and typed in my answer.

· · ·

ow does this weekend sound?

I remained standing, my gaze at the calm, blue water of pool as I waited for her response to come in. A few seconds later it did.

This weekend sounds good.

"He didn't sound too excited about taking me out. Okay, excitement might be a bit much to ask. I would have been happy with eager, but he just sounded … I don't know, almost cold. As if he was arranging a business meeting."

"'What do you expect? He's the dark and brooding type. I like that in a man."

I had very little experience of men, knew next to nothing about how to please them, and nothing about how to intrigue them. In fact, most men found me unapproachable or boring. I chewed my bottom lip nervously. "Or maybe he's not looking forward to the date."

Sandra looked up from the jacket she was lint rolling for me, a disapproving frown on her face. "You've been saying that since Wednesday. Stop it. Please."

"Well, that's because he hasn't even texted me since Wednesday. Is that normal? Does a man just stop making any contact once you've agreed to a date with him?"

"Maybe he's busy. Maybe he's sick. Maybe he lost a toe. A thousand things could have held his attention beyond texting you every minute to say how excited he is about your date."

My hand tightened around my phone. "Be honest with me, Sandra. Wouldn't he have tried to at least get to know me better if he was really interested?"

"Not necessarily. Every man reacts differently so stop over-thinking this or you'll ruin it for yourself. I always look at the worst-case scenario before I go into any situation and decide if I can live with it. In this case, he's not interested in you and he just wants a one-night stand." She shrugs carelessly. "So what? Bang his brains out. Trust me, a man like him will make a fantastic one-night stand. Those muscles. Those big, strong hands. Those thighs. And that bulge. Hell, he has a big bulge in his pants. You can go all night long with a bulge like that."

I knew she was trying to make me feel better, but she didn't understand. I would die if all he wanted from me was a one-night stand. Even thinking he only wanted a one-night stand with me made me feel sick to my stomach. "You shouldn't have asked him for his number. Maybe he's not trying so hard now because I didn't make him work for it."

Sandra straightened then, and turned to me. "You did not just say that."

"I did." I sighed. "My brain's starting to malfunction, but then again it could be the truth."

She came to the counter and handed the jacket over. "Relax, babe. This isn't a marriage proposal. Didn't he contact you about the location and time? And he got your opinion on it before he went ahead with arrangements. In my book that's adequate effort. He's interested. Plus, he's taking you to The Ivy. No man is going to spend that kind of money on a one-night stand. So... go on the date, and if he turns out to be a jackass looking for a wet hole, then come back to me with the story. Just remember if you don't want to oblige, I'll be happy to be his very wet hole." She grinned broadly.

I shook my head at her, some of the tension leaving me. Sandra was a good egg. She'd always been there for me. And me her. "You're bad, you know."

"Bad? I'm downright wicked. Maybe I'll teach you some moves you can make on him."

I giggled as I placed my phone on the counter, and began to slip my arms into the jacket. "I'm still waiting for him to send a text to cancel."

She searched my face, her expression serious. "Oh, my God, you think you're not good enough for him."

"It's not that exactly, but I can't help feeling he is out of my league. To start with he looks like a movie star and he's obviously super successful. I mean, what's he even doing in this town when LA is just around the corner?"

"Well you can ask him these burning questions on your date tonight, can't you?" She came over then to pull me away from the counter. "And plus, you're not out of his league. I would kill for your hair and your eyes. I would do even worse things for that body of yours. And you're real smart. This flower shop will become successful one day and you'll make a shit ton of money, most of which you'll send to me as an allowance for being such a good friend. But let's not talk about the future yet. Right now, it's past seven and you need to get going, or you'll be late to the restaurant."

"I could get stood up," I muttered as I grabbed my purse and walked towards the door.

"In that case grab a cab and come right back here. I have Champagne. We'll make our own party."

I stopped at her statement, fear gripping my stomach. "Really, that's your response."

"What else do you want me to say? No, Willow, you're too good to be stood up. I've been stood up at least five times in my life while you haven't, even once. You can't live your life as squeaky clean as that, so go strut that virgin pussy of yours out in the world and be disregarded like the rest of us. Have you called an Uber?"

"I'm taking the van."

Her mouth fell open. "You're going to arrive at the date in this hideous van? You're wearing a four-hundred-dollar dress. *My* four-hundred-dollar dress!"

"You bought it in a sale for a hundred and fifty dollars,' I threw over my shoulder as I hurried outside before she could stop me. She followed me out.

'I'm not going to waste my money on an Uber when this

works perfectly well," I said, as I jumped into the rickety, washed out van and locked the doors so that she wouldn't be able to open it.

She grabbed onto the door handle and tried to pull the driver's door open. "This is why he's going to dump you after the first date. Open this freaking door. I'll pay for the damn Uber."

I started the engine, rolled the window down, and stuck my tongue out at her before pulling away.

"Willow!" she shouted at the top of her lungs in the street.

I waved at her through the rear-view mirror, and continued on my way towards the restaurant.

14
Caleb

I arrived at the restaurant twenty minutes early. I could have gone in and had a drink, but I felt too restless to sit down. I paced the ground next to the valet, who discreetly kept throwing me strange glances.

We'd agreed to meet at 7:30pm, and it was now exactly fifteen minutes past. If it had been anyone else I would have already walked off, irritated to have lost that time, but when it came to Willow, twelve years had been nothing. What was another hour or even two?

When we were young she was always late. Even then I didn't mind waiting. I remembered her worried little face as she ran towards me. Breathlessly, she would apologize, "I'm sorry I'm late, Caleb. I was (insert reason, usually reading) and the time just flew away from me."

"Caleb?" I heard her voice call out to me, and turned around towards the street. I thought she would arrive and use the valet parking service like I had. Instead, she was heading towards me on foot, in a light, pale pink dress that billowed in the soft evening breeze.

Her hair was not as straight as it had been the last time, and it took me back to the past. Back then, she used to have light waves and curly ends, and I could vividly remember my fingers gently sifting through the golden strands. It saddened me that it would be a while again before I was allowed that privilege with her. I went forward, and met her; she was slightly out of breath.

"I'm sorry I'm late. I was at the shop and the time just flew away from me."

I was speechless at the nostalgia that hit me in the guts. Everything had changed and yet nothing had.

"Why are you looking at me like that?" she whispered.

I shook my head. "Someone walked over my grave."

Her eyes widened.

"Shall we?" I asked, my hand beckoning for her to walk on.

She nodded and went ahead of me. I watched as her petite body, balanced on high pink heels, swayed to the unhurried, seductive pace of her walk. A fire flared in my loins and I hardened immediately at the sight. I could watch her forever. She wasn't mine yet, but I couldn't help the fierce pride of possession roaring inside me.

I was determined to make her mine again.

I reached over and pushed open the door for her. Maybe she

was one of those women who wanted to open their own doors, but fuck it, until she told me otherwise, I was going to treat her like the princess she was. I had asked for a secluded table and we were given one in an intimate corner.

This place itself was particularly cozy with white blossoms on the walls, candles on the tables. Soft, romantic music filled the air.

"I can smell roses," she said, wrinkling her nose.

I took a deep breath and indeed there was a subtle scent of roses in the air. "Hmmm."

"I've never been to this restaurant."

I smiled at her. "Neither have I."

She smiled back as we settled in and I felt my heart stop. I had to look away to regain my senses. This woman had absolutely no idea of the hold she had on me. I tried not to stare too hard as she picked up the menu and looked at it. In the light of the golden candlelight her skin seemed to glow like marble. A small willow tree necklace gleamed between the soft skin of her collarbones. I stared at it. She had saved it. She saw me staring and touched the necklace, self-consciously. "It's just an old trinket, but I'm insanely attached to it." Our eyes met. Her teeth sank into her plump bottom lip and I felt my cock jerk.

"Would you like something to drink?" I croaked.

She nodded and tucked her hair behind her ears. She was

nervous. It was an old habit of hers. Whenever she didn't feel confident she did that.

"A glass of wine would be nice. The ..." As she moved her finger down the list, I signaled to the waiter and he began to head over to us.

"The Skinnygirl Moscato will do," she concluded.

Thankfully, the waiter arrived so I placed her order and then mine, simply opting for a bottle of the Moscato wine she'd ordered. Spending the last twelve years in prison meant I knew nothing about fine wines or great dishes.

"I have to drive home," she murmured, "so I'm having to limit myself to only one glass."

"Don't worry," I assured. "If necessary I can always send someone to bring your car to you in the morning."

Her smile was nervous. "I'd rather just drive home."

I nodded in agreement, but didn't cancel the bottle order, then regretted it when the wine came. It was so damn sweet I nearly spat it out. She laughed at my expression. "Don't you like it?"

"No." I put it to one side and ordered a neat whiskey.

15
Caleb

For our meal order I took charge. When she was young she had always loved crab and I saw the crab dish on the seven-course starter meal for two. I knew she would never dream of ordering it herself so I ordered the seven-course starter meal for both of us. As soon as the waiter slinked away she leaned forward.

"There were no prices on my menu. I hope that seven-course meal was not too expensive."

"Don't worry I can afford it."

"It's just I feel so extravagant having seven courses."

"I've never had one before, but I believe it's made up of tiny portions," I said honestly.

"I wouldn't mind a bigger portion of crab though. It's my favorite."

"I know."

Her head tilted. "You do?"

Damn, I was no good at this lying game. "I meant you look like a girl who loves good food."

She grinned cheekily. "What does a girl who loves crab look like?"

"She looks like a girl who loves life. She uses her fingers to eat, laughs a lot, loves the wind in her hair, wears comfortable shoes, cries at movies, sings in the shower, is loyal to a fault, and will defend the people she loves to her death."

She leaned back in surprise, her eyes twinkling. "You got all that from the fact that I love crab?"

"I'm a good judge of character."

"I'm terrible at reading people," she admitted.

"You may be better than you think. Go on, take a shot at reading me."

She took a sip of wine and gazed at me from above the rim of her glass. She placed the glass back on the table, her eyes never leaving mine. "Okay. I think you're the strong, silent type and very brave. I also get the impression you're very resourceful. If I had to be stuck on a deserted island with only one other person I would chose you, because I just know you would figure out a way for us to survive. You'd climb the coconut trees and find a way to break the fruit open without a knife. You'd make a fire so I can cook the fish you've caught, and you'd find a way to build us a shelter and some kind of shower contraption. Who knows, give you enough time and you might even fashion a raft for us to leave the island on."

I laugh at her description. That was exactly what I would have done too. I heard my own voice laughing and I realized I hadn't laughed like this for a long, long time. In fact, the last time was when I was with her.

She frowns. "You're tough and successful on the outside, but inside you've got some great pain. Some hurt that you are hiding from the world."

Suddenly the atmosphere between us changed. Electricity crackled between us. That was too close to the bone. "That necklace," I whispered, grasping on the first thing that came into my mind. "Where did you get it from?"

She traced the delicate gold pendant. "My father gave it to me on my tenth birthday."

I thought of the Powerpuff watch sitting on my night stand. There was a time she had refused to take it off. But of course, she probably couldn't recall any of that time. I watched her face, my heart heavy with sadness for all that she had been through. If only I had realized earlier. I could have done something. I wanted her to remember me, God, how much I wanted her to, but if it meant remembering those dark, painful memories, then I was okay with her not remembering us. The way we were. It was a special type of torment, but I had broad shoulders. I could bear it for us.

"He died in a car accident," she said softly. "Both my parents did."

"I'm sorry." It sounded lame. Stupid. I wanted to reach across the table, take her in my arms and rock her until the hurt fell out of her, but I couldn't. I could just sit opposite her and make inane platitudes.

"It's okay. It happened a very long time ago. I was incredibly lucky. I was adopted by two wonderful human beings. You have to meet them one day. They are truly amazing. I even switched out my middle name for my adopted mother's."

"What is it?" I asked.

"Sabrina. My full name is Willow Sabrina Rayne."

"It's a pretty name. It suits you."

"Thank you." She bobbed her head awkwardly. She had always been lousy at taking compliments. Even something as mild as a pretty name. "What about you?" she asked. "Do you have a middle name?"

"Nope."

"Caleb's a great name," she said. "It suits you."

"Thank you," I replied gravely.

The waiter arrived with our first course then. Salmon Tartare, and we got right into it. It was delicious. I was more than content to sit silently there with her eating the most delicious thing I'd ever had in my life, but I was no longer at the canteen. I was out in society, where civilized conversation was part of the ritual of eating.

"Did you just move into town?" she asked.

My nerves tightened in my stomach at the line of questioning that was approaching. The salmon in my mouth suddenly felt flat and tasteless. I didn't feel good at all about the responses I was going to have to give her. "I did."

"Where did you come from if you don't mind me asking."

"New York," I replied, "and no, I don't mind you asking. I wanted a change of pace."

"Well, if a change of pace is what you wanted, then you've made a 180° tilt. Things move at a snail's pace here in Folsom compared to New York."

I watched as she lifted a small piece of fish to her lips and slipped the tiny morsel between her lips. Lust uncoiled like a serpent in my belly. It had slept for many, many years, but it was well and truly awake now. "You don't like it here?"

"Don't get me wrong," she said. "New York sounds like an exciting holiday, but I love it here. I have the flower shop and my parents. I could never live far away from them. I owe them everything."

She put her fork down.

"My mom is a breast cancer survivor. We thought it was over and done with, but she had it return. After her last round of chemo, she became a shadow of herself. My dad took her to Florida for a holiday."

"I'm sorry about your mom."

"She's getting better. What about you?" she asked. "'What will you be doing here in Folsom?"

I swallowed my drink of water, and used the napkin to wipe the corners of my lips. "I run a brokerage firm so I'm going to bring that down here to see how it can perform."

"That's great. I wish you all the best here in Folsom. I should have brought a congratulatory bouquet with me."

I shrugged. "You weren't to know. How about you? How long have you been in Folsom?"

Her eyes moved away from me. I needed to know what she remembered about her past. Up till now, most of it had been hearsay so it was best to confirm it from her very lips.

"I moved here from a small town called Bitter Creek. It's about an hour and a half away. That's where my uncle used to live until he was murdered and his house burnt down by a kid with social problems. Apparently, it was just a random act of evil. No one knows why he did it. He never told anyone."

She shuddered. I was gripping the fork so hard I was afraid I would bend it. I forced the words out. "I'm sorry for your loss."

"It's okay. I have almost no memory of him or that night." She gives an awkward laugh and picks up her glass of wine. "It would seem I probably saw the killer and ran away from the murder scene. Unfortunately, they say I must have tripped along the way and fell, hitting my head. When I woke up I had lost two years of memory. Those two years have never come back."

Little glasses of lemon sorbet were served. I let the cold sweet ice melt on my tongue. Ah, how much I had missed locked away in prison. I stared at Willow and felt like the luckiest man alive.

The evening continued on with light, pleasant conversation. She smiled easily, and the conversation flowed. It was during our third course of steak *au poivre* with scalloped potatoes that she asked me a question I wasn't ready to answer.

"Why did you ask me out to dinner?"

I took my time patting the corners of my mouth with my napkin as my brain scrambled to search for a response. I couldn't tell her the truth, but I didn't want to be nonchalant in my response either.

"I felt a deep attraction to you, and I wanted to get to know you better."

She blushed. "Oh." She lifted her glass to her lips. I detected a hint of disappointment in her tone and it near drove me crazy.

Soon, the dinner began to wind to a close, and the time came for dessert. I knew that she would especially enjoy the cherry *clafoutis* baked with chocolate pieces. Back then, she'd loved everything that had chocolate in it.

I watched as she enjoyed the sweet, the deliciousness of it all made her eyes close and her shoulders roll up to her ears.

And I. I just sat there and savored the wonderful warmth that filled my heart at the sight.

16

Willow

https://www.youtube.com/watch?v=lcOxhH8N3Bo

I had parked my van one street away because I didn't want to use valet parking. After dinner ended, he insisted on giving me a ride to my car in his. When his car was brought around he opened the passenger door for me and I slipped in.

His dark green, top of the line sports Mercedes was like him. Lean and dangerously luxurious. From the gleaming exterior to the pristine interior. It even smelled of a sophisticated, rich blend of spices. Once again, I was reminded that I was a struggling entrepreneur working her butt off in a flower shop in a tiny town, while he was a wealthy, shining bachelor from New York. He could literally have anyone he wanted. Why was he pursuing me? Was it something to while away the time, or did he see me as a quick and easy conquest?

We soon arrived at my van, and instead of waiting in the car while I got out he jumped out of the car and in a flash, was around my side to open it. Honestly, I never had anyone behave in such an old-fashioned, courtly way to me before, and I had to admit that I actually liked being treated as if I was something so precious and important.

After I thanked him, we walked to my van in silence. I tried not to feel embarrassed about the sad state of my van as I climbed into it. I thought that he'd be on his way then, but he insisted on following me back home. Maybe he did just want me for sex. But I realized that somehow strangely I was okay with even that.

The man was irresistible.

Actually, from the moment I spotted him waiting outside the restaurant, I'd been immediately floored by just how breathtakingly handsome he was. He wore a dark gray suit, with a simple, fitted, black T-shirt.

But the way the suit framed his shoulders, or was it his shoulders framed his suit, was absolutely mesmerizing. All through the night, I hadn't been able to take my eyes off him, his arms, those tattooed fingers touching my skin. I had relished the sultry way he had focused on me through the night, as though he wanted to know everything there possibly was to know about me.

However, at the parking lot, he hadn't even leaned in for a kiss. Instead, his face had turned serious as he looked around at the surroundings before insisting on escorting me home. Well, in front of my father's house nothing could happen, but in front of Sandra's apartment, the possibilities were endless. I chose to head back to Sandra's apartment.

When we arrived, I parked in front of her apartment building and got out, wishing I had taken Sandra's advice to use an Uber. Getting down from the van in three-inch high sandals was not very ladylike I imagined.

He got out of his car and he walked over to me, his gaze on the building.

"It's Sandra's place," I explained when he reached me. "I'll be spending the night with her."

It suddenly occurred to me that the statement sounded quite provocative, as though I was extending an invitation for some sex and for a moment I panicked. However, he only regarded me coolly, his ocean blue eyes, sharp and attentive.

"Goodnight, Willow," he murmured. "I had a great time tonight."

I was stunned. Wasn't he going to make a move at all? "Me too. But I'm not happy you didn't let me split the bill with you."

He smiled, his perfect teeth flashing brightly in the dark. "Maybe next time."

My heart jumped in my chest. *Next time?*

"I'll wait here until you get in," he drawled in that sexy voice of his.

"Ok," I whispered, and to my surprise, my voice was hoarse.

Instantly, his gaze went to my lips and remained there. The look in his eyes was incredibly similar to what I imagined was in mine. Longing ... potent desire. Something that charred our insides.

But with it seemed as if with great effort he dragged his gaze away from my trembling mouth and started walking away.

The question slipped out of me before I could stop it. "Why won't you kiss me?"

He froze, then turned around slowly.

I felt horror grow inside me at just how brazen I sounded. "I'm sorry, I don't know what came over me. I didn't mean to say that at all. Must be that one glass of wine I drank. It was really potent," I babbled. I was so mortified I would have carried on humiliating myself too if he hadn't taken a step towards me. The words dried in my throat. I could only stare up at him

He took another step closer. "Don't you know?"

My brain was glitching. "Um ... uh ... don't I know what?"

"Why I didn't kiss you?"

He took another step closer to me, and it forced a response out of me. "No, I mean, isn't that how a date is supposed to end? The boy takes the girl home and kisses her good night?" I was trying my best to turn it all into a joke, but no one was laughing.

He took the final step that closed the distance between us, and I felt like I was going to pass out. Now, he was deliberately and wholly teasing me, and I relished every second of it.

"I wanted to be careful," he said, his low, deep voice washing over me. "I don't want you to feel uncomfortable with me for even a second."

I smiled in response and opened my mouth to speak, but before I could, he curled his big, strong hands around my waist. He pulled my unresisting body forward, till I was pressed against him. My face tilted up to stare into his eyes.

Dang, he was beautiful.

I couldn't help but reach out to touch him. My fingers lightly stroked the supple skin of his cheek, and then for some reason my finger moved over to stroke the bridge of his nose. I should have been more nervous with him ... more guarded, but I wasn't. I wanted to ask him why he felt so familiar to me, but before I could even string a single sentence together in my head, he leaned forward and sucked my bottom lip into his mouth.

No one had ever done that to me. I had expected something light and simple, but the moment we touched, it was as though we had been created specifically and solely to kiss the other. I closed my eyes with pleasure. This, oh God, this. I had been waiting for this my whole life. Slowly his mouth worked my bottom lip. My whole body responded. I felt as if my bones were melting. I was being one with him.

His taste still had a slight hint of whiskey and the dessert we had shared. It melded magically with the taste on my own tongue. Heady. I felt his arms tighten around me as he moved on to capture both my lips. The kiss ... was *searing*.

I felt as if I was falling. My hands fisted around the front of his shirt to keep me stable, and I gave back as much as he took, slanting my head in sync with his, as he took the kiss even deeper.

Tremors coursed through my body as his tongue slipped into my mouth and began a sensual dance with mine. He stroked and sucked and teased me, and by the time we parted for a breath, I couldn't believe the ride he had taken me on.

I stood boneless in his arms. For what seemed to be a life-time, all I could do was stare into his stunning eyes.

In the distance, a dog barked.

It startled me and brought me back to reality. Instantly, I pulled away from his embrace. I felt shocked and disorien-tated. My knees wobbled with the sudden movement, and I would have gone sprawling backwards on my ass if he hadn't reached out and caught me. Only when he was sure that the strength had returned to my legs, did he let go of me.

I almost couldn't look at him. I was that shaken. I bent my head and pretended to straighten out the imaginary wrinkles in my dress. When it was clear he was not simply going to walk away and I wasn't going to be able to carry on straight-ening out wrinkles that weren't there, I lifted my gaze to his. He was waiting. There was patience in his eyes, as if he would have stood there all night waiting for me to get myself in order. He made me feel like his attention was solely for me, and that he had all the time in the world for me.

The light evening breeze blew at his hair, dropping it down on his forehead. He pushed it back impatiently and I realized then I was truly at the risk of falling madly in love with the unreal man before me. It was crazy because I knew nothing about him. He could be a serial killer for all I knew.

"I ... uh ... I should get going," I mumbled.

He nodded and slipped his hands into his pockets as he waited for me to make my next move.

"Thank you for dinner," I said, and clutching my purse in hand, I started to walk away, my palm pressed flat against the body of my van until it could no longer support me. I did not look back even though I was dying to. As I got into the building and closed the door, I heard his car start up and roar away into the night. I leaned against the door and took deep calming breaths. By the time I arrived at Sandra's door, I felt almost normal again.

I had my own key, so I let myself in, walked over to her couch and collapsed on it.

From the next couch Sandra said, "Wow, that must have been some date you were on."

"It was," I whispered.

"I'll go get some wine. Start talking."

17

Caleb

There was someone on our tail.

I had noticed the car as we turned at the first set of traffic lights after we left the restaurant.

My fists were clenched at my sides as I watched Willow go into the building, and when I was certain that she was safe inside, I got into my car and drove away.

I took a longer route home. The seconds morphed into minutes as I discreetly watched the rearview mirror, and soon enough the cream Honda that had been following us since we left the restaurant came back into my line of vision.

I had tried to see its plate number, but it was too dark to make out, so I decided to lead him down a quiet street. A few minutes later I put on my seatbelt and began to speed up, and the driver did the same so that he wouldn't lose me. As we got to a lonely stretch of road I accelerated even more so that I had him on a dangerous enough momentum. Grabbing my steering wheel tightly, I slammed on my brakes, and my car screeched to a sudden stop.

Behind me, I heard the violent screeching of his vehicle as he slammed on his breaks to avoid the crash, but he hadn't a hope in hell of stopping the collision. My halt had been too abrupt. His sedan crashed into the back of my car. The impact was brutal, my airbag burst into action as the sound of metal crunching with metal reverberated around me. I didn't have time to dwell on the state of my car or myself.

I kicked my door open and ran towards his car. I could see the smoke emanating from the engine of the car behind me, and his windshield was shattered. I could hear his agonized moans from within the car, but when he looked up and saw me advancing, he scrambled around pathetically as he tried to get out of the car from the passenger side.

Just as he managed to wriggle out, I grabbed him by the back of his collar like he was a dog, pulled him out, and *threw* him against his car. His body hit the metal hard and his scream of pain pierced the night.

"Fucking hell," he cursed as he slid to the ground.

I pulled him up, slammed his body back against the car, and grabbed him by the shirt, forcing him to stare at me. He was a thug with an unkempt stubble covering his face.

"Who sent you?" I snarled.

"You know who did," he muttered. "I'm just meant to send the message that they have their eyes on you. They want you to let them know when you are set up so they can send their man over to your office for the ... apprenticeship."

I felt black rage grip my insides. I was so furious I wanted to kill him. How fucking dare they? How dare they ruin my life?

"You hurt me and you're dead," he said.

I let the anger go. He was just the messenger boy. Even so, I just couldn't leave without taking my anger out on him. He had to pay for the damage he did to my car. I threw my fist and it rammed into his jaw.

He collapsed to the ground with a howl.

I looked down on his sprawled body and sent my own message. "Tell them this," I said. "I am yet to make my decision, so they should wait to hear from me. However, if before then, I find out that I or anyone around me is being followed, then there will be no fucking deal. And no fucking apprenticeships. I will see this thing through to its fucking end. Let's see who will be left alive after the dust settles."

He moaned and I kicked him in the gut and he curled his body into a ball. "Did you get that?"

"I got it! I got it!" he sobbed.

I returned to my damaged car. I turned on the ignition and it roared into life. That was the beauty of German engineering. I sped away into the night.

18

Willow

Two days later

"That phone is going to melt if you keep staring at it like that," Sandra mocked.

I lifted my head from the screen I had been peering at, and slipped it moodily back into my pocket. I was ashamed I had once again been caught staring at it, but it had become my very annoying habit over the last two days. I picked up a broom and began to sweep away the soil and bits of stem from under the table where Sandra had just repotted three plants.

Sandra came over with a bowl of cereal in her hand, and sat on the table I had been sweeping under. "Since he hasn't contacted you, then why don't you contact him?" she asked, as she deliberately and noisily slurped the cereal off her spoon.

"Will you stop slapping your lips like that?" I scolded.

She laughed. "Hey! Hey! Don't take your irritation out on me just because you're too chicken to call him. This is the twenty-first century, you know. You don't have to sit at home and wait for him to call you, you *can* call him."

I sighed deeply, turned away, and continued on with my sweeping.

"Oh for God's sake, just freaking call him," she shouted, exasperated. "You were forward about the kiss right, and see what happened? This is just the next step of your journey into his bed."

"Why do I always have to be the one stepping out first?" I burst out, whirling around to face her.

At first, she had been taking the matter very lightly, the way she always handled her own romantic life, but as she noted the pain on my face and voice, she placed her bowl down and straightened her spine.

"He hasn't even sent one text?" she asked, her voice quiet.

The reminder was painful, and his behavior, absolutely puzzling. We'd had a great time that evening so what had made him lose interest afterwards? Was it because I was too forward? Maybe he was some kind of Alpha, hunter type who preferred to make all the moves.

"Look, maybe he's just been really busy," Sandra said. "Didn't he tell you that he was working on setting up his office here?"

"No one's ever too busy to send a text, Sandra. You've said that yourself a thousand times."

"I know, I know, but maybe he's not into texting. It's very annoying and the practice shouldn't be legal, but unfortunately there are people like that. I usually give them a wide berth, but I will make an exception if they look like Caleb." She grinned.

The phone began to ring and she jumped off the table nimbly and went to the counter to answer it.

"Hello," I heard her say, and my mind immediately tuned it all out. She didn't understand. I couldn't take Caleb lightly. He was not a little romance that I could indulge in and then move on to the next. He was too important to me. He was the man I had dreamed of, waited for all my life. While I continued with my chore, my mind went in never-ending circles as I tried to figure out what I had done wrong, or all the reasons why Caleb had not called, until Sandra rushed over to me. In her haste, she knocked over a pot. I turned around to see soil spill out into the very section I had just cleaned.

My brows drew together in a frown. "What the hell, Sandra."

"Don't worry about it. I'll clean it up," she said, waving her arm dismissively. "You'll never guess who just called."

A small flutter started up in my chest. Almost like the flapping of delicate butterfly wings. "Who?"

"Someone with an order, but a very special order."

The butterfly wings grew in span and strength. They were like the wings of a great eagle inside my chest, and suddenly it was hard to breathe. I became afraid I would once again be disappointed. I kept my expression neutral, but my voice sounded choked as I asked the question. "What flowers did they ask for?"

"Daylilies, but that's not the important part," she said, coming to stand in front of me. "What's important is the person was his lawyer."

I almost couldn't breathe. "Whose lawyer?"

She crossed her arms across her chest. "You know very well whose. Anyway, she said she absolutely loved the bouquet he purchased the other day from us, and that she would like another. However, this new purchase isn't for her, but for him because he has just opened his new office, and she would like to congratulate him on it."

Her smile was wide and filled with excitement, but I just stared blankly at her. I was horribly disappointed. It was not him at all. It was someone else wanting to buy flowers for him.

"How is this good news?" I whispered.

The smile instantly disappeared from her face. "This is good news because I'm going to prepare the bouquet right now and you're going to deliver it."

"I'm not doing that," I said, shaking my head. No, I can't run after a man like that. No way. If he wanted me he would have to make the next move now.

"You're acting like you have a choice," she scoffed. "I'll prepare the bouquet, but I'm not delivering it. It will just rot in here if you don't take it. You decide what's going to happen to it, *boss*."

She turned around and walked away, and I tried to calm my racing mind.

Was this a ploy between him and his lawyer? Was he the one that had told her to order the flowers? What if he wasn't? Wouldn't it be strange if I went to deliver the flowers and he didn't know anything about it? Wouldn't I be unwelcome? Perhaps he didn't even want me to know anything about him beyond what he'd revealed on our date.

I pushed these thoughts out of my mind, and went on with my work. A few minutes later, Sandra called out to me. "I'm done with the arrangement."

I ignored her, but when I didn't hear anything else from her after about fifteen minutes, I went out front and saw the bouquet sitting next to the cash register while she lounged behind the counter, smiling at something on her phone. She hadn't even put the flowers in the cold room.

"What are you doing?" I scolded. "Those flowers are going to wilt."

She didn't even bother looking up at me. "I said I wasn't going to go and I meant it. Anyway, I couldn't go even if I wanted to. I have a severe headache. I'm sorry, boss, I can't help you today."

She giggled then at something she saw on her phone.

Defeated, I sighed and went back into the office to pick up my purse.

I was wearing a pair of shorts and a simple white t-shirt, which although quite casual, I deemed decent enough to go on the errand with. I ran a brush through my hair, reapplied my pale pink lip gloss and slung a satchel purse across my shoulder. Then went back out to the floor. "Where's the address?" I asked, avoiding her eyes.

"All the details are on the envelope by the bouquet's side," she said, laughter in her voice.

With a glare at her, I went over to the bouquet filled with daylilies and carnations. It was a beautiful bouquet, but it needed something more to really lift it. I headed over to the table and added some purple statice and green pitta negra.

After including them, I stood back to judge the completed work.

"And that is why I do repotting and you are in charge of flower arrangements," Sandra called quietly from behind the counter. Her voice was no longer fake-strict or mocking.

I glanced back at her. "Are you sure it doesn't need anything else?"

"Nope. It's absolutely stunning. Perfect, in fact. I think we should take a photo of it and add it to our Collection Album," she said with a smile.

19

Caleb

There was a brief knock to my door, before it was pushed open. Without looking away from my computer screen I could tell by the hurried, heavy footsteps that it was the new derivatives portfolio manager I'd recently hired, Maxwell Garrett.

"Here they are," he said excitedly as he dropped a stack of papers on my desk. "The S&P 500 price return histories for the last five years, as received from Citigroup. I sent the rest of the data from 1926 to your email so it should be in your inbox by now."

I gave the stack a glance. That was going to take me all night to get through. "Thanks."

"Why do you still insist on me printing these out. It would be so much easier to handle them digitally, would it not?"

"I'm using both mediums, but physical copies help my focus." I did not bother to mention how drastically the world had changed while I was locked away. All I had in the prison was one old computer, which I had gotten quite attached to. This dizzying array of new technology was as foreign to me as Chinese or ancient Greek.

"Okay, I also came to remind you that the second round of interviews for the senior investment officer position will be starting in ten minutes. Would you like me to give you a call when we're ready so you can make your way over?"

"No need," I replied as I flipped to the next page. "I'll be there."

He went out and I buried myself in numbers again. I was good at this. This was the only thing that could take my mind off Willow when I was inside. Knowing these numbers would one day be the passport to giving Willow the life she deserved.

Ten minutes later I got up from my chair and without bothering with my suit jacket, I picked up the files of resumés, and was out of the office. When I arrived at Anne, my secretary's table, I found her signing for a huge bouquet of flowers. She looked up at me with a vague smile.

"This came for you. It's from Marie Spencer," she said, but my gaze and senses were completely riveted by the woman standing next to her who was refusing to look at me. My heart lurched.

"I should go," she said to no one in particular, and turned away.

"Willow," I called sharply.

She stopped, and turned around to face me. "Hello," she greeted, stiffly.

The air in the room seemed to freeze over, as for a few seconds afterwards neither of us said a word. Even Anne.

"May I see you for a few minutes?" I asked.

"Uh ... actually, I'm in a rush to make another delivery so maybe ..."

"It'll just be a few minutes," I insisted. I had been behind bars for so long I had not learned there were rules in the dating game. You called a girl back when you were interested. I should have called her. How would she know that in my head she was already mine and everything I was doing was to remove any obstacles standing between us and hasten our coming together? I had fucked up.

"Um ..." Willow looked uncertainly between the speculative expression on Anne's face and mine.

"Anne, please let Garrett know I'll be a few minutes late. This way, Willow," I said decisively and turning around started to return to my office, listening intently for the sound of foot-steps following me. I walked through the door and held it open for her. When she passed through, I shut the door, walked over to my desk and deposited the resumés I was still holding in my hand. Then I leaned a hip against the desk and faced her.

Her beautiful face was expressionless, but I knew she was hurt. I kicked myself for being so insensitive, so stupid. I didn't beat around the bush. "I'm sorry," I apologized. "For not contacting you. Things have been hectic—"

"There's no need for that," she interrupted. "It was just a date, not a marriage proposal or anything. It meant nothing. You're not obligated to contact me."

It was only hurt talking. I had disappointed her and I richly deserved the cold treatment. I stared at her steadily until her gaze faltered and she looked away. I threw all caution to the wind and went towards her. Startled at my sudden approach, she retreated until her back hit the door.

"What are you doing?" she called out hoarsely.

I halted, just two steps away from her and forced myself to take a deep breath. "I'm really sorry, Willow." I apologized, hoping that she could see how much I meant it. "I've been swamped with work. All my focus has been on opening up this office."

My explanation was a partial truth, but it would have to do ... for the moment. Ever since I became aware of being under surveillance, I knew it was better to stay away from her until I got these men off my back. And the only way to make that happen was for me to deliver a viable financial product to them. I'd been knee deep in the research that would confirm if I could actually create what they were asking of me. Once I had that information, I could negotiate harder. I would have the power to demand they stay the fuck away from Willow and me while I created their financial instrument. To that end I had abandoned all else and worked day and night to handle that.

"Alright," she murmured. "I understand."

I took another step towards her and this time she didn't retreat. There was nowhere for her to go anyway with her back pressed defensively against the door.

With a tight smile at me, she turned around and pulled the door open, but I was faster. My hand reached above her head and snapped the door shut again.

She stilled, and so did I. I could see her hand tighten so hard around the handle, her knuckles showed white. Her gaze locked onto mine.

"I have to leave," she announced, breathlessly.

Without taking my gaze off hers, I slid my left arm around her waist, she laid both her palms against my chest and pushed me away. The strength in her arms was puny, futile, useless. I pressed her body hard against mine and she melted into me. There was no more struggle.

"I ... I ... really have to leave," she repeated, her voice thick and hesitant.

I leaned down and buried my face in her neck, deeply inhaling her scent: flowers. Always. Even before she had the flower shop. She always smelled of flowers. Intoxicating, wild flowers she would pick from the fields. I wanted to cry with the memory. Us, lying in a field. It was summer. She was tickling my nose with a flower.

"Caleb," she breathed. It was a protest. I knew that, but I couldn't stop myself. The heat that rolled off her body melded with mine and it was as though I was once again, in the past. I was back in a big open farmer's field. The sun was shining on my face. The baked ground underneath me was hot. There was the sound of a bee buzzing. Willow was laughing. Her golden hair was like the halo of an angel. I was content. I was king of the whole world then.

"Caleb," she called again, and I was back in my office.

I parted my lips and placed a gentle, sensual kiss on the skin just beneath a wildly beating pulse in her throat. Her breath came out in a rush. I felt something inside me weaken and break. How long could I hold myself back? I closed my eyes and savored the heady rush of her taste, before I pulled back, and behaved like a civilized man again.

"I'm sorry," I whispered. It took everything I had to pull away and take a step back. I couldn't rush this. She needed time. Time to fall for me all over again.

She stared straight into my eyes. "Why didn't you call me?"

"I was too occupied," I said lamely. I prayed she would believe me despite how unimpressive the excuse sounded. "I have a project that I need to figure out immediately, so for the last two days I have focused on it completely."

"You could have sent me a text."

That would have been the most convenient option, but it hadn't even occurred to me to do that. I'd been out of the world for too long. "I will," I replied sincerely. "From now on, I'll send you messages every chance I get."

She smiled suddenly and it warmed my heart. I had been forgiven. That was her all over. No matter how bad someone was to her, she was quick to forgive. All they had to do was say sorry. And her bastard uncle knew that.

"Okay," she said and turned around once again to pull the door open.

I knocked it back shut and a frown appeared on her smooth forehead. I only had one question for her. "Why won't you kiss me?"

The scowl fled and she smiled at the reminder of her exact question to me two nights ago. "Are you mocking me?"

"No, but I'm wondering how you thought you could leave without kissing me."

She flattened her hand on my chest, right over my heart. I was certain she could feel the erratic thumping. Then she lifted herself onto her toes and inched closer to me. Our lips touched.

Her kiss was warm and sweet, and I completely lost myself.

She groaned softly into my mouth as I tightened my hold around her waist and pressed her into my hardness.

I kissed her passionately, sucking desperately on her tongue, and drinking in as much of her essence as I could. She tasted like heaven and I could have gone on forever, a knock on the door startled her and she gasped and pulled away.

I couldn't take my eyes off her. "Mr. Wolfe," Maxwell's voice came through the door. "We're waiting for you."

"I'll be right there," I said, never taking my eyes off her. I waited until the footsteps went away before I took a step back. The loss of contact brought a chill to me.

"I'll send you a message," I promised.

She nodded, ran her fingers through her hair, and quickly exited my office.

Outside, Anne and Maxwell were waiting, no doubt curious as to what business I could have with the flower delivery girl. She didn't look any of them in the eye. I watched her almost sprint through the door, and hurry towards the elevator. Only when she disappeared from sight did I return my gaze to the two employees standing before me.

Anne seemed to be fighting back a knowing smile, but saying nothing she turned around and returned to her desk.

Maxwell coughed delicately and I focused on him.

"The file of resumés," he said. "I gave them to you earlier."

"Oh yeah," I replied, dragging my attention away from Willow. "It's in my office. I'll go grab it. You go on ahead."

"See you in the conference room," he replied and went in the opposite direction Willow had gone.

Willow

I received his text just as I got to the first intersection on my journey back to the shop. As I waited at the red light, my heart thudding in my chest, I tried my best to restrain myself from checking it, but I could only wait until I stopped at the next red light. I grabbed my phone and the moment the home screen lit up, I saw the golden words.

Hello Caleb here.

I put the phone down and grinned to myself. Who sends a text like that? But the sensation of joy that flooded my chest couldn't be denied. He made contact. He said he would and he did. I was dying to reply, but I had to wait until I got back to the shop. By that time another message had pinged its way into my phone.

The moment I cut the engine, I unlocked it and read the next message he'd sent.

Sorry for not keeping in touch. I do want to get to know you better, but I have to work late tonight at the office for the next few days. Any ideas?"

I wanted to wait a bit more, to settle my heart before I replied.

"A message like this one will do."

His response came lightning fast.

You got it.

I tried my best to control the smile that was stretching my lips into what must be the biggest, goofiest grin, but the muscles of my face refused to cooperate. I slipped the phone into my pocket, and stepped out of the car onto clouds. I couldn't feel the ground anymore. I was on such a high that it felt like I didn't even need to breath.

When I got into the shop Sandra rushed up to me. I tried my best to keep things neutral, but by the twinkle in her eyes I had not succeeded.

"How did it go?" she gushed.

"It was alright," I replied, heading towards the office.

To my surprise she didn't follow me. I sank into my chair and sighed with delicious contentment. Life was good. At least it was ... until Sandra came in a few seconds later with a broom in her hand. Like a banshee she moved to attack me with it, and I had to jump up from the chair and rush around the other side of the desk.

"What the hell!" I yelled.

"I send you out with all the love and support that you'll need and you come back to me with a pathetic thing like 'it was alright?' What's wrong with you? Don't you know you're not supposed to do that to your best friend?"

"Oh for God's sake," I half-complained and half-laughed, as I caught the broom before she could use it on my face. I dragged it away from her grasp, and put it aside.

She took a seat on one of the chairs in front of my desk. "All right I forgive you. Now, start talking," she said. She raised her eyebrows. "I don't have to remind you we have three more brooms in the storage room."

I laughed and returned to my seat. "Well,' I said, "his secretary was accepting the flowers when he walked in ..." By the time I finished my story her eyes were saucers.

"Now what?" she breathed.

"Now the ball is in his court," I murmured.

21

Caleb

From the moment she left, it became impossible to concentrate.

The candidates we'd invited for their second interviews came in one after the other, but I could barely pay attention to them. All I could think about was the woman that I'd just kissed in my office. It had just dawned on me how easy it was to contact her. I had lived twelve years with her at the forefront of my mind, but unable to see or speak to her. It could now all happen at the press of a button. I was almost overwhelmed with excitement.

"Er ... Mr. Wolfe?"

I looked away from the blank wall that my gaze had been locked on, and found the other two men watching me curiously.

"Do you have any more questions for him?"

I cleared my throat, and made a super-human effort to

concentrate on the task at hand. "Yes, yes, I do."

A few hours later, I looked up from the mountain of research in front of me to realize that the day was gone. Our office was on the eighth floor of one of the few high rises in town. I swiveled my chair around. Behind me were floor-to-ceiling windows that gave a beautiful view of the city's skyline. I had paid big money for this view, but after twelve years staring at a brick wall I knew the value of a view like this. It was price-less. I gazed at the striking sunset, and for a few minutes, I drank in the majestic display of the orange and red hues across the horizon.

It was breathtaking.

There was only one thing wrong with it. I couldn't share it with Willow. Rising, I headed over to the window. I leaned my forehead against the cold glass. Where are you Willow? What are you doing? She was so near and yet so far. I wanted to speak to her. To hear her voice. I pulled my phone out of my pocket and called her.

She picked up after a few rings. "Hello."

"It's me, Caleb," I said, my stomach tightening.

She gave a soft laugh. "I know. I have your number saved on my phone."

I swallowed. I hadn't really thought of what I wanted to say to her. Always in our relationship, she talked and I listened.

Once again, she stepped in to help me. "How has work been so far?"

"Good. What about the flower shop?"

"Things have been good here too," she said.

I couldn't help my smile. I'd never had such a mundane conversation with anyone for the last twelve years, and I loved every single second of it.

"You should be closing soon, right?" she asked. "Or are you working late tonight too?"

I sighed. "I have to. I won't be out of here until past midnight."

She sucked in her breath. "That late?"

"Yeah."

"What about dinner? Don't you have to stop for dinner?"

"I'll order something in," I replied.

"What do you usually get?" she asked.

I tried to imagine her. The only place I could think of her being was at the flower shop. I imagined her at the table where she made her arrangements. Had she stopped working to take this call, or was she working as she talked to me. I imagined the expression on her face. That soft smile.

"Caleb?" she called.

"Uh, sorry. It usually changes. Anne, my secretary, usually asks me what I feel like having, and then orders it before she leaves for the day." I lifted my arm to check my watch. "That should be in about thirty minutes."

"What do you feel like eating today?"

"I have no idea. Most of the time I just let her choose. Food's not that important to me," I replied.

"Do you like Chinese food?"

"Yeah, I like Chinese food."

"There's a place close to my flower shop that makes the best *Lo Mein* and dumplings I have ever tasted."

"I've never had *Lo Mein*," I said softly.

"Should I order some for you then?" she asked.

I had a better idea. Fuck work. I could always get back to it after dinner. "When do you get off work? Why don't we head there together for dinner?"

Silence.

The seconds ticked away, and I began to sweat. Was she going to turn me down?

"No, I don't want to distract you from work. Here's what we'll do instead. I'll get a take out after I close the shop, and come over to your office. We can have dinner there. What do you think of that idea?"

A massive grin broke out across my face.

"That, Willow Rayne, is a brilliant idea."

She laughed and her laughter was like music to my ears.

22

Willow

The security guard was expecting me and he waved me towards the elevator. I thanked him and rode the elevator to Caleb's offices. When the doors swished open, I stepped out into the reception area.

It was a very different scene from the bustling, busy place I had come to earlier. Everyone had gone home, and the network of cubicles beyond was eerily deserted with the lights dimmed. I walked down the corridor, past the glass demarcated meeting rooms on either side, until I reached his office. My shoes had made no sound on the dark gray carpet.

I was nervous and there was a slight tremble to my hand as I lifted it to knock on the door that led to his secretary's office. As I expected I got no response, but I pushed it open and walked in. Her room was empty, and on her table sat the flowers I'd delivered earlier.

I frowned slightly. After all my hard work, he hadn't taken them into his office.

I walked up to them, curled my free arm around the glass vase, and headed towards his door. As my other hand was occupied with holding our dinner I wasn't able to knock. I had just thrust my head forward to lightly bang on his door, when it was pulled open, and I nearly fell through.

Water splashed out of the vase and drenched both of us as he caught me in his strong arms. His eyes moving to the things I had clutched to my chest. His eyebrows flew upwards when he realized what my plan had been. I flushed red with embarrassment.

"Sorry," I mumbled, lowering my eyes.

Laughter flowed from his lips. I lifted my gaze towards his face. He was unbearably beautiful when he laughed. It didn't even seem like he realized the front of his shirt was soaked.

"Were you just about to knock with your head?" he asked, shaking his head.

My cheeks burned even further as he stared at me like he couldn't believe my logic.

"My hands were occupied," I tried to defend myself.

His gaze suddenly softened. It was of course, bizarre and impossible considering we'd just met and hardly knew each other, but that look made me feel as though he adored me to an almost unreal proportion.

"Let's eat before the food gets cold," I muttered.

He took the vase from me and put it down on the coffee table that was in the seating area.

I placed the food on the table next to it, and couldn't help but ask. "Why didn't you bring the flowers into your office?"

He glanced at the bouquet. "Honestly?"

"Of course."

He took his seat and shrugged. "I'm not a huge fan of flowers."

I took my seat next to him. "Really?"

He nodded.

"So why did your lawyer send them to you? It's a strange thing to send to a man if you don't know for sure he loves flowers?"

He smiled at me, my brain began to glitch once again. I wished that I could tell him not to do that too often, or at least without warning because every time he did, my self-control slipped a bit more. Naturally his eyes were cold and hard, but when he smiled like that, he was suddenly transformed into some sort of God, that I wanted to touch, stroke, and just ... just ... lick. Oh God, what was I turning into?

"I think Marie ordered it from your shop because she knew you'd deliver it," he said.

I had been about to unpack the food that I'd gotten us, but I stopped. His statement sounded a bit peculiar ... for several reasons.

"She knows about us? I mean, not us, I realize there is no real us yet, but our date."

"She does." He entertained me patiently, like he had all the time in the world just for me.

Something else bothered me, but I couldn't for some reason, place the worry at that moment so I continued with unpacking the takeout boxes of food. He joined me. We worked silently, with my mind processing the revelation of his lawyer's involvement. I was trying to figure out why it caused that unsettled feeling inside me.

"Why would she want me to come over?" I asked finally.

He met my gaze full-on. His eyes intense. "She knows that I am attracted to you."

"Oh." The uneasy feeling still plagued me. "You seem pretty close to her."

"Not really," he replied. "But I've known her for a long time."

"I see," I said, but I didn't. It was weird. All the boxes of food were finally laid out before us so I handed one to him and picked one for me.

"There's no fork?" he asked as I handed him a pair of chopsticks.

"Don't you know how to use these?" I asked.

He shook his head. "Nah."

I smiled, finding his admission a bit amusing. "Don't worry, I got some forks too, but I thought since you lived in New York you would be an expert at using them."

He put a piece of the chicken into his mouth, leaned back, and chewed on it.

I watched his face, waiting for his reaction. "How is it?" I asked.

"Delicious. You made a good choice," he replied sincerely.

Pride warmed my chest.

23
Willow

We went on eating, and when he asked to taste some of my dumplings I held out the box to him.

"Can I taste yours?" I asked, looking at the carton of pepper beef he was holding.

His lips stretched in amusement. "Haven't you already had it just now?"

I was caught. All I'd really wanted was to share something that was his without even realizing it. My head lowered in embarrassment. "I ... I'm just a bit greedy today."

He offered the box to me, but I was too embarrassed to even look at him, so he turned my face to his and brought a piece of dark meat to my lips. "Be a devil. Have some," he drawled.

I looked into the gorgeous sunburst of blue and ice and black speck in his eyes and my lips automatically parted.

I closed my mouth around his fork, savoring even more than the food, the fact that the white plastic had been in his mouth. Sharing made me feel intimate with him, and it was what I most enjoyed. I barely even tasted the food.

"Another piece?" His voice was thick, and his eyes suddenly veiled.

I shook my head. Words were gone from me. I looked away, needing to collect my scattered thoughts that had scattered like fallen leaves in the wind.

The atmosphere had changed and I had lost my appetite, but I pretended to put another piece of food into my mouth and chewed mechanically. *Stop it, Willow.*

My gaze went over to his big oak desk, and the mess of papers that were strewn all across it. I could never work in such a mess. It would do my head in, but it obviously worked for him. He probably made more money in a day than I did all year.

"You mentioned that you're working on a project. Can I ask what it's about?"

"Of course," he said. "I have a group of overly greedy bastards as clients."

My head whirled around. The expression on his face made me laugh and a bit of food went down the wrong pipe. I started coughing. He leaned forward, grabbed a bottle of water and held it out to me. I accepted it, drank it down quickly. "I'm sorry," I apologized. "It's just your expression ..."

He was leaning back against the sofa, to all intents and purposes in a relaxed pose, but his eyes were strangely alert. I wiped my mouth with the back of my hand and again his gaze became disturbingly sultry.

"I love it when you laugh," he whispered. "Never apologize for it."

It felt as though he was speaking from the depths of his heart which I couldn't understand since we barely knew each other. I felt absolutely speechless. How the hell did we get here so fast? As it stood I was ready to sell my soul to him. I took a deep shuddering breath and forced my gaze back to my food. I felt slightly better when I was not directly looking into the starburst in his eyes. "You were telling me about your project," I croaked.

"Do you know about stock options?" he asked.

"Not one bit," I replied honestly.

"Well, I'm trying to create a type of financial product that will give returns of at least two percent a month."

"Two percent doesn't seem too greedy to me," I ventured.

"It doesn't sound like much, but when you are talking about the kind of volumes they want to attain it becomes a metric that's almost impossible to achieve unless ... it's some form of Ponzi scheme."

I frowned. "Don't they know that?"

"They are aware," he said softly.

My jaw dropped. "They want you to create a Ponzi scheme for them, don't they?"

He nodded slowly.

"And how much are we talking about?"

He sighed. "Millions."

"Wow!" I stopped suddenly. "Ponzi schemes are illegal. Couldn't you go to prison for setting it up?'

"Yeah," he agreed grimly.

"So why are you doing it? Why take the risk? Don't you have enough money already?"

"It's complicated, Willow." His lips twisted into a bitter smile. "They have leverage on me ... for now. But I'm going to clean it all up. I have a plan."

I was suddenly frightened for him. All my dreams of us being together felt fragile, breakable. What if he ended up in prison? I had so many more questions about his background to ask him about, but at the same time, I didn't want to pry too much and make him feel like he was being interviewed. A strange coldness invaded me. I hugged myself and rubbed my arms.

"Trust me. I know what I am doing," he said softly.

"Okay,' I said softly. I looked at him. Suddenly, I was sorry. I had harbored such harsh thoughts about him when in fact, he was being squeezed by people who obviously had something on him. What, I didn't know. But whatever it was it was bad enough to make him do something that could land him in prison. "Now I can see why you've been so occupied. You're completely forgiven for not contacting me in the last two days."

There was a gentle smile across his face. "I wasn't completely forgiven earlier?"

"No," I replied shyly, as my teeth bit down on my bottom lip. I couldn't even look at him.

"That kiss this afternoon, didn't do it?" he teased.

"Really? You thought one kiss should have been enough to obtain my complete forgiveness?"

He turned those incredible eyes on me. I was so painfully aware of him it was becoming harder and harder to breathe.

"What would it have taken?"

I swallowed the lump in my throat and let my eyes slide away. "I'm not sure yet. I'll have to think about it."

He leaned forward and his scent filled my nostrils. It was some expensive cologne, but underneath it there was something familiar. The smell of earth. On a hot summer day. "You smell familiar," I whispered.

Something flashed in his eyes, but it was gone so fast, I thought I imagined it. I felt I was dangerously close to losing my mind. Before I could tell what he was going to do, my chin was in his hand. Then he kissed me. It was fire.

I thought my heart had stopped beating. Molten desire pooled between my thighs, and I lost my head. The box I'd been holding left my hands and tumbled to the floor. I jumped up with a gasp, my heart lurching at the sight of the food that I had spilled onto his new carpet.

"Oh my God! I'm so sorry."

"Don't worry about it," he said.

"Where's your cleaning supplies closet?" I asked, jumping up in a panic. "I'll take care of this right now."

"Willow," he called as he stood and clamped his hands around my arms. His gaze bored into my eyes. "Calm down. It's not a big deal."

"We can't let the food soak into the carpet or it'll leave a stain. Please, just tell me where the cleaning supplies closet is."

"I have no idea where the cleaning supplies closet is," he admitted, "and I have no intention of letting you clean my carpet. If it stains, it fucking stains. So fucking what."

I chewed my bottom lip. "You really don't care."

"No, I really don't care."

"Okay. At least, let me clean it up with a tissue."

He let go of me and stepped away. "Okay, if it's going to make you feel better."

I quickly picked up the food and cleaned up using the paper

napkins and water. Fortunately, it was only lemon squid so I managed to get it looking almost back to what it was. Hopefully, when it dried it wouldn't show at all.

"There," I said, with satisfaction. "That's better."

"Feel better?" he asked, watching me expressionlessly.

"Yup." I popped myself back down on the sofa. We still had some dumplings left and they must be cold by now and the last thing I wanted to do was eat, I leaned forward and reached for them. Through it all I could feel his gaze on me ... watching me, and it made me burn.

"Do you enjoy working at the flower shop?" he asked.

I nodded. "I do. I'm afraid I'm not very ambitious."

"Why do you care about ambition?" he asked. "You should care more about being happy."

I turned to face him, absolutely loving the conviction in his tone at his words.

"I know," I said. "But the expectations of your loved ones are a heavy burden to carry. Plus, I'm adopted, and I know I shouldn't be saying this, but I feel a bit more indebted to them than I probably would have if they were my biological parents."

"I completely understand." Then he leaned forward and without a word, tucked my hair behind my ears as though it was an abominable obstruction to his view of my face. Then he gazed at me with such love in his eyes that I couldn't hold back any longer.

"Why do you look at me like that?" I asked.

"Like how?" he asked.

I forced myself not to hold back. "Like you ... adore me."

24

Willow

https://www.youtube.com/watch?v=WjqYTpE6Qdg

"I do ... adore you," he said quietly.

His answer shocked and confused me. I distinctively *felt* as that was not the first time I was hearing those words from him. He'd said those exact words to me before and I had said something similar back. But of course, he hadn't and neither had I. I must be mistaken, but I couldn't help feeling as if I was dealing with something I couldn't understand. There was also the sense of danger, as if I was stumbling about in the dark and there were monsters prowling all around me.

"I'm done," I said, jumping to my feet. "I should leave so that you can get back to work."

He rose with me, and began to assist me in putting away the

used boxes. He wrapped it all in a plastic bag and as he headed over to a corner to deposit it in the wastepaper basket I headed over to his windows. I wanted to leave, but I couldn't help myself. The view was so striking. I had never seen Folsom from this high up before.

"This is beautiful," I said.

"It's even better when you look at it with the lights off," I heard him say from behind me. The monsters were waiting in the dark. I didn't turn around to face him.

"Could you turn the lights off then? I want to see it."

A second later, I heard a click and the entire room was thrown into darkness, offset only by the illumination of the town's skyline beyond.

I heard him come up to me. Just as I had expected and hoped, he stood behind me. He was so close I could feel lovely heat from his body.

As though programmed to respond, I took a step backwards, and leaned my frame into his.

His arms encircled my waist, and I couldn't ignore the fact that I felt more at home in his embrace, than I ever had in my own body. We both watched the skyline lit by thousands and thousands of little lights, and didn't say a word. Simply content to bask in each other's presence. But as my awe at the splendor of the skyline before me began to fade into the background, I became more and more aware of the hard solidity of his body. I had never leaned on a man like this and it felt so damn good.

The sweet ache in my core that had made my nerves taut with tension all evening, began to intensify. My fingers began to stroke the skin of his arms, and in response his arms tightened around me. I didn't know how to ask for what I wanted. I wished I was Sandra. She would have just turned around, wrapped her arms around his neck, and kissed him naturally, but me. I was frozen to the spot.

I battled internally with myself: how to delicately let him know that I wanted him to fuck me out of my mind, and when I couldn't find the guts I gave up with a sigh.

It was time to leave anyway. I tried to pull out of his hold, but he wouldn't let me go. His arms were underneath my breasts now and with the way they were bunched up, he might as well have been touching them.

Suddenly, I found my courage. What did I have to lose? I began to slowly grind my ass into the bulge in his pants, and before long, my effect on him was apparent. He became as hard as rock.

I moved my hands from his arms and wrapped them around his neck. My chest jutted forward, as my gyration against his groin continued. My intention couldn't be clearer.

"Touch me," I groaned.

He leaned down to place a soft kiss on the skin that shielded the pulse in my neck. Then his arms loosened, and began to move up the outline of my body towards my breasts. The sinking of his hands into the soft swells of my breasts was so intimate and erotic, I was convinced that it was enough to make me orgasm right then, but I bit my lip and hung on.

He ran his palms lightly against my hardened nipples.

The agonizing ache between my legs intensified, and my whole body began to pulse with anticipation. When his hands covered my heavy and tender breasts through the cotton material, I felt as if I was being pulled into a trance of pure arousal. The pads of his thumbs circled and stroked my nipples as I writhed helplessly against him. I was beyond logic or rational thinking. Instead a primitive, almost animal instinct took over.

Which was good because if I had thought about what I was doing I would most probably talk myself out of it; I didn't know him enough ... it was too soon. The attraction I felt to this man was overwhelming, and the build up inside me was agonizing, excruciating, almost unbearable. I needed some sort of release, and he was the only one that could give it to me.

I found the courage to turn around and meet his gaze.

The dark made it easier, easier for me to watch him as boldly as I wanted to. The shadows in the room fell softly on his face, but through it all, the ocean blue of his gaze remained piercing, boring into the depths of mine.

I slanted my head and kissed him, deeply and passionately, until it felt as if my bones had begun to melt inside of my body. I clung to him just for the ability to remain on my feet. As my breathing grew harsher he fanned my clawing need with the sensual languid strokes of his tongue.

Our breathing filled the quiet room, the pattern harsh and

ragged, and it turned me on even more. When I pulled away from his lips, I traced hot, needy kisses along his jaw and down to his neck. I couldn't think. I was like an animal. Feral. Shameless. Greedy. I needed to have his bare, heated skin on mine. My hands went to the first button of his shirt and began to desperately unfasten it. His hands closed around my wrists and stopped me. He couldn't speak immediately, so I watched his lowered head and shut eyes as he tried to get himself under control enough.

I was just as flustered, my heart pounding violently in my chest.

"Willow," he whispered. "Let's not go any further. Anymore, and I won't be able to control myself."

My heart skipped several beats at his words. He was restraining himself on my account. "I don't want you to control yourself. Do whatever you want to me."

His eyes shot open to meet mine. They were dark with longing, and somewhat filled with lust at the explicit permission I'd just granted for him to do whatever he wanted to with me.

"Are you sure?" he asked softly, as if he didn't believe his own ears.

I nodded. "I am."

But he still hesitated, his hands tightening around my wrists. "You're sure we're not moving too fast?"

I took a step back away from him, and the moment he let me go I grabbed the ends of my shirt and pulled it over my head. In the dimness of the room, I caught the hunger in his eyes. It glittered. I could never have in a million years realized then what I'd just signed up for. Before much could register, I was caught in his arms and my feet cleared off the floor. I gasped with shock at the suddenness of his attack.

"Hold on tight," he said, his voice deeper and raspier than I had ever heard it. With his hands firm underneath my thighs, he locked my legs around his waist. My entire body tingled. I could feel the heat of his body through our clothes. It made my open, wet pussy tingle.

He began to move, with me clinging to him and with his eyes heavy lidded with sensuous anticipation. He carried me to his desk and without taking his eyes off me, he swiped away the crazy mess on it, and deposited me on the surface.

His hands worked the clasps of my bra and the lacy material was unceremoniously tugged down my arms.

A little fear struck my heart then. I had the sensation I'd been put on a desk before. Not by him. Someone else, but I didn't know who. It felt real, but maybe it was just a dream. A bad dream. I was crying and saying no. I swallowed hard. Some of the lust was suddenly gone, but I couldn't really say no. It was too late to go back. I wasn't a cock tease. His mouth closed around one of my breasts and the memory or dream of ... of being raped on a desk went away.

I completely lost myself.

My head fell backwards as he sucked hard on the hard bud. I wanted to call out his name, but I'd forgotten it, and mine for that matter. It was as though my brain had disintegrated, as I gradually lost control over my own body.

His mouth moved from one breast to the other, molding the supple flesh in his hands and sucking feverishly as though he worshipped me. He bit them and I moaned. Waves of sensation washed over me. I knew I was close to climaxing. When I thought I was close to orgasm, he moved away from my nipples altogether and began to trace kisses down my torso. I watched as he headed downwards. I was completely overwhelmed with the need to come. When he reached the band of my shorts, he returned his gaze to mine and gave a low but sharp command.

"Lock your arms around my neck."

I immediately obeyed, and without taking my gaze from his he lifted me just slightly off the table. In no time, the band was unfastened and the pull of my zipper rang out across the room. This would be my first time. Well, the first time that I would be aware of. As I had grown up, I had come to realize that I'd been touched before. I instinctively knew how things worked, but I couldn't remember any of it. Perhaps I'd lost my virginity to some boy during the time my memories were lost.

"You will never regret this," he muttered, and the emotion in his words struck me.

Tears stung my eyes at the promise, and I couldn't understand why.

"I will protect you," he swore as he pulled the shorts from the curve of my ass. "I will take care of you, and I will make sure that you're the happiest woman on earth."

I was so shocked by his intense promises I couldn't speak. He pulled my shorts down my legs, and tossed them aside. My legs were jerked apart, and all I had on before him was a lacy white thong, and I knew that the thong had moved while he was carrying me and it was now stuck between my pussy lips. I wanted to pull it out, but I couldn't move. My heart was pounding so hard in my chest I could barely breathe. He stared down at the quivering, wet flesh in front of him as if he was mesmerized. Finally, he raised his gaze up to me.

"Oh, Willow. How beautiful you are," he breathed.

He lowered to his knees, and my heart lurched when I realized what he was about to do. He was going to do that thing that Sandra loved. He was going to eat me out.

My legs instantly tried to close shut but he grabbed the underside of my thighs, and kept them wide apart.

"No, don't. I've been dreaming of this."

He began to trace hard, heated kisses along the insides of my thighs.

Soon he arrived at my pussy and he pressed his face hard and shamelessly against it. Then he took a good, hard inhale of my sex. Surely, this was not normal. Surely men and women didn't smell each other like this. I felt myself begin to unravel.

25

Willow

"Caleb?"

"You smell like heaven, Willow," he said to me, his voice gruff.

Gripping the lace he pulled it to the side, and I was fully exposed to his hungry eyes. I felt the cool air in the room brush across my sex, and the exposure made me shudder. I had never been so glad then that he had turned the lights off before all of this began. Without warning he opened his lips wide and sucked my entire sex into his mouth. I wanted to shut my legs. This was too intimate ... too unnerving, too incredible.

But my sex was trapped inside his mouth, and from the look of things he wasn't going anywhere. For a while I just felt nothing but pleasure at the sensation of his hot mouth working my entire pussy. My hands violently gripped the edge of the table and my eyes rolled to the back of my head, as intense tremors coursed through me at the erotic stimulation.

"Caleb," I rasped, but he was just starting.

He moved back slightly and his tongue shot out. He started licking me from the base of my sex, all the way to the engorged bud at the top. He licked me diligently, like a dog licking a plate, as if he was savoring the liquid pouring out of me, as if it was the sweetest thing he'd ever tasted.

His lips closed around my clit and that was my undoing.

The intensity of his suction, coupled with the diligent stroke of his tongue across the immensely sensitive tip, made me almost fly off the table. I grabbed onto his head, trying my hardest to push him away, but at the same time caging him in place with my legs and grinding my pussy into his face.

He ravished me with an insatiable hunger, until my body arched into a deep bow and my hands clawed into his silky hair, as the rolling waves came and swept me away. I saw stars, I saw colors. It was indescribably beautiful. It was like nothing I'd ever experienced. The ecstasy was so intense I felt as if I was outside my body and flying. But eventually, my body collapsed onto the desk and my hips jerked like a caught fish at the aftermath of his onslaught.

With my body spread out across the surface, I slowly became aware of the rapid rise and fall of my chest. "Oh God," I gasped. He straightened and loomed over me.

I licked my lips. There was a smile across his face as he made quick work of the buttons of his shirt. I watched as he peeled the fabric off his strong, lean body and then once again gripped my thighs.

"Wait, Caleb," I started to plead. I didn't think that my body could contain the extent of pleasure that he was wreaking through it. I was going to lose my mind.

But before I could say another word, he ripped the tiny soaked thong from my body and flung the scrap of material behind him. One sharp tug and I was hanging just off the edge of the table. To my shock, once again he returned to his knees.

His tongue rimmed between the folds of my sex, and then proceeded to suck feverishly on the pulsing opening of my sex. I cried out when he dipped his tongue into me. Whatever reservations I'd had disappeared like a wisp of smoke in a tornado.

God, I wanted this.

I moaned when the pad of one of his fingers replaced the assault of his tongue and stroked up and down the slit of my sex. Then he thrust it into me, gently and carefully, before pushing it all the way through.

My hips bucked at the delicious intrusion. Lazily, he finger-fucked me. It was maddeningly good. But as I prepared myself to enjoy the sensation, another finger was thrust in. It was a tight fit, but it felt good.

"Yes," I gasped.

Then he inserted a third.

"Caleb," I cried out, my head rising off the table.

"Shhh ..." he said. "I'm just stretching you, baby. Getting you wet and ready for me." With three fingers inside me he rose to his feet and swung one arm around my waist to hold me firmly in place.

His fingers began to move expertly inside of me. I was clenched so tightly around those digits I could feel every curve and protrusion of his fingers as he thrust them into the depths of my core. He began with a gentle, lazy motion but then his pace quickened. My hips writhed of their own volition, pumping to meet the rhythm of his drive, then he leaned forward, and began to ram into me fast and hard. My back flew off the table.

"Holy fuck!" I cried out at the heightened burst of pleasure, but he had no intention of stopping or slowing down.

To my horror, I began to gush liquid.

"Caleb, stop!" I half screamed, but he wouldn't listen. And it was a good thing he didn't because the waves were already coming for me. I grabbed his shoulder and held on for dear life, my nails digging into his skin.

I was mere seconds from an explosion when he lowered his head and sucked my clit into his mouth. He was sucking and ramming mercilessly into me.

Pleasure washed over me in brutal waves and I came with a piercing scream, my hips jerking and rocking maddeningly into his relentless tongue. But still he didn't stop or move away until I collapsed back onto the table.

"Oh God," I cried out, tears burning my eyes. I could register nothing beyond the violent trembling of my body and the erratic pounding of my heart.

He lapped at me, greedily licking up every bit of my cream. The velvety pressure of his tongue, prolonged my torment. Still, he knew to keep away from my clit. It felt so swollen and sensitive I could feel the warm air he exhaled as he breathed over it. When he had cleaned me up he rose to his feet, and grabbing my arms, pulling me to him. I wrapped my arms around his neck.

"How was that, Willow?" he asked.

I wanted to bite him, to cause him some sort of pain because of how raw he had just made me. "You're dangerous."

He laughed and crushed his lips to mine. The smoky-sweet taste of my sex still lingered on his tongue.

"Hmm," a deep moan flowed out of me as I kissed him back. Reluctantly, I let him pull away.

He looked at me as if I was a juicy piece of steak and he was starving. I thought of the condom Sandra had put into my purse. I knew I should take it out now, but I had waited for this man all my life and I couldn't bear the thought of something even that thin between us. He was a man of the world. Maybe he would bring it up, but even though I just met him this was no casual thing for me. He was the first and only man I'd ever wanted in my life, and I felt as if I'd known him for a lifetime. In fact, it already seemed as if he held my soul in his hand.

"What now?" I whispered, as my hands gently caressed the myriad of inked designs on his smooth, sculpted chest.

With his scorching gaze on me, he began to work the buckle of his belt. In no time his pants were undone. Smoothly he pushed the material, along with his briefs, down his hips, and his cock sprung free.

Now I understood why he had said he needed me to be really ready and wet first. His cock was eye-wateringly massive. Stunningly thick and erect, it was pale in the dark with light green veins snaking along its surface. Those snakes pulsed making it look angry and beautiful.

Like a child examining a new toy I reached out to touch that beautiful cock, my hands circling around the base. He let me. I sized him up with my hands, my fingers running across the bulging veins that ran down the length. I wished now that the lights were on so that I could see him properly. As I stared at his cock in fascination it jerked and a drop of pearly cum appeared on its eye.

How strange. I wanted to lick it. To taste him. To close my mouth around the thick head and to suck it hard. I let my eyes drift upwards. "Can I suck your cock?"

Something flashed in his eyes. A need so strong it looked like it was tearing him apart. Shocked, my hand reached up, as if to comfort him.

But he clenched his jaw and shook his head. "No. If you do I won't be able to control myself any longer."

"Do we need a condom?" I blurted out.

"I'll use one if you want to, but I'm clean as a whistle. I haven't been with anyone for twelve years."

I blinked. "Twelve years?"

"Yes, twelve fucking years," he growled as he pulled me toward him suddenly, and covered my mouth with his. I felt his thick, hard cock press into my stomach.

That desperate need in his eyes made me assume he would immediately thrust into me, but, and as I was slowly beginning to find out, he was obsessed with teasing me until I danced on the point of madness.

He changed his position and stroked the mushroom head of his cock up and down my slit, smearing his cum on my sex, then he rubbed the entire shaft between my pussy lips until his whole cock was completely coated from root to tip in my slickness.

The heat rolled off him in waves, and I could feel my own sex spasm in anticipation of being filled to bursting by him. I couldn't wait any longer. I licked my lips, eager to have him inside of me. The need to be filled and stretched by him was almost violent.

"Fuck me," I rasped out.

His eyes were so dark they were almost black as he took hold of his cock, and positioned it at my entrance.

Excitement buzzed through me like a drug. He started to push into me, and my eyes fluttered shut. God, he felt unbearably big, much bigger than I had imagined. If I had not been looking down and watching his cock enter me I would have thought someone was trying to thrust a freaking football into me. It felt as if he was splitting me in two. For a moment, I doubted it would be possible for him to go any further. And yet I was desperate for him to fill up that empty hole inside me.

"You okay?" he asked, concern in his voice.

I nodded.

"I'll go slow," he promised.

My hands went to grab the clenched cheeks of his ass and he took his time, filling me inch by excruciating inch until he was about halfway into me. The discomfort was gone. I felt beautifully stretched. It was wonderful.

Then he gripped the underside of my thighs, and with a hard thrust, rammed the rest of his length into me. My sex convulsed around him, greedy and ecstatic. The moment I had waited for all my life was here. I was finally complete.

26
Caleb

I almost couldn't believe it was happening. To her, this was probably just a great time with an attractive stranger, but to me this was everything. For twelve years, all I'd been able to think about was the day I would be joined to the missing piece of me that had been torn away all those years ago.

And tonight, it had finally happened. I had always imagined it would be in the most lavish of places, befitting of the treasure she was to me, but looking at her now spread out on my desk, it seemed perfect.

As she shuddered against me, I looked down at her in awe. This was the woman of my dreams. The one that I had given up everything for. My Willow.

I had my dick in her, but I still didn't feel worthy of her. She was too fine, too good, too precious for me. But there was no one else worthy of her either. I told myself, I didn't deserve her but no one else in the world could love and cherish her the way I could. And that was that.

"Caleb," she breathed as if in wonder, and raked her nails down my back.

How I loved the sound of my name on her lips. I began to pull out of her, and the sensation of my flesh moving along the tightness of her walls almost made me lose my mind. She was so fucking tight, even more so than I had imagined. But I caught myself. This was all for her, and I needed to make it as amazing as possible. And I needed to make it last for as long as I could.

I stopped the moment my tip reached her opening. I felt her arms tighten once again around me as she readied herself for another thrust. I heard her low whimper, and was glad that she couldn't see the raw, exposed, and completely vulnerable expression that must be on my face.

This went way beyond sex for me. This was love, and my heart almost couldn't take it.

I lifted her slightly off the desk, and in one fluid thrust, slammed back into her.

She bucked at the force of my plunge, her back arching at the agonizingly sweet torment.

"Holy cow!" she yelped. "Jesus. You're so deep."

I had reached the end of her, so I began to writhe my hips slowly to find the exact spot that would blow her mind.

Judging by the moans and the tightening of her grip around my neck, I got an inkling of where the best angle of my lunges should be directed to and got to work.

My hips settled into a delicious rhythm that was a mixture of slow and fast plunges. My thrusts would be leisurely long with pauses, then when her teeth were almost on edge with frustration I would attack her with a burst of crazed, merciless drives that completely unraveled her. She was struggling for air as she clung to me.

I savored every single movement of this dream so I could replay it in my mind over and over again for the rest of my life.

I watched the range of emotions that ran across her face, from frustration, to pleasure, to joy and bliss. Then to pure wonder.

And all the while I fell more and more in love with her mesmerizing beauty. I wanted to forever be the only man she allowed in her body, the only man she showed this side of herself to.

Without warning a remembrance of her abuse from twelve years earlier came to mind, and a scorching wave of anger overtook me. I wanted to erase every trace of him from inside her. I pounded harder and harder into her, and suddenly tears were pouring down my cheeks.

"Caleb," she called.

But I couldn't stop. I had lost total control of my own body. I was exorcising the horror of him from her body. I had to. For my own sanity. I fucked her with every iota of strength I had inside of me, and when it still didn't seem nearly enough, I plopped her down on the table and grabbed her thighs.

"No," she panted, her skin slippery and slicked with sweat as she tried to get away from me, but I couldn't let her go. Like a man possessed I couldn't stop.

"*Caleb!*" she screamed.

Finally, her voice got through the fog in my brain and I froze. I stared at her in shock. "Have I hurt you?" I gasped, horrified by what I had done.

Her hand reached out to touch my wet cheek. "No! I ... I just thought ... I ...you looked like you had ... I don't know ... lost control," she whispered. Her eyes were enormous.

I took a deep breath. "I had," I admitted. I forced my lips to twist into something that looked like a smile. "You have that effect on me. Do you want me to stop?"

Her cheeks were flushed and her eyes never left mine as she shook her head and said clearly, "No. I want you to continue. In fact, I want you to lose control again."

I pulled her forward until her ass was just on the edge. The heavy desk scraped across the floor in protest with every violent ram into her. I thought I wouldn't lose control again. I thought I would be able to handle myself, but I became possessed again with need to own her. I fucked her like a wild beast.

I drove into her, as she rode the storm of ecstasy that I knew was going to completely knock her out. I was hanging by a thread, but I ignored my own enjoyment, just to be sure she had the best fuck she possibly could.

"Oh God," she moaned as she began to quicken.

She crushed her lips to mine as her body shattered.

I felt the orgasm tear through her body with the force of a storm. Her head wrenched away and I watched in wonder as her trembling body arched into a tight bow. Her breasts jutted out and her head fell back. In soft light the whites of her eyes gleamed, as she fought against the unraveling of her body and soul. As she flew among the stars I continued to fuck her. I wanted to prolong her orgasm for as long as possible.

Then I felt my own climax begin its approach. I rode on until I was a breath away from exploding, and quickly pulled out of her and let a violent stream of my semen burst out of me and spray on her belly. I couldn't hold back my growl at the earth-shattering pleasure of watching my seed all over her belly. One day it would be growing inside her, but today I was content to paint her with my cum.

I relished the continued spill of my release as the pleasure continued to pump out of me.

My hand went to my cock to milk the rod of every bit of molten lust that remained and sprayed her breasts with it. It took me a few more minutes to come to my senses. When they finally did, I lifted my gaze to see there was a smile on

Willow's face as her body continued to jerk at the orgasm that had just rocked her. At the sight of her so spent and smeared with my cum, I couldn't help the burn of pride that filled my chest.

My Willow. My woman.

27
Willow

I returned home in a daze.

For the first few minutes after Caleb had wrecked me, neither of us had been able to move. I had laid sprawled across the table and he'd collapsed next to me. I was too drained to even care that my legs were wide open and I had his cum all over my body. Without thinking, instinctively, I rubbed his seed into my skin. Then I brought my fingers to my mouth and tasted him. He tasted of strength and musk and wood and leather. He tasted beautiful. I turned my head and saw him watching me. And I didn't care. We said nothing.

"Play with yourself," he whispered.

It never even crossed my mind to disobey. My hand moved to my pussy and I began to circle my swollen clit. It felt unbearably erotic to be masturbating on his desk while he watched me. He rose and switched on a desk light. I didn't care that I would be completely exposed to him. He came and stood in front of me so he had a clear view of my open pussy and what I was doing to it. I played with myself gently. It was more of a show I was putting on for him than anything else, but to my shock I felt my climax begin to rise inside me in seconds. He slipped his fingers into me and finger fucked me as I came. Right there, in front of him, my body went into multiple orgasms. Again and again the waves came. Each more beautiful. Then I felt his mouth on my clit, his tongue greedily lapping my juices. And I came again. All I could feel was his tongue, drinking from me. As if he couldn't stop. As if I was a cool brook of sweet water he'd found in a harsh desert.

Slowly, the exploded fragments of my brains began to come back together.

When he cleaned me up with his tongue, he rose and stood over me. I would never be able to forget the raw emotion in his gaze.

"You're mine. You know that, don't you?"

I'd nodded like a controlled puppet. All my feminist views flew out of my head. I wanted to be his. I didn't know what would have happened next if my phone had not rung. I jumped off the desk like a startled cat. I knew it would be my mother, wanting to know where I was. I'd promised her we'd clean out the linen closet together. I didn't want to lie to her so I told her I was leaving without saying where I was leaving from and ended the call.

We didn't speak as we dressed. There was no need for words. Anyway, I was too mind-blown to make small talk. He walked me out of his office building right to my van and waited until I got in.

"I ... I had a ... a good time," I mumbled lamely. It felt sacrilegious to reduce the experience to a good time, but I didn't know what else to say.

He smiled softly, and I knew he understood. "So did I."

I saw him in the rearview mirror standing there all alone watching me and part of me hurt to leave him. It wanted desperately to turn the van around and go back to him, but I didn't. I just kept on driving. My mother was waiting for me. Anyway, I needed to get my head together. I was a mess.

When I arrived home my dad was having his second dinner of the evening, and my mom was busy putting together a pumpkin pie. "There you are," she said cheerily.

I forced a smile to my lips as I went over to give my father a hug.

"How was business?" he asked.

"It was not bad," I said, nodding absentmindedly. There was some more light chatter, but I couldn't stay with them for long. I had memories to revisit and process.

"Mom, call me when you're ready to tackle your closet," I told her and hurried up the stairs. When I got to my room, I threw myself onto my bed and closed my eyes. I thought of the orgasms that Caleb had wrung out of my body. I could still feel light tremors of it buzzing through me. I'd never thought sex could feel this amazing.

I had never been particularly taken with the idea of sex. The idea of a man pumping away into me filled me not with curiosity, but slight revulsion. The whole thing seemed dirty to my mind. Whenever Sandra or my other friends went into detail of the men they'd had sex with, I cringed inwardly.

I never told anyone, but secretly, I thought I was frigid.

But with Caleb, I had unraveled without a second thought. I should have been intimidated by him, by his sophistication, that aloof air that hinted at danger, instead I felt at home with him, as though I had known him all of my life.

Why?

My phone vibrated with an alert, and my heart lurched into my throat.

Have you reached home?

I read the message over and over again, wishing with all of my heart I'd just stayed with him like my heart had told me. Maybe I would be in his arms or fucked once again into oblivion.

I sent my reply.

I just did. Thanks. (smiley face emoji)

Almost immediately afterwards, he responded.

Good. Sleep tight. We'll speak tomorrow.

He was ready to call it a night or maybe he was going to continue working, either way there was something I had to clarify.

You said something earlier ... maybe it was just the amazing sex talking ha, ha (laughing face emoji). But you said that I'm yours. What did you mean exactly? (confused cat face emoji)

I wrung my hands anxiously after I sent the message and waited for his response. It came in seconds.

I meant exactly that. You're mine.

I couldn't control my smile as I read his response, but it was still somehow vague. I wanted him to spell it out but I didn't want to look too attached. I sent him a goodnight message with a kissing face emoji, and put the phone away from me. My mother called up to me and I went to help her re-arrange the linen cupboard. At least three times, my mother stopped, and with amusement asked me, "What are you smiling about?"

"Nothing much. Just happy," I said.

～

The next day, Bradley brought some magnolias to the shop and when Sandra wasn't paying attention, I quickly cornered him outside and asked my question.

"What does it mean when a guy says that you're his?"

He paused for a moment, as he pulled his soil stained gloves from his hands. "Hm... it generally means exactly that."

"So, like a girlfriend?"

He narrowed his gaze. "Yeah, but it's a bit more. It's more of a passionate claim. Well, that's my opinion, anyway. It's how I would use it. Why are you asking?" His eyes were filed with curiosity. "Did someone say this to you?"

"Umm ... no," I lied. "I read it somewhere and was just curious."

"Phew," he let out a deep breath. "I thought I'd have to go fight someone. You and Sandra are mine," he joked.

"Umm okay ... Bradley," I said, but I cringed inwardly. I didn't need pity from him. Instead of messing about with me he should stop being such a coward and go say those words to Sandra.

"What are you two whispering about?" Sandra asked, coming over.

"I was just telling Willow you and her are mine."

She laughed. "In your dreams."

The phone rang then I went to answer it.

28
Caleb

Taking a deep breath I took the call. I reminded myself that I was doing this for Willow... for us. So that we both could be left in peace. I said nothing while he introduced himself as Finnegan. He had a slimy voice that made my skin crawl. I'd met hundreds of men like him inside. Psychopaths.

"We'll send our guy over on Monday," he slimed.

I felt my free hand clench into a fist, but my voice was quiet. "No."

Willow might decide to come to the office, and I didn't want her anywhere close to these bastards. Besides, I knew men like him and his lot. If you give them an inch, they will take a mile. As soon as I allow one person into my premises they'll start to behave as if they own me and the business.

I laid out my own demand. "I work alone and I don't want any of you hanging around here. I've made headway on the product, so in about a week I'll meet with whomever you want wherever you want, and show you the ropes of how it works. And then we'll be done. You just make sure it's someone with a brain because I'm not going to repeat myself."

"Sure, sure," Slimy said.

I ended the call and turned to stare unseeingly out of the window. I didn't trust that oily voice. "Sure, sure," was always bad news. I already knew giving them a powerful vehicle to cheat the system would never be the end of it. It would just be the beginning. They would always want more and more until I got caught and sent back inside.

But even more than that I didn't want to have another Ponzi system that ruined the lives of thousands of innocent people on my conscience. When I had created my first one I had been a naïve kid. I had actually believed Frank when he said it was simply a learning tool. A way for me to learn the ropes.

"Once you have created such a vehicle, you will understand exactly how the market works," he said.

Well, he was right about that, it was indeed a great teacher, but the thing I'd created was so brilliant he sold it behind my back. The people he sold my monster to unleashed it on the public. Five years later, I read about my creation in the news. The thing had sucked millions into it, and it was called the worst scam in the history of the stock market.

That was the day I fell out with Frank.

No one knew I was the creator and no one pointed a finger at me, but the guilt of seeing the frightened, lost faces of those pensioners who had lost their life savings haunted me for years. Some chosen patsies went to jail and their fortunes were confiscated, but there was no way to claw back the bulk of the hundreds of millions that had simply disappeared. There was nothing anyone could do for those unfortunate people. I swore that day I would never again be so careless with my talent with numbers.

Never again would I put myself in that position.

I had bought myself a week to find a way to free myself and even though I felt angry and frustrated that I was again in a position where I was being asked to do something that would definitely land me back in prison, I was determined to find a way to beat them at their own game. I was a smart guy and one way or another I was going to find a way out for me and Willow. I had to.

I turned away from the window, I couldn't lose the faith. I had Willow to think of. Who would take care of her if I was inside? I had programmed her number on speed dial and before I knew it my finger had already pressed her name.

"Are you alright?" I asked as soon as she picked up.

"Yeah," she replied, slightly out of breath. "I'm sorry. I was outside."

"Have you had lunch?"

"Not yet."

"I'll come over. Let's eat together."

"Really?" She was breathless once again.

A smile slipped onto my lips. It was the Willow effect. No matter how bad I felt she always made the sun shine again in my world. "What do you want?"

"A burrito bowl, from that village bistro opposite your office building. They have another branch at Berkeley and it's the best burrito bowl I've ever tasted."

I didn't even know there was a bistro opposite my office building. "Alright. I'll be there soon."

I picked up the food and drove to her shop. The door tinkled when I pushed it open. Inside it was quiet so I went past the counter, and headed out back. The back door was open and it led out to a fenced, small concrete courtyard that she had turned into a garden.

It held an impressive array of flowerpots and hanging baskets. I found her on her knees, a big sunhat on her head, and her face turned in my direction. She had been planting seedlings into a wooden trough filled with soil.

"Hey," I called softly.

I felt my heart slam against my chest. The past tumbled into my head. How many times had she looked at me like that, with that same expression. It saddened me that our wonderful past was lost to her, but I reminded myself that it was better this way. I watched her face light up with excitement.

"Hey," she greeted shyly, jumping to her feet.

I went over to her, and without even hesitating pulled her

into my arms. I captured her lips in mine and quickly lost myself in the kiss. This was what mattered. Only this. I could beat those men. I was smarter than them.

The trowel she had been holding fell from her hand, but neither of us paid attention to it. The kiss was intense. Her gloved arms wrapped around my neck, while I grabbed onto her leg and raised it up so she could feel my hardness against her sex.

With my hands on her ass to hold her in place, I bent my knees and ground my cock into her. Our tongues swirled in a passionate dance, as we shared without words just how much we had missed each other over the last two days.

When I finally broke the kiss, she was panting, struggling to catch her breath.

I waited as she leaned her head against my chest, and when she was finally recovered enough, she lifted her eyes up to mine. In the bright sunlight, I could see the golden patterns in her lovely brown eyes.

"I missed you too," she said with a smile.

And I kissed her once again. I wanted to take her back into the shop, lock the doors and take her right there, but I forced myself to exercise some control.

"There's no one manning the shop," I said.

She grinned. "Oh, Sandra is meant to do that, when she heard you were coming she suddenly realized she had to run an errand in town that could take up to three hours."

"I like the way your friend thinks," I murmured.

She blushed a delicious pink.

God, she was so beautiful she made my heart ache. "Don't you worry someone would come in and steal your stuff while you're out here, though?" I asked, because I couldn't tell her what was in my heart.

She started taking off her gloves. "I'm listening carefully. I run out every time the bell rings."

"You didn't when I came in." I pointed out.

"That's because I knew it was you." She held up her phone. "'I can view the camera's display from my phone."

I nodded. "Do you want to eat now?" I asked, "or do you want to round up first?"

"How long do you have?" she asked.

"As long as you want."

She stuck her finger in my chest. "I'm serious."

"Alright, about an hour and a half, but I can get away with two."

"There's twenty minutes of work left to do here, so I'll just leave it until you've gone."

I looked at the seedlings she was planting and rolled up my sleeves. "No, you won't. I'll help you."

"But you have to go back to work. You'll be all sweaty."

"I like getting sweaty with you," I mocked.

"Stop it," she warned sternly, but her cheeks were flaming.

"Or what?" I drawled.

She wasn't playing that game. "Just wait a few seconds then," she said and hurried away. She returned with a large pair of gloves, a kneeling pad and a straw hat that had seen better days. She handed the gloves over to me, dropped the pad on the ground, and placed the hat on my head. Then she leaned away to admire her work.

"There!" she cried. "You're protected."

"Thank you," I replied, as I thought of the men I had lived with in prison and how they feared me. If they could see me now. I tried to get my hands into the gloves, but they were too small, which was a good thing because I wanted to feel the soil on my hands. It had been too long since I felt good, honest soil on my skin.

After briefly instructing me on what to do with the seedlings, we worked together in silence. She would never know how much I appreciated working with those seedlings. The thin velvety stems, the cool feel of the dark earth between my fingers. The heat of the sun on my back, the total peace of being next to her.

It was over too soon and she stood and surveyed our handiwork.

"Let's go wash up," she said.

We went together to the big butler's sink at the back of the shop. We took turns washing our hands. She went before me and after she was done, she moved back and stood behind me wiping her hands on a towel.

There was a mirror over the sink and I watched her reflection through it, her heat flushed face adding a vibrant sheen to her complexion. It gave me an almighty erection just to see her like that.

"Are we officially dating?" she asked, meeting my eyes in the mirror.

"Of course we are," I replied. "I thought I made that clear the last time." I turned with my hands still wet, and approached her threateningly. "Or do you need a refresher?"

With a laugh, she took several steps backwards until her back hit the closed door and she was caged between my hard cock and the unyielding wood.

I grabbed the hand towel from her and dried my hands, while she licked her lips in anticipation. Her chest rose and fell rapidly. I pressed my body against hers and her eyes widened when she felt the hardness of my dick.

"You didn't make it clear," she whispered. "You only said that I was yours."

Our faces were just inches away. "What else was I supposed to say then?"

"You were meant to ask me, officially ... to be your girlfriend."

I looked at her curiously. If she knew what I felt. If she knew what we had promised to each other. But of course, she had forgotten everything.

"Don't worry," she said quickly, mistaking the look in my eyes. "I'm going to say yes."

I ground my hips against hers. "Willow Rayne, will you be my girlfriend? Officially."

She bit her lower lip in an effort to control her smile, her eyes were sparkling. I stared mesmerized by them. I had lost twelve years of this.

"I'm not sure," she teased.

"Let me help you make up your mind," I growled. Reaching under her skirt, I pulled her panties down her legs. When they pooled around her feet, I grabbed her from under her thighs and lifted her off the ground.

29
Willow

A second later, my legs were tightly wrapped around his hips, and he was mercilessly pounding into me.

I couldn't believe we were doing this in my shop, where at any moment anyone could walk in and clearly hear our bodies slamming against the door. It was madness and I should stop him, but the working next to him in the sun had turned my brain to mush. I had watched his fingers caress the soil and dreamed of them on my body. That sense of déjà vu was overwhelming. If I didn't know better I would think we had done it before. Kneeled on the bare earth and planted flowers together under a burning sun.

"Faster," I panted, digging my nails into his ass as I swung my hips to meet his wild thrusts. His cock filled me, the delicious friction driving me out of my mind.

It wasn't long before I felt myself begin to climax. My core tightened at the impending release and when it crashed through, I cried into his mouth. "Oh God." I shuddered. "Oh God!" It shook me hard, so I hard I heard him coming as if from far away.

His burst came with a guttural groan. The violent slam of his fist against the wall almost made my soul leave my body, but I understood him. I was as shaken as he was, the frantic, desperate pace of our mating meant even my blood hummed with excitement. But once again, I noticed that he'd pulled out of me before he came and it was his fingers that were pumping inside me. I knew I should have appreciated him for the precaution, but I wanted his seed in me. I wanted those seeds to grow inside my body like those pale seedlings we'd planted together.

I'd orgasmed so hard my juices were still spilling out of me. My legs felt as if they had locked into position and I couldn't unhook them from around his hips.

"I don't think I can stand," I gasped.

He straightened then and I watched completely mesmerized, as he licked his lips and with the back of one hand patted the sweat away from his forehead.

He then pulled the bolt on the door and carried me towards the sink, he positioned me next to it.

"What can I use?" he asked.

"There are some wipes in that drawer," I told him, and he headed over to retrieve it after which he began to carefully wipe me down. I watched as he set about taking care of me, as if he had long accepted me as his responsibility.

He was extremely quiet as he cleaned me up, and I knew that his silence was nothing bad and I shouldn't break it. Not that I wanted to. I too was in a contemplative mood as I replayed the sheer magic of our joining. No matter how fast and furious it was I never felt dirty or soiled. It felt right. I felt good.

As he pulled my skirt over my thighs I heard myself blurt out, "Have you ever felt like this with anyone else?"

Realizing how idiotic I sounded I quickly hurried to explain. "I'm just wondering. I don't have that much experience." Or any for that matter that I was aware of.

His gaze softened. "Never, Willow. Never."

My breath left me with a rush. Every time he said things like this, it should have been impossible to believe, and it should have made me suspicious of him because it was too much too soon for a man to be saying these things. It almost made him seem emotionally careless.

But for some weird reason I believed him. Maybe it was his temperament. He was quiet and watchful and serious. He didn't seem like the kind who could be emotionally careless, and moreover when he said the words, it didn't seem like he was trying to impress me or mess around with me. It seemed as though he was speaking from the very depths of his soul.

I didn't want his apparent sincerity to persuade me into completely letting my guard down, and giving all of myself to him. I had visions of being left high and dry. I unlocked my legs from around him and slid down until I was on my feet.

His cock was still hanging outside his pants and I grabbed some of the wipes with the intention of returning the favor, but before my hand could reach him, he seized my wrist.

"If you touch me," he warned. "Neither of us will leave here for at least twenty minutes."

"The burrito must be cold by now anyway," I whispered.

And instantly his cock jumped to attention.

At that moment, I heard voices from beyond the door. My heart lurched into my throat. We both stilled as we listened, and it didn't take long to realize that Sandra was outside with Bradley.

"Where is she?" I heard him ask.

"Willow," I heard Sandra call out my name. "Willow," she called again loudly.

I knew she was giving me a heads up so I could get myself decent. When she started to head our way, I slapped my hand across my lips and to my surprise Caleb looked as if he was unable to control his laughter. I threatened him with my gaze as I hurriedly straightened myself. If Sandra were to catch me right now in the state I was in, I would never hear the end of it. Even before I was ready Caleb had straightened himself.

"I'll go first, then you can come out later," I whispered to Caleb. He stole a quick kiss from me, and then began to nibble on my lower lip, reluctant to let me go.

Realizing that he wasn't going to stop, I pulled the door open and almost fell out in my haste. Both Sandra and Bradley were watching me with confused expressions on their face.

"What's going on?" Bradley asked watching the stupid smirk on my face.

"Nothing," I replied as I glanced nervously at the door, then glanced at Sandra. "You came back early?"

She raised her eyebrows. "Yes, then I met Bradley in town and he said he had a delivery to make."

"Oh," I said and began to head towards the counter in order to divert all unnecessary attention away from the backroom. "Well, Bradley. You can just leave the bags over there." I tried my best to get behind the counter and pretend to look for something on the shelves behind it. A few seconds later, all of our heads turned, as Caleb walked in from a direction he was not supposed to be coming from.

Bradley's eyes nearly popped out of its sockets and Sandra winked at me.

"Hello," Caleb greeted. "Great to see you again, Sandra."

She raised her hand to wave slowly to him. I avoided all of their gazes and kept my eyes on the computer screen.

"He said he wanted to use the bathroom," I explained airily. When I raised my head I was shocked to catch the murderous scowl on Bradley's face.

Caleb was fully dressed. His white shirt was tucked neatly into charcoal pants and his sleeves were folded to just below his elbow. Even his hair had been arranged back into place, but one look at our flushed cheeks, swollen lips and glazed eyes, and there was no doubt of what we had been up to in the restroom. I was fooling no one. But even so why was Bradley so angry with me? What business of his was it if I chose to have sex with someone in my own damn shop?

"Well, I've got to get back now," Caleb said.

I nodded. "I'll see you out. Sandra, I'll be right back."

"Wait!" she suddenly called. "Bradley please pass me that lucky bamboo plant over there. I heard that you just opened your office downtown. This is a gift from us to you. We wish you all the best."

She reached out to take the vase from Bradley but before she could reach it, it left his hand, and headed straight for the floor. Sandra immediately jumped away, but Bradley didn't move an inch.

"Hey!" Sandra yelled as the ceramic vase shattered into pieces.

The soil and plant it had contained burst out, soiling the floor. We all looked to Bradley in shock, but even more stunning was the black look of fury on his face.

He was glaring furiously at Caleb!

What the hell was going on? A strange fear slithered down my spine. Whenever I saw a man lose his temper something happened inside me. I felt like running away and hiding somewhere dark and small, like a closet.

Bradley turned to look at me with hurt eyes, then he stormed out of the shop. Caleb watched him leave without a word before he turned to me. "Is that your delivery guy?"

I was also taken aback by Caleb's tone. I stared at him in shock. He almost seemed like a completely different person. Everything about him was changed. His demeanor, his voice, the tension in his body, the color of his eyes.

"Yeah, he is," I replied, confused and shocked.

"Do you know him well?"

"Yeah I do."

Sandra clicked her tongue. "Don't mind him, Caleb. He's just a little upset. We've known him for a couple of years now and in that time he's always had his sights set on Willow. But she's never really been open towards him. I guess seeing how you two are now, he got a bit um ... disappointed. He'll get over it. I'll get you another plant."

I turned to Sandra in shock. "What?"

She jerked her head in my direction. "You mean you didn't know?"

"No, he's not interested in me," I denied. "He likes you. He told me himself."

"Bullshit. He has no interest in me at all. We're just friends. It's you he's had his eye on, but you were too blind to see."

I shook my head. I felt ashamed. All this time I had leaned

on him for support and he had been nursing this huge crush on me, and I never even suspected.

Sandra turned to Caleb. "Look, don't worry about it. It was just a little tantrum, but he's harmless. And he'll get over it."

I looked at Caleb. He was staring at me, his eyes veiled. I couldn't tell what he was thinking. "I guess you should get going," I whispered.

"Yes, I should. I'll call you," he said, and walked to the door.

"Ooo, do I smell burritos?" Sandra asked from behind me.

"Yeah. Caleb and I didn't get a chance to eat them," I replied automatically, even though I felt dazed and shocked by everything that had happened.

"Can I have his then?" she asked.

I turned around to face her. "Yeah, go ahead. Sandra, why didn't you tell me about Bradley?"

She shrugged and moved towards the bag of food. "Two reasons. First, I thought you knew. Second, he's not right for you."

"I feel so stupid and guilty. All this time I thought he was into you."

"Listen, it's not your fault he didn't have the guts to tell you from day one he was interested in you. If I were you, I would be happy this happened because finally it's all out in the open and he can move on. I've been hurt by guys loads of times and look at me. I'm stronger and better for it. Now come and eat with me."

I moved towards her even though my appetite was completely gone.

30

Caleb

I t was Friday, and Willow had agreed to a date at my place. She had initially suggested a take-out at the office, but I'd practically lived at the office for the last week and I needed a bit of downtime.

I had a lavish home in the hills that hardly ever saw me. I would have opted for a condo in the city center, or preferably even in my office's neighborhood, but the house was in a gated community with considerably more security. And security was a good thing.

The downside was, after my tiny cell, the house made me feel quite irresponsibly extravagant. Especially since I had no one to share it with. Yet.

"Wow!" she exclaimed, her eyes large with wonder, when I opened the door. "I knew this area was exclusive, but this is the biggest house in the complex."

"So you like it?" I asked, with a smile, as my eyes ran over her. She looked especially delectable today in a sun dress, and with her hair pulled into a messy bun. I couldn't wait to wrench it free into the cascade that made her look nothing short of a living goddess.

"What's not to like?"

I laughed and catching her hand, pulled her into our home. She just didn't know it yet.

With a hand to the side of my face, she buried her face in my neck for a moment as though to breathe me in, before placing a quick kiss on my lips and slipping out of my grasp.

As she walked away all I could do was stare after her. I didn't know how long I could keep the knowledge to myself about the absolute hold this woman had over me. I wanted so badly for her to know she was irreplaceable to me, that my happiness was in her hands.

She took a good look around at the neutral shades in the expansive living room that an interior decorator Marie knew had selected. Then we went out through the French doors towards the pool and spa. She stood for a moment looking down at the view of Sacramento, Folsom Lake, and even the Sutter Buttes.

She turned to me. "This is breathtaking. You brought me here to show off, didn't you?"

I smiled. "Actually, I invited you over to take advantage of you."

"Well there *is* that." she laughed.

The joyful sound filtered into the house. This was what I had wanted, what this house lacked. For her sounds to wake the house with vibrancy and spirit.

She came into the house and I tried to control my intense expression, so that it wouldn't scare her away. To her, things must seem to be moving too fast between us, while for me it was twelve years too slow. Things were touchy in other ways too, and I couldn't wait till they weren't.

"Want something to drink?" I asked casually.

"Sure." Her voice was equally casual.

I walked over to the kitchen and she followed me. I pulled the refrigerator open and removed the pitcher of water my housekeeper had prepared for me. It contained refreshing slices of lemon and kiwi in it. During one of our conversations, Willow had told me how much she liked fruit infusions, and I took note of it.

"Did you prepare that for me?" she asked as she took her seat on one of the stools at the island's counter.

"My housekeeper did," I said as I poured her a tall glass, and slid it over.

She accepted the glass and drained it in an instant. "You took classes on how to make a girl fall in love with you, didn't you?"

I grinned at her. "Are you falling in love with me?"

"Answer the question. You have, haven't you? Tell the truth. Otherwise, how the hell do you know to be so attentive to a woman?"

"Maybe it's because I'm crazy about you," I said softly.

For a moment I thought she was going to be serious with me, but she shook herself and laughed again. "Or maybe you've been married, or at least been in a long relationship. You failed at being attentive in the past and now you're making sure you don't make the same mistakes with me. I'm not complaining, but I'd like to know if that's the case."

I took a sip from my glass as I watched her curiously. She had been just like this in the past, chatty and making up entire stories in her mind. Of course, I had been an all too willing audience.

I placed my glass on the marble counter, and locked my gaze on hers. "I've never been married, or been in a committed relationship either."

She narrowed her eyes in suspicion. "Sandra says you might have a secret family in New York, and you're here to get away from a nasty divorce."

My eyes widened with surprise.

Her hands shot up in defense. "You can't blame us for trying to figure you out. You're a mystery. How can you be so great in bed, be that good looking, that successful, that attentive, and yet still be single? It doesn't make any sense."

A memory of her as a young girl popped into my mind. She had walked in the rain to my house. 'What are you doing?' I had asked, shocked to see her soaked to the skin. 'I brought you this,' she replied holding out a bunch of wild flowers. 'I had already picked them for you and it didn't make any sense not to bring them over.'

"She's right, isn't she?" Willow demanded, pulling me out of the memory of that rainy day. That was the first time I kissed her.

I cleared my throat. "You're beautiful, and you're considerably great in bed too. Why are you single?"

Her mouth fell open for a couple of seconds as she probably struggled to decide on what part of my comment to respond to first. Eventually, her finger went up in the air. "First of all, I'm twenty-three so it's quite normal that I am still single, and secondly, I'm considerably great in bed? I should be offended at that, but I think this is the first time you have teased me so I'm honestly more affected by the discovery that you have a humorous bone in your body. I thought you were just calm and serious and not much fun."

I laughed again. "You didn't complain about me not being much fun when I was inside you."

"Oh, and now you're out-right bragging too. I'm not sure I like this side of you."

I headed over to the counter, lifted myself onto its surface and studied her. She was so beautiful when she glared at me like that.

"Are you smiling so sexily now because you think it's going to placate me?"

"Is it working?" I mocked.

She paused. "Yes, God freaking damn it."

I laughed out loud then and she looked stunned. The laughter died in my throat. "What?"

"I've never heard you laugh like that. You're always so guarded. Come to think of it, you're completely different today. Is it because we're in your home? Are you more comfortable here?"

"You could say that." I nodded.

Her eyes softened. "All your life you've had to act stable and unfaltering on the outside, haven't you? I know the feeling."

"How so?" I asked.

She shook her head. "No. You have to tell me deeper things about yourself first."

"I'll tell you whatever you want to know. But first I need to know what you want to have for dinner. I'll talk as I cook."

"You know how to cook?"

31

Caleb

I thought back to all the prison noodle meals I had managed to put together due to my skills with an electrical outlet, clippers, and the guts to drop a live wire into a cup of water. And then there was the years living with my dysfunctional parents, of course. I'd learned how to survive on pasta made with butter and tomato puree.

Today however, I had all the ingredients that I could possibly need to make it a great treat for her.

"I do," I replied. "Is spaghetti okay with you?"

"I'm not okay with spaghetti, I love it."

I grinned. "Good."

"Did you learn how to cook from your mom?"

I was silent as the dark memory came to mind. "No."

The sound of my voice was like the shutting of a door and her face fell. To build the kind of intimacy I wanted with Willow, I couldn't hold back any part of myself from her.

"She was an alcoholic," I said softly. "My stepdad drove her to it, with his cheating, and his problems with substance abuse."

To give her time to process it I jumped off the counter and set about putting a pot of water on the stove to boil.

She appeared by my side and slipped her hand through mine. "I'm really sorry, Caleb," she said softly.

"It's okay. I haven't seen her in a very long time."

"What do you need me to chop up for you?"

"Do you like spring onions?" I asked and she nodded with a smile.

I retrieved them from the fridge along with a bunch of bell peppers, carrots, mushrooms, and the ground beef we would need. She began to rinse them in the sink.

"Do you like shrimp?"

"I do," she said, amused. "But that's already a lot of meat. You want to add shrimp too?"

"I want to make sure you have a great meal."

She rose on the tip of her toes to nibble lightly on the tip of my nose, and I couldn't believe the audacity. I hadn't completely got used to someone being so liberal with me and my body. I enjoyed every moment of it though. When we were younger and my hair was much longer she used to pull out her hair ties and use them to style my hair. When she was finished, she used to lean back and say, "You're too beautiful to be a boy, Caleb." My hair was much shorter now, but I wanted her to be as mischievous with me as she had been then.

"When did you last speak to your mom?" she asked, as she picked up a knife and began to chop the vegetables.

I thought of my mother swinging her fist into my face. "It was a long, long time ago."

"Do you ever plan on seeing her again?"

"Can't. She's dead."

A heavy silence filled the room, and I sensed she regretted her line of questioning. "I'm sorry," she apologized in a small and breathy voice.

I went to her, encircled her waist with my arms, and pressed my body into hers. "There's no need to be. It was a long time ago." Then I pressed a kiss against her cheek. She turned in my arms. "Are we going to cook or fuck?"

I laughed. "Fuck?"

"That's the wrong answer, my boy. Back to your station now."

I walked away from her towards the fridge.

"You know, I told you I lost my parents," she began.

I sensed her turn to glance at me, but I wasn't prepared to meet her gaze and act like I had no clue of what she was about to tell me.

"I also lost some of my memories," she continued. "I woke up one day in a hospital in Bitter Creek, and two years of my life, from a couple of days before my parents died, was gone. I haven't been able to recall any of it since."

I felt myself tense as I turned to her. I couldn't feign surprise. That kind of audacity to pretend just wasn't in me and every cell in my body rejected the idea of lying to her, so I made sure that my gaze on her was soft and consoling.

"You don't seem surprised," she said, her head tilting to one side.

"It's a very unusual story. What happened?"

She returned to her task. "Apparently, after my parents died, I was sent to live with my uncle in Bitter Creek. He was the priest of the Catholic parish there. But then something happened one day, and the church was burned down, he was murdered, and I was found unconscious on the street not far from the house. They think I was running away from the scene when I fell and hit my head. They were hoping I could tell them something, but when I woke I couldn't remember a thing, and it's been that way ever since."

My heart was pounding so violently I was sure that she could hear it. I forced myself to keep my tone as neutral as possible when I asked, "Did you ever find out what caused the fire?"

"It was a teenage delinquent from my school." she said with a shake of her head. "Maybe he was trying to rob the house, and my uncle interrupted him. I was taken away by Social Services. They told me that he was sent to jail."

I felt that old anger that made my blood boil. The reminder of what I had walked in to find her own uncle doing to her.

"You know what's really funny about all this?" She turned to me.

"What?"

"Of course, I missed my parents like mad, and I felt sad for the way my uncle had died, but I didn't actually grieve for him because I hardly knew him. He only came to visit my parents three or four times. But I always grieved for my lost memories. I felt as if there was someone important standing in that dense fog. And I've been looking for that person who sometimes comes in my dreams as a figure that I am running toward, but can never reach. Even though reason tells me if that person was that important in my life he... or she, even though it feels like it is a he, would have come to find me."

"Maybe that person couldn't come to you."

She sighed. "At first I clung to that hope, but it's an extremely unlikely scenario. The story was so big it was all over the media. I even remember reporters from a few cities were camped outside the hospital. If the person existed, he would have found some way to contact me. Phone, write, e-mail."

"I'm sorry, Willow," I whispered.

I wanted to hold her. To tell her she was not wrong. That person did exist and had longed for her as much as she had longed for him, but I realized I never wanted Willow to remember the past. I wanted Willow as I found her in her flower shop. Willow without those horrendous memories. Why put her through that hideous time again?

In my head it was like yesterday that she arrived at our school like a lost angel. She was so sad, so inconsolable. I wanted to wrap her in cotton wool and never let the world hurt her again. How could I know her uncle, the priest, the man who smiled so kindly at her, was breaking her wings in secret at night?

"Never mind," she said with a smile. "I know it seems unlikely after all this time, but deep inside I have a feeling that someday my memories will come back."

I didn't want her to see my face. I turned away and pretended to look for something in the cupboard. I grasped the bottle of olive oil so hard my knuckles showed white. Deliberately, I loosened my grip. *Calm down, Caleb. Calm the fuck, down. It's all in the past now.*

She brought over the vegetables she had sliced for me and stood by my side as I began to fry them.

I asked her about her shop and the mood of our conversation lightened up. When she asked for a taste when I tasted the sauce, I took the spoon towards her mouth, and the sight of her lips and tongue tasting the sauce from the same place my own lips had been, sent a jolt of heat to my cock.

I wanted to pull her on the kitchen table and fuck her until she screamed, and she must have seen in the look in my eyes, because she leaned forward and wrapped a hand around the back of my neck. Pulling me down, she slipped her tongue into my mouth.

The taste of the sauce and her mixed erotically in my mouth. When she moved back a few seconds later, her eyes were glazed with lust. "It tastes great," she said as she licked her lips.

"You don't want us to eat today, do you?" I asked and without taking her eyes from me she reached down and grabbed the rock-hard bulge straining against my pants.

She grinned cheekily. "Actually, I do, but I've always wondered what it would be like to tease a big cock and now I know."

I inhaled deeply. "Ah, that. We have the whole night for you to understand what teasing a big cock gets you."

32

Willow

After that huge dinner, like two pythons who had each swallowed a goat, we collapsed on the big, modern couch that looked like it never seen a butt in its life. I thought about giving him that blowjob Sandra had taught me to do in detail, but nah. Too full. Later. We had all night. Sprawled next to Caleb I monopolized the remote and surfed the TV channels.

As I paused a moment on a Modern Family scene I recognized and loved. That was when he made a shocking admission that he had never seen the hilarious family sitcom. That was it. I immediately tossed out our plans to watch a movie together and settled on that instead.

I was very comfortable. Caleb had even thrown a blanket my way which was nice, but when I looked over at him he looked like he would make an even better pillow for me, so I lazily shifted myself over until I was wrapped around him, and his big, powerful hands were curled up around me. And there I stayed, a warm blanket over me and his delicious heat under me. I had never felt more content or more at home in my entire life.

I loved the gentle rise and fall of his chest, and intoxicating scent of spices and wood. It was like being inside a gorgeous dream.

I could have stayed like that forever, but my phone began to ring. My first thought was to ignore it, but what if it was mother? What if something had happened at home? I quickly peeled myself from him and hurried over to get my phone from my purse.

Just as I found the phone, it died on me. "Damn." I took my phone with me and returned to the couch. I knew Caleb had an i-Phone too. "Caleb, my battery is out of juice. Can I use your charger?"

He was in the kitchen, pouring a bag of popcorn kernels into the microwave to be popped. "Sure. It's in my bedroom. Just go up the stairs, first room on the right. You'll find it on my nightstand."

"Thank you," I replied, my heart warming all over again. Ever since I had got here he'd done all he could to ensure I felt at home in is house. And even though I knew that it wasn't the case, it was almost too easy to believe that this was my house too. I'd even caught myself earlier on rearranging items on the shelves of his refrigerator door, and bagging all his leeks, and putting them neatly in the vegetable drawer.

I passed the staircase, lined with art, but no pictures of his family, and thought back to the account he had given me about his mother. After what he said about her I hadn't had the backbone to ask about his father. Someday when we're closer and when he was comfortable enough to trust me, maybe he would tell me himself.

Caleb seemed like the kind who bottled everything inside and stayed aloof. I wanted him to express himself, to reveal himself to me, but I was patient. I wasn't going anywhere. I could wait as long as it took.

I arrived at his bedroom and walked in. It was decorated in the same neutral tones as the rest of the house. It was somewhat soothing to me, but it was completely without personality, the way expensive homes usually are. Not a thing out of place, everything color coordinated to death. Soulless but so what, it was Instagram worthy.

Only one side of the bed was slightly rumpled, and it made me smile. It was kind of a small confirmation that I was the only one he had eyes for. At least, at the moment.

I didn't find his charger where he said it'd be, so I pulled the drawer open, hoping that it would be there, and to my relief it actually was. I rose with it and was just about to turn away when I realized that amongst the odds and ends, was something that looked somewhat familiar.

That made me stop.

Why would anything in his room look familiar to me? I'd never been here before. Almost in a daze, I leaned down and reached in, and pulled out a bright pink watch. I stared at it. I had never seen it in my life, and yet for a moment there, something had tugged at me. Not a whole memory, but the scent of one.

I wondered why he would have something that should belong to a little girl. Did he have a little sister or cousin?

I glanced at the door and back at the watch. I turned the watch around and something struck me.

At first it was just a light pressure in my chest, then tears filled my eyes. I reached up in awe to touch them as they rolled down my face. It was the strangest thing. What the hell was affecting me in this way? I looked again at the watch in my hands and something flashed in my mind.

A memory had escaped from the impenetrable fog.

I felt my knees buckle as I collapsed to the ground to a crouched position.

I had never ever had a memory return like this. Yes, little fragments in my dreams that I couldn't piece together when I awakened. Never like this, when I was fully awake and conscious, and never with such vividness and clarity.

I was in an unkempt backyard and I had a red water balloon in my hand. I was running, my high pitched little voice was filled with excitement and laughter. I was chasing someone, so I couldn't see his face. I threw the balloon at him and it hit his back, and exploded, drenching him.

"I've won," I was screaming. "I've won." But my words were cut short by a balloon hitting me right on my chest. It took my breath away.

A woman's gruff voice said, "Don't let him off that easily, hon. There's more balloons right here."

Then the fog that had lifted, allowing that one memory through, closed in on me again.

"Wow!" I breathed and blinked. To my shock another image suddenly came to me. It was like dropping a stone into a lake and watching the ripples spread.

I was seated in a bus and I was hugging a backpack tightly to my chest. There were other people sitting around me, but I was all by myself, and I was heading somewhere. I couldn't tell where.

On my little wrist was the pink watch I was now holding in my hand.

The memory went as quickly as it had come, but that flash of the past came with feelings. The little me was sad. She was very, very sad. The crushing emptiness and loss inside her was so all-encompassing I could feel it even now in my bones. The inexplicable sadness was so stunningly real I suddenly found I couldn't breathe properly. I took short gasping breaths.

I shut my eyes and urged more memories to appear, but it seemed there were no more. I didn't know how long I stayed there, waiting, hoping and praying for more, but tight fog was letting no more out. I looked up when my senses picked up on the sound of footsteps on the hardwood floor. He burst into the room and stopped when he saw me sitting on the floor.

He froze and I was able to make out the terror on his face. It was almost as jarring as the memories had been. I felt as if I was in a dream. Why was he so terrified? I tried to rise, but it seemed every iota of strength in my body was gone. I felt as weak as jelly.

"I'm okay," I wanted to say but the words would not form in my mouth.

He rushed to me, and pulled me into his arms. "What's wrong, baby? What's wrong?"

I opened my hand and showed the watch to him. "What is this?"

33

Caleb

Fuck, fuck, fuck.

I had screwed up. Royally! Without a thought, I'd told her to come to the room to get the charger, but when she had not returned after a few minutes, I knew instinctively what had happened. She'd found the watch. I'd fucked up.

My heart felt as if it had fallen out of my chest then.

I had dashed up the stairs and froze. It was my handiwork. I'd brought the past back into her life. My carelessness had hurt my baby. Her eyes were filled with tears. Her mouth was open but no words were coming out. She was trying to rise to her feet, but she couldn't.

She was in shock.

I'd done the one thing I'd sworn to myself I'd never do. Trigger her memories. I wanted to fix it. I wanted to go back to the time before I told her to go look for the charger in my bedroom, but fate had never cared what I wanted. Even as I ran to hold her in my arms I already knew I couldn't fix this. Nothing would be the same again.

I wrapped my arms around her. I wanted to rock her to sleep, back to before she found the watch. Instead, she grabbed onto me in desperation. "What is this?" she asked.

I bought myself time and shifted my gaze towards the pink watch she held in her trembling hand. What was I going to say? How much did she know?

"Caleb," she whispered breathlessly, "I used to have a watch like this when I was young. Why do you have this?"

Her eyes showed her hope and fear at the same time. That perhaps I was someone from her past that she didn't recognize.

I felt sick to my stomach.

I longed to tell her the truth. I wanted it so much, I had to bite back the words, but it was clear from her question that she had not remembered her uncle and what he had done to her.

Tears rolled down her cheeks. "I remembered sitting in a bus. I felt grief... terrible, terrible grief. I never... I never have before. It was horrible. This is the memory of the grief I forgot. And a balloon fight. I remember playing with a boy."

I couldn't look into her pained eyes anymore. I knew what she was asking. Was I the boy?

Yes, Willow. I was that boy. I threw the balloon at you.

I crushed her to my chest and ran my hands softly down her back to soothe her the best way I could, then I lied to her. I lied to my baby. As I lied tears burned my eyes. I blinked them away fiercely. This much and more I will do for you, my little Willow.

"This watch used to belong to a close friend of mine when I was younger. It's not you. It's not yours," I lied.

My words made her body go limp. She was disappointed. She wanted it to be me. She didn't know it, but she had been waiting for me. Waiting to fulfill the promise we had made to each other that night of the fire.

I continued to hold her as she recovered. When I became concerned about the twisted position she was in, I lifted her into my arms and carried her down the stairs. She hid her face and hands in my chest. Gently, I laid her on the couch and wrapped us both in the thick blankets. I left the TV on so that she could listen to it to distract her. For a long time neither of us spoke. She stared blankly at the flickering TV screen even though I knew she was not watching it.

It must have been at least twenty minutes later, when I heard her small voice say, "That memory must have been from when I first arrived at Bitter Creek because I was so full of sorrow. I must have been mourning for my parents."

"Yes, probably," I murmured.

"My psychologist told me not to force the recollection of my memory. That my mind was protecting me because the pain and trauma of what happened was too great. And as time went on, and as I became stronger I would be able to remember things, but I never have. Not until today. Not until I saw that watch. Maybe I had one like that."

I placed a kiss on her sweetly scented hair and held her even tighter to me.

"That watch ... I guessed it must have been a gift from them. It felt like something I'd lost a very long time ago."

She lifted her head to mine. "This might be too much to ask but, do you mind if... if... I have it? Just for a little while. I promise I'll return it to you. It's the first thing that has been strong enough to trigger a memory for me and maybe having it with me will trigger more memories."

I had vowed that I would protect her, and instead I had inadvertently led her into this pit. I felt as if I was being ripped to shreds from guilt and remorse. I was a fucking selfish bastard. As if I needed to see that watch every night. I should have locked it away.

"Do you have to remember?"

"I want to," she said simply.

"Why not let the memories come slowly, when they want to? Why force them?"

"You cannot understand what it's like to know there is something there behind the veil. Something... I can't explain it, but it feels as if there is not only sadness, but something sinister. Something dangerous. Often, it makes me feel I'm not living like everyone else. It's as if I'm waiting for something... or someone. Like I am just existing, or going through the motions until I find it. I don't want to be stuck in limbo anymore. I don't want to run anymore. I want to deal with whatever is hidden in that fog and move on."

"You can have the watch," I said.

She reached up to plant a gentle kiss on my cheek. Then she pulled out of my hold, and stood to her feet. "I want to go home," she said. "Will you take me home?"

34

Willow

"Aren't you going to work today?" my mom asked from the door.

At the question, I raised my head from my pillow and turned towards her. I never wanted my mom to worry so I put on my best smile. "I feel a bit lazy this morning so I asked Sandra to come in early today."

"Well, you rest as long as you like. You've earned it," she said as she shrugged her arms into her robe. "I'm making blueberry pancakes. I'll bring some up for you."

"Thanks, mom, but you don't have to do that. I'll come down for them."

She half-shut my door and went down the stairs. I returned my gaze to the window I had been staring out of ever since Caleb had dropped me off last night. I hadn't been able to get a wink of sleep, and it was just making everything worse.

I stayed in bed, until the whiff of pancakes cooking in butter wafted up the stairs and into my bedroom. I jumped up then. As I was making my way to the bathroom, my phone vibrated with an incoming text.

I picked it up and saw Caleb's message.

Feel like a quick trip away today? I'm thinking Palm Springs. We could be on a plane Friday, and I'll ensure to get you back by Sunday evening, or Monday morning at the latest.

I stared at the message bemused. So this was what it was like when you had a boyfriend. They cooked large meals and invited you on weekend trips away. Before I could reply, another text arrived in my inbox.

Come on, Willow. I've been having a hard time too. Let's forget it all for a day or two and just relax. If you feel bad about being indebted to me, you can pay me back later.

I couldn't help responding then. With a smile on my face I typed back:

You're my boyfriend. Why do I have to pay you back?

Calling him my boyfriend felt quite strange to me, but it also brought with it a sense of joy and contentment.

Fantastic! We have a date then?

I laughed, and sent my reply.

I have to tell my parents about you first. Let's see how that goes.

The answer was immediate.

Don't worry. I'll turn on the charm. They'll love me.

I was grinning when I answered him.

Very sure of yourself, aren't you?

His answer made my toes curl.

It's very hard to resist a man who is crazy about your daughter.

I felt almost light-headed with joy as I headed off to take a shower, and by the time I got out, all I could think about was spending time with Caleb on a beach somewhere, and allowing my mind to roam freely.

I got ready and went downstairs to the kitchen. It was filled with everything that was familiar to me. The pancakes were warming in the oven and both my parents were there. My mom was laughing hard at something, and my dad grunted at me. He was not a morning person. I felt great love for him at that moment. I would always miss my biological parents, but I owed these two kind souls everything. They had taken me in when I was confused and lost and loved me unconditionally.

I sat at the table.

I didn't want to lie to them anymore, not even by omission. "Mom," I called.

She wiped the tears from the corners of her eyes and turned to me. "Yeah? Can you believe your dad is adding sardines to a peanut butter sandwich?"

"Oh, weird," I said.

He sent a scowl my way.

"I ... uh ... I wanted to say that I'm going on a short trip today."

The idea was no doubt surprising. I never went anywhere. Ever. I waited for the few seconds it took both parents to process it.

"That sounds great," my mom said cautiously. "Who are you going with? Sandra?"

"No... um..."

"You're going alone?" My dad interjected, his voice slightly raised with alarm.

"I don't think that's a good idea, sweetie," my mom said at the same time.

"I'm not going alone. I'm going with a... uh... with a friend."

They turned to look at each other, then turned back to me.

"Friend? What friend?" my dad asked.

"You're going with a man?" she asked.

I nodded again, and the room was thrown into silence.

"You have a boyfriend?" my mother asked incredulously.

I nodded again. I guess it was safe to say I ruined my father's peanut butter and sardine sandwich.

35
Caleb

I didn't expect to meet Willow's parents so soon, but I was ready. I had been planning this day for twelve years.

I gave myself a clean shave and dressed simply in light tones. A white shirt paired with an unthreatening dove gray suit. I had long understood that I gave off an aura that was dark. It served me well inside, but it was the last impression I wanted to have on the people who had so graciously and beautifully raised Willow on my behalf. I was filled with gratitude and admiration for them and I had big plans for them too. I planned to change their lives so it was unrecognizable to them. New house, new furniture, new bank accounts, and lots of travel, anywhere they wanted to go.

I stood at their door, with a very large bouquet of red roses in hand. Willow answered the bell, a sparkle in her eyes. It made me so glad to see the vibrancy that had returned to them.

Her eyes widened at the bouquet. "For me?"

"No, your mom," I replied.

She pretended to pout and my heart skipped several beats at how cute that expression was. I quickly reminded myself that she wasn't the one I was trying to impress tonight.

"What did you get for my dad?"

"What?" I said stupidly. My nerves tightened.

"You got flowers for my mom, what did you get for my dad?"

I blinked. I'd been in prison so long I had not realized things had changed. "I ... Am I supposed to get something for him too?"

"I thought you wanted to impress them both."

I couldn't believe I had fucked up again. I looked down at my shoes and thought quickly. I had lots of new things that I had not even opened yet, and I could give him one of those. "I'm about ten minutes early anyway. I could quickly go get something for him. Just make up some excuse. I'll be back in about twenty minutes," I muttered.

As I turned away, her small hand settled around my wrist. I raised my head to meet her laughing gaze.

"Hey, I was only messing with you."

I stared at her. "Oh. You were?"

"Yeah. You sounded so cock-sure about impressing my parents I decided to tease you. I didn't really expect you to fall for it. Where have you been living all this while. Under a rock?"

"Yeah, you can sort of say that." I straightened my spine.

Her lips twitched with amusement. "You really like me, don't you?"

I looked deep into her warm eyes. She looked happy again and that warmed my heart. "Have I not made that crystal clear?"

She looked behind her, noted no one behind her, but turned back to me and dropped her voice to a whisper anyway. "I know you like to have sex with me, but I didn't think you'd be willing to meet my parents so soon, yet here you are .. nervous out of your mind. To be honest I never thought it was possible for you to get this nervous."

"I'll stop being nervous, when you stop teasing me," I said.

She reached up to nibble on my lip just as there was the sound of a polite cough behind her. Hell, she threw herself away from me so fast she knocked over an umbrella stand. It crashed to the ground, which made her jump like a cat finding a cucumber behind it. It was quite adorable to see her flustered. I glanced away from her flushed face towards her mother. She was smiling at me, but her eyes were wary.

It was the first time she was laying eyes on me, but it wasn't mine. Over the years, I'd been sent several photos of both her parents as they lived their quiet, unremarkable lives and raised my Willow.

Her father ambled into the foyer. He was a tall, gaunt man, and the epitome of a good provider. He spoke little and cared deeply for his family. He looked between us expressionlessly, then he turned to his wife. "What happened?"

"Willow almost broke her neck trying to hide herself when I caught her kissing her new boyfriend," her mother explained tactlessly. I fell in love with her then. I knew we'd get along just fine.

Her father's face darkened at the words, and I didn't blame him for one second. I'd have done the same if I'd been in his shoes.

"Mom," Willow groaned under her breath.

I stepped forward then, and introduced myself. "Hello, Ma'am. I'm Caleb Wolfe."

"Well, it's nice to meet you, Caleb. You can call me Sally."

I turned to her father and held out my hand. "Sir. Good to meet you."

He accepted the gesture, his expression still hard. He jerked his chin towards the bouquet in my hand. "Is that for me?"

"No, sir," I said, as heat rushed into my neck. Watching my inept, clumsy performance, no one could possibly imagine I had practiced this for twelve fucking years.

Her mother lightly slapped him on the shoulder. "Stop it, George." She turned to face me. "They're for me, aren't they?"

"Yes ma'am."

She took the flowers from me, sniffing the fragrance delicately. "Thank you, they're beautiful. Please come in. Willow, why don't you unpeel yourself from that wall and come and join us too."

I winked at Willow and she raised her eyebrows at me before I went with her parents into the living room. Her mother disappeared into the kitchen and her father offered me a drink. I asked for whiskey and he nodded with approval.

"Ice?"

I shrugged. "Sure."

Once a glass of whiskey was in my hand, the interrogation began.

"Willow tells me that you're from New York."

That was absolutely not true, and I carefully couched my words. "I'm not, but I've worked there for a number of years, Sir."

"Stock trading?"

"Yes, Sir."

"I also hear that you're quite successful at it."

I took a sip of whiskey. It was cold and smooth. "I've been quite fortunate, yes."

"Hmmm..." He then nodded a few times as if he approved of something. "So why forsake the bright lights to move to this sleepy town?"

I glanced at Willow. "I'm not a fan of bright lights, Sir."

"It can get very boring here. There's little nightlife to speak of."

"That's okay. I like a quiet life."

He stared into his own whiskey glass. "My daughter is very precious to me. If you think you're going to come here, hurt her and move on, you better think again." He raised his head and looked me full in the eye. I wanted to rush over and hug him hard and call him Dad. That was how much I respected him at that moment. He didn't care I had more money than him. He just wanted me not to hurt his daughter.

Next to me I could feel the tension in Willow's body. "Dad! We just started dating," she burst out.

Before I could open my mouth to answer, the door opened and Willow's mother came in. The delicious smell of food cooking wafted in with her. She clapped her hands to get our attention.

"Okay, everybody. The meal is ready. We're having meatloaf. Stop everything and come to the table now. I've been slaving over a hot stove all day and I want to make sure it's served at its best."

Everybody obediently stood and followed her out to the next room, where a table was set for four. My heart warmed when I saw how much trouble she had gone to. There were flowers, candles, linen napkins folded into swans, and crystal goblets, and gleaming silverware.

"What a beautiful table setting," I complimented.

She blushed with pleasure. "Thank you." She gestured towards my seat and I moved towards it. I waited until her father was seated before I did.

The meatloaf was brought in and my stomach rumbled. I just about stopped myself from rubbing my hands together. The last time I had meatloaf was at Mrs. Steven's house. She often invited me for dinner because she knew my mother's idea of a meal was either a chicken bucket from KFC when she was feeling generous or a pot of macaroni and cheese from a box. I watched Willow surreptitiously as her mother served me a thick slice of meatloaf and piles of vegetables and potatoes. When I caught her eyes, I smiled softly at her. She smiled back.

Then it was time for grace. I closed my eyes and let her father's words wash over me. We never said prayers at home and when I was in prison, I was downright angry with God, but hearing her father's simple words of thanks, felt good and right. Yes, my life had been shit, but it made me the man I was today. Hard, resourceful, resilient, unbreakable. And because of it I could better protect and care for Willow, her father, mother, and our children when they came into this world.

"You're a very handsome man. Can you believe Willow didn't mention you at all until today?"

Willow choked and sprayed out the water she had just sipped. "Oh, my God! I'm so sorry."

She then shot up from her chair, and the force of her movement sent it crashing down. And then she reached to grab it, but her elbow knocked over her glass of wine. Fortunately, my reflexes were fast and I managed to catch it before it spilled on her mother's snow-white, flawlessly ironed tablecloth. I quickly rose and helped her pick up her chair.

She froze, and clenched her eyes shut. "I'm so sorry, Mom."

"It's okay, honey. There's no harm done. Sit down and eat your food."

Both her parents watched silently as Willow sat and I followed. I picked up my knife and fork.

"This looks wonderful, Ma'am," I said with a smile.

"Call me Sally, remember." Her smile was warm and genuine and I knew I had passed her defenses. She approved of me. There was only her father left to conquer. I cut up a piece of meat and forked it into my mouth. It melted in my mouth. It left Mrs. Steven's dry meatloaf in the dust.

"Mmm ... this is the most delicious meatloaf I have ever tasted," I told Sally, truthfully.

Sally beamed with pleasure. There was a twinkle in her eyes, when she said, "Good, I'm glad you like it. It's my mother's special recipe. I'll pass it on to Willow so she can make it for you."

"I really appreciate that," I said with a chuckle.

"What are your intentions towards my daughter?" her father asked suddenly. "You never answered my question from before."

I turned to him. "I'm not a player, Sir. Never have and never will be. I'm here to stay. My intentions are utterly and completely honorable."

He stared at me as if trying to decide how sincere I was.

"Willow says you have a quick trip planned for the weekend?"

I nodded. "That's right."

"You'll keep her safe for us, won't you?"

"I'll guard her with my life, Sally," I promised.

It was the absolute truth to me, but I could feel the others in the room were startled by my words. I could only hope I didn't come across as too good to be true.

I lowered my head and returned to my food.

For a while we ate and made small talk, but her father was not finished. He put his knife and fork down and looked at me seriously. "Willow said we shouldn't ask about your parents, but she didn't have any information on your father. I hope you'll understand that I need to know at least that much about you before I approve of ... *this trip*."

"I completely understand, Sir. My father wasn't very stable when I was growing up, sir. He was a bit abusive and quite the alcoholic. He left home when I was fifteen and I haven't seen him since."

The room went quiet.

There was an odd expression on her father's face. "So ... you raised yourself?"

"Pretty much, Sir."

He frowned. "Where did you go to college?"

"I never did, Sir."

"How did you get into investment—?"

"Dad?" Willow protested, but I placed my hand on hers to reassure her that I was fine to answer any questions her father wanted to ask.

"Willow, why are you interrupting me? Don't I deserve to know the background of the man who is about to whisk you away for a weekend?"

"You do, Sir," I replied. "Please go ahead."

"Investment securities. How did you get into it?"

"I met a man who was a wizard with numbers, when he found out I was quite good with them too, he took me under his wing and mentored me. Things progressed from then." I had told no lies.

A silence ensued then, but luckily her mother stepped in to break the ice. "Would you like some pecan pie?" she asked and I sent her a smile. "I would absolutely love some, Sally."

She pressed her husband's shoulders as she headed into the kitchen.

Willow

"I am so sorry about my father giving you the third degree."

He only laughed as he clicked his seatbelt into its latch. "There's nothing to be sorry for. I would have done the same. He's a great father."

"He is," I replied dreamily, and relaxed into the first-class seat. This was life. Being whisked away from it all with a tall, hot man for the weekend.

I felt his large warm hand rest on mine, so I slid mine underneath and linked my fingers with his. He turned to me with a smile, and as I watched his beautiful face and gentle eyes, I couldn't understand how and why this angel had just appeared out of nowhere.

"Isn't it weird that I feel as if I know you from the past?"

Instantly I felt him go tense, and I hurried on to explain. "My mom mentioned it," I said. "Her words were 'he acts like he's known you forever'."

He seemed to relax then, a small smile teasing the corners of his lips. "Perhaps I have. In another lifetime."

I wasn't completely dismissive of the idea. "Perhaps you have," I said. "I wouldn't know, would I?"

At the seriousness in my tone, he turned to me. "No, you wouldn't."

His grip tightened on mine and something sparked in the air between us. "But we haven't met in this life, have we? I mean before, in the past?"

He smiled, but he looked away. "You haven't."

"Are you sure?" I pressed on. I was aware it must be irritating for him that I kept asking if he was connected to my forgotten past. I'd even told myself I should give it a rest and stop trying to make him fit into my drama, but I simply couldn't help myself. He was so familiar. He *felt* like the man I'd been waiting for. The man from my dreams.

He returned his gaze to me. "Why do you think you have?"

"Well, the way you act. We've only known each other for a short time but you seem so ... decided on me."

"I take my commitments very seriously. And I'm not decided on you yet. We're going away together and I'll be watching out for horrendous habits I can't accept."

I laughed. "Well, I'll be watching you too. Who knows if you secretly have some fetish that you hide under all this cool, infallible exterior."

His response surprised me. "I do," he said. "And that's why I'm especially looking forward to this trip. I can't wait to fully unleash myself at you."

A bolt of excitement zapped through me. I wanted to have his fetishes unleashed on me. "Why do I believe you?" I whispered.

He shrugged. "Maybe because you know I always say what I mean."

"Uh, oh. I shouldn't have agreed to this trip, should I?"

His smile almost made my heart burst. It was full and gleaming like a wolf's. "Maybe you shouldn't have."

When we arrived at our hotel room a few hours later, I was stunned by the splendor and luxury all around me. I was a simple girl from a small town. This, I had only seen in movies. I didn't even dream of it, because it seemed as unreachable as marrying a prince.

The hotel lobby was all marble and chrome, and when we got to our suite I gasped. What an expansive, beautiful room, with a glorious four poster canopy bed, and an oversized lounge. Out on the terrace was our own swimming pool and Jacuzzi, and it all overlooked the panoramic view of the ocean.

"Wow!" I exclaimed as I took it all in.

He tipped the young man who had brought our suitcases for us and followed me towards the windows. I turned to him with eyes brimming with excitement. "This is very, very extravagant. I'll have to work a whole year and some to pay my half."

"Don't worry about it. The moment you're able to I'll ensure that you pay me back."

I laughed. "Don't you need some kind of collateral?"

"I do," he drawled. "I'll collect it tonight."

My eyes widened, especially as his 'friendly' threat on the plane came to mind. "You're not one of those charming serial killers, are you?"

He chuckled. "Nope."

Then he turned and headed into the bathroom. I walked out onto the balcony, and after soaking in the magnificent scenery around me, I shut my eyes and breathed in the cool night air. A light breeze brought the scent of the ocean. I let the memory of the boy with the balloon play in my mind, but no more would come. Immediately, the hollowness in my heart that I had been trying my best to ignore came back.

I opened my eyes and decided then. On this brief break I would not think of the past. I gave myself the permission to relax. I'd leave all my troubles and concerns behind me, and to do my best to be present enough to enjoy my time with Caleb.

I hadn't heard his footsteps. I only sensed his presence when the spices and warm vanilla in his aftershave enveloped me. He slipped his arms around my waist and pressed a kiss to my neck. His hands slid down my sides before curving around my ass. Then he grabbed it and pressed me into his somewhat hardened groin. He was usually always gentle with me but I especially relished times like this when he was aggressive and just a tad bit rough. It gave me a glimpse into a dangerous side of him that he didn't let out very often, and it thrilled me.

"Do you want something to eat?" he whispered into my skin.

I closed my eyes and savored the sensuous silk of his lips against my neck. I wanted him to show me that other side of him, but I told myself to wait. Somehow, I knew it would come later, closer to midnight, when beasts come out to play.

"I'm not super hungry," I murmured, "but I'm sure that there'll be some light food and entertainment downstairs."

"Alright," he said to me. "Let's go."

37
Caleb

We ended up at a nightclub.

After an interesting Japanese meal of blow fish and sake, we'd been on our way back to our suite when a cacophony of excitement and loud music had grabbed Willow's attention from across the beach. She stopped and glanced at the venue's colorful flashing lights and listened to the squeals and shouts of its patrons from afar, then she looked up at me with enormous eyes. "Shall we?"

I'd never been to a club before.

I hadn't exactly been a model teen before I was incarcerated, but I had missed all of the official rites of passage into adulthood. No 18th birthday, no 21st birthday celebration. Instead I'd spent those years locked away with bullies who were three times my age and size, hardening my heart even further. The only softness inside me was my love for Willow.

As we got closer the sound became deafening. I could feel the music beating inside my head, even in my veins. It was exciting and something I'd never experienced before. Inside it was a humid fest. Willow tightened her grasp of my hand and led me through the unending onslaught of pressing human bodies.

We passed the dance floor and arrived at the bar. There was an enclosure marked VIP with a plush empty seat. I walked up to a waiter, ordered the best champagne in the house, and gave him the biggest tip of his life. He opened the velvet ropes and let us through. We sat on the plush sofa and watched the mayhem while we waited for our bottle to arrive. People stood in clusters drinking and shouting above the music, but most were dancing wildly on the floor. The champagne arrived and we clinked glasses.

"To tonight," I mouthed.

"To tonight," she mouthed, her eyes filled with a wild light. She leaned closer. Her lips were touching my ear, and her hand on the side of my face.

"Let's go dance," she yelled, above all the sounds around us trying to drown her voice.

I didn't know what to say. I was a fighter not a dancer. There had been no opportunity for dancing where I'd been. I was sure I had two left feet and I didn't really want to humiliate myself just yet. Maybe once I had seen what everyone else was doing. "Maybe later," I shouted back.

She responded with an adorable pout and a hard tug at my

shirt. Frowning, she pulled her phone out of her purse and wrote something into her notes app.

Then she held the lit phone screen forward so that I could read her words.

> *I've always wanted to come to a club*
> *with someone I cared about.*
> *So that I could thoroughly let loose.*

I wanted to say yes and oblige, but the more I watched the dancers bouncing around violently as if they were boneless the more convinced I became that dancing was just not for me. As a matter of fact, most of the dancers looked like they were juiced up on drugs. Perhaps if it had been a different kind of music. The kind where I could mold her to my body ...

I watched her subtly from the corners of my eyes. Her head was bobbing to the music as she sipped her champagne. When she was done with her glass, she set it down and turned to me once again. I looked straight ahead and pretended to be engrossed in the dancers.

"You're really not going to come with me?"

I took the phone from her and typed in my response.

> *This doesn't look like my kind of thing.*

She took her phone back and typed in another message.

> *Oh, come on.*

I shook my head in response.

"Just for a few minutes," she mouthed.

She must have seen from my expression that I wasn't exactly excited by the prospect so she jumped up and tried to pull me off the sofa. When her efforts proved completely useless, she scowled at me and joined the crowd. I didn't feel good about rejecting her. I was torn between wanting to be with her and not making a complete fool of myself.

I drained my glass and decided to keep my eyes on her, and on everyone that came even remotely close.

When she got on the dance floor, I noticed she kept to a corner so that she could dance as freely as she wanted to, but then men slowly began to eye her. I noticed them, and scowled. One eventually went up to her and joined her in a dance.

She ignored him and carried on doing her thing, and I realized what she had meant when she said she had always wanted to dance with someone she cared about. Another man, it seemed as if he knew the first guy, came up and began to dance on the other side of her. She was sandwiched between the two bastards. I saw the discomfort in her face as she tried her best to pretend these two men were not on either side of her.

I didn't think. My body moved and suddenly I was pushing bodies out of the way, on my way towards her.

One of the men came so close to her that one of his hands brushed her hip. She pushed it away, but clearly did not want to make a scene. Then the other one moved in and brought his face close to hers. Her reaction was to lean away, which served to bring her closer to the other dog behind her.

Both men were smiling widely, trying to make light of the fact that they were taking advantage of her. She turned in the direction I'd been sitting in, and there was almost a hurt look on her face, but I was not there, I was already more than halfway across the floor. That look on her face twisted my heart. Made me lose all reason. I was no longer in a nightclub where people went to have fun. I was in a bear pit fighting rivals off my woman.

As I reached them they ignored me. There was no reason for them to think I mattered to them.

I grabbed Willow's hand and pulled her out of the circle of their bodies. Only one of them had a brain. He saw the look in my eyes and immediately started to back away.

The other thought that it would be an idea to challenge me.

He had no idea. No fucking idea.

It was like sending a two-year old toddler into the ring with a heavyweight boxer. I grabbed him by his scrawny neck. Before he could even figure out what was happening, I'd thrown him forward. He flew across the floor and landed on his ass.

The crowd gasped and screamed at the altercation and moved out of the way. The man immediately jumped to his feet, incensed, while I stood my ground and stared menacingly at him. I didn't want to fight him. He was just a kid.

But when his companion found the guts and came for me too, I let Willow go. Slowly, I began to fold my sleeves up my arms in preparation for them. In a fight confidence is everything. Both men exchanged a look and in that look I already knew I had won. I didn't blink. My eyes had kept me safe inside and I knew how intimidating they were when I was riled. They waved their arms aggressively and cursed loudly before they walked away.

Willow grabbed my hand. "Come. Let's dance somewhere else."

Willow

After Caleb had tossed a fully-grown man across the floor as if he was nothing more than a bowling pin, and without even seeming to have to exert himself, my desire for dancing dissipated like smoke.

I wanted him inside me! It was strange though as the very thought of violence would have repulsed me before, but now seeing Caleb switch from his usually calm demeanour was an aphrodisiac like nothing I'd ever known before.

I pulled him along towards the hotel. He followed without complaint all the way to the elevator. He stood next to me as we silently rode up. The bud between my legs was throbbing with excruciating arousal.

"I thought you'd always let me get my way," I said.

He turned towards me.

It was incredible, but I felt no shame, I wanted to climb him right there.

"Most of the time I will," he said.

I moved to stand in front of him, and slightly lifted myself to the tips of my toes so that the top of my head could come close to his neck. He had his hands in his pockets, sporting that deceptively cool pose, but tonight I'd found out given the right motivation, he was as dangerous as a tiger protecting its dinner.

I put my face as close to his as was possible and stared into those beautiful eyes. I got lost in the starburst inside them. My voice was a whisper. "I wanted to dance with you because I wanted to grind against you tonight."

His expression didn't change, but his pupils opened like the shutter of a camera. It was amazing to watch.

"The night is not over. You *are* going to grind on me," he growled.

There was so much promise in those words, I felt a flutter in my chest. I moved away when the elevator dinged at its arrival on our floor. I looked up at him flirtatiously from under my lashes. "What's the fun in that? It's more exciting when we're surrounded by other people."

Then I swayed out of the elevator.

He had the key so when I got to our door I leaned on my hip against the door frame and waited for him. Suddenly, I felt the forceful thrust of his hips against me at the same time his big hands came around my body.

"Hey!"

He kissed my neck, which immediately made me go weak at the knees. Before I could protest his hand slipped into the band of my skirt. I was powerless to put a stop to whatever he planned on doing, nor did I want to. My head fell backwards as his hand slid into my underwear to grab my sex roughly. It had been my intention to do exactly this to him the moment we got back to the room, but he had beaten me to it. I jerked my hips restlessly to and fro to relieve the tension between my legs.

His fingers slipped between the already damp folds of my sex. Then he began to move in a delicious circular rhythm. He teased my clit at just the perfect tempo, and my whole body shuddered. I could only gasp when he slipped a finger inside of me.

"What if someone comes?" I muttered hoarsely.

"I thought you said you wanted people to watch," he said as a second finger joined the incursion. They curved and stroked, and I was certain that I was going to come right there, in front of our door when anyone could pass at any moment and see us. He was right, I didn't care. After all I would never see them again.

He, however did. There was a sound behind us and he immediately pulled his hand out of me, slipped the card key into the card slot, and pushed open the door. There was a look of extreme protectiveness of me in his eyes as he led me in. He closed the door and leaned against it.

"Who's the coward now?" I mocked.

He didn't react, just looked at me, as if he was about to devour me.

I began to walk backwards. "I'm of the mind to refuse you right now. Just like you refused me with the dance."

He threw the key card across the foyer's console table. There was no expression on his face at all. "Sure. I can respect that."

I stopped. In that moment, I truly wanted to strangle him. "Caleb!" I groaned.

A small laugh escaped him. His laughter surprised me. It was in times like this when the less controlled, spontaneous part of him came out that I melted. He was usually attentive and watchful, almost wary, almost as though he was expecting a bomb to go off somewhere close. I always wondered what he had gone through in his lifetime to make him so guarded and non-expressive.

I cocked my head, and decided then to try my best to understand him so that I could better respect his limits. "Why didn't you want to dance with me?"

His response however, once again surprised me. "I wanted to, badly."

"So why the refusal? Why are you so averse to dancing in public?"

"If you want me to dance with you in public, you're going to have to teach me first ... in private."

"Ah, you need lessons?"

"Many."

"How come you've never learned to dance?"

He shrugged. "Never had the desire or the opportunity."

"Do you want your lessons to start tonight?" I asked mischievously.

"Since we're not having sex, we might as well dance."

I felt as if I wanted to punish him for it and there was only one way that came to mind.

I untied the sash that cinched my green velvet wrap skirt around my waist and stepped towards him. He slipped his hands back into his pockets at my approach, and stared at me, his lips twisted with wry amusement.

"Are you going to strangle me with that?" he asked.

"Why? Do you want me to?"

39
Caleb

I stood my ground as she approached, unblinking, electrified, and hard as fuck. She was beautiful, sexy and vibrating with vengeful ideas ... and I loved every bit of it.

Willow, Willow, Willow.

From that first day she had arrived at school, alone and sad, she had me twisted around her little finger. I would have become an angry, psychopathic thug if she had not come. I was already halfway there. I carried a knife inside my jacket and I very nearly used it on someone. But after our gazes touched across the canteen, everything changed.

She became my lifeline, coloring my life with sweetness, excitement, and hope. Taking my mind off what always awaited me at home.

But that was also when it started, the irresistible desire to dedicate myself to ensuring she was safe. The feeling never went away. Ever. Not for one moment. Not even when I was banged up inside, I used to sit in my cell and worry about her.

I watched her now, as she came towards me. All grown up, confident, sexually powerful, and unbelievably beautiful.

As she neared me I had to hold myself back from grabbing her. I knew she wanted to tease me so I let her take her time. Her breasts were full and straining against the low neckline of her top. I was dying to take the creamy mounds in my mouth, but ...

Patience, Caleb, patience

My cock swelled painfully inside my boxer shorts.

She threw the sash around my neck, her eyes boring confrontationally into mine. "How offended would you be if I used this to pull you along with me?"

I wanted to laugh at how serious she sounded. "I wouldn't be offended at all," I replied gravely. "But you won't be able to unless I decide to take a step from this spot."

"You keep throwing your weight around," she said softly. "You love intimidating me, don't you?"

"Are you intimidated?"

She puffed. "Of course not."

"Exactly."

She took another step closer to me and moved towards me until our faces were only inches apart. Her body lightly brushed against mine and her sweet scent swirled around me. Maddening me. I couldn't even think straight. I wanted her that bad.

"I want to know the extent of the power I have over you."

"You can do whatever you want whenever you like," I said hoarsely. And it was the truth.

Her pupils dilated. "Whatever I want?"

I nodded slowly. She was killing me.

She smiled, and slowly it widened to reveal her small even teeth. Then she pulled at the sash and my head lowered to meet hers. Her tongue slipped, licked my bottom lip, then she lightly nibbled on it.

It was taking everything in me to keep from taking charge, from moving past the tease and having my way with her. With every second that passed I could feel the screws in my brain that held me tightly in control come loose.

"I want to suck you off," she whispered.

I swallowed hard. "It's your show, babe."

Turning around, she pulled me along with her and I went like a hypnotized slave.

A few minutes later, I was horizontal on top of the bed and my hands were tied above my head to the bed post. She was positioned between my spread legs, and working the buckle of my belt. She pulled her panties off and twirled the lacy material on her index finger.

"Promise me you won't use your hands."

"They're tied," I pointed out. The anticipation she had built inside me meant I was barely able to speak by this time.

"You know very well you could easily break away," she said. "Remember, don't grab or stop me. I just want you to lie there and be tortured."

I gave the promise. "I'll do my best."

She shook her head. "Nope. Doing your best is not enough. You have to promise you will not stop me no matter what."

"Fine," I agreed, from between clenched teeth.

She deliberately took her time to unfasten my slacks.

"Lift your hips," she ordered.

When I obeyed she pulled the fabric down and my cock popped out, thick, hot, and heavy. The warmth of her breath against it made it throb. She moved to sit astride me, taking most of her weight onto her knees as she lightly settled her sex over my engorged cock.

Then she began to stroke her wet pussy all over my dick. Watching her do that made me breathless. I could see that it had the same dizzying effect on her too; soft moans flowed from her lips as her eyelids drooped with lust. A part of me wanted to shut my eyes so that I could thoroughly savor every bit of pleasure she was teasing out of my body, but I couldn't take my eyes off the seductive writhing of her hips.

I couldn't see any part of her and I couldn't see myself either as her skirt was gathered around my groin, but that just made it even hotter.

I wanted so badly then to put my hands around her waist, but as I moved to do just that I remembered my hands were tied up. She opened her eyes just in time to note my attempt, and it brought a satisfied smile to her face.

"How does it feel to be bound?" she asked breathlessly.

If only she knew about the handcuffs I'd worn in my lifetime. "Don't worry I'm going to return the favor."

With a laugh, she got off me, and standing on the bed began to undress. One by one it all came off until she was fully naked. She sat astride me again. I stared at her mesmerized.

"Show me your pussy," I growled.

She leaned back and, resting her palms behind her, opened her legs wide. Really wide. And she was so fucking beautiful I thought I would come right then and there. I stared hungrily at the open pink flesh between her legs. Her little pussy was dripping with excitement. I could feel her sweetness leak onto my belly.

"Let me have a taste," I begged.

She straightened and leaned forward till her face was bare inches away from mine. Then she grinned wolfishly. "You have to deserve things like that." Then she crawled up my body and held her sweet pussy just over my mouth. The scent of her drove me wild. I could feel my mouth begin to water.

When I tried to lift my face and lick that juicy peach, she pulled away with a mocking laugh.

She turned around so her ass was on view. Deliberately, she got on her hands and knees so I would have a glorious view of her swollen pussy hanging between her ass cheeks. With one hand, she grabbed my cock and guided it between the wet folds of her sex.

My breath came out sharp, and fast. She let my cock impale her slowly. Her tight slickness sent a delicious heat spreading from where we were connected, all the way to every nerve-ending in my body. I was beginning to sweat, and my heels were digging into the mattress. I wanted her to move, but she gave a sigh and lifted herself off me.

It was like a kick to the gut. I was so desperate and turned on I wanted to beg, but I knew begging would be no use.

She turned around and kissed me. Hooking my tongue into her mouth, she began to suck it hard. It was wild and sensual. No one had sucked my tongue before let alone like that.

Slowly, she began to trace the heated kisses down my torso. Her lips on my skin burned, but there was nothing I could do to soothe the ache beyond remaining still, and helpless to her assault.

She began to slide down my body as her kisses went lower and lower. My whole body felt like it was on fire. Until she was at my groin. Then she lifted her head, and with a flip of her hair to the side grabbed the base of my cock.

Her hands were small, but their hard grip on my cock was

firm. She slipped her tongue out and licked the pre-cum oozing out of me. I couldn't take it anymore. The restraint was going to drive me crazy and she hadn't even fully begun.

"Willow, let me go," I said, barely recognizing my own voice. "Untie this fucking sash."

"Absolutely not," she replied.

I pulled at the pathetic tie of her sash, and sat up. She was too startled by the sudden movement to be able to move away quickly enough. My arms locked around her body.

"Caleb," she complained. "You promised that you were going to play along."

"True, but I'm not ready to lose my mind in the process."

"Well, you don't have a choice. That's my triumph and you're going to let me have it. And moreover, you've made me lose my head in the past too, and I didn't complain."

I held out my hands and she retied my wrist using the same pathetic knot. Well, let her do her worst, next it will be my turn and won't she be surprised at what my fetish is. I let myself fall back on the bed.

"Be a good boy," she said approvingly as she lifted her arms to wrap her hair into a messy bun on top of her head. Watching her elegant, fluid movements was beyond mesmerizing. She was just a dream come true. She tapped on my lower stomach, which made my cock jerk in response.

Fisting me firmly she lowered her head and slid her tongue up and down the shaft, and licked from base to tip and all over as if I was a quickly melting Popsicle she was slurping on a hot day. At her leisure she moved down to my balls and after sucking on them returned her lips back to my head.

My hands fisted the bed sheets at the tease, as I fought to keep my breathing under control.

"Willow," I swallowed, unable to remain still. My body became too agitated for me to control as she hollowed her cheeks and once again pulled me deep into her mouth until I reached the back of her throat. I felt her gag, then smoothly move forward. She tried it again, and gagged once more. She let a second pass, then she took me deep into her throat again. Gagged again. Tried again. I knew then she was learning to take all of me into her mouth. I let her practice. I loved watching my cock disappear into her luscious mouth. It was just beautiful. It seemed as if my cock stayed longer and longer in her throat before she pulled upwards.

Until she pulled up completely. She looked at me with swollen lips. "I just found out I love sucking cock." With the tip of her tongue she dug at the entrance of my cock, as if trying to tease out my cum.

"Fuck, Willow. Are you trying to drive me crazy?"

Her head began to bob up and down in the most luscious rhythm, and I moved my hips to meet her pumps. She milked me deliciously. It wasn't long before the great rush of pleasure came and I was emptying myself down her throat. I thought she would take her mouth off my cock, but she sucked even harder.

In that delirious moment of pleasure, my hands broke free of the sash and went to hold her head in place as my hips fucked her mouth, and my mouth called her name. Again and again. Until the storm subsided.

"Willow," I breathed when every drop of pleasure had been sucked out of my cock. I flattened against the bed. I heard her soft laughter as she moved up my body until her face was poised just above mine.

"Feel better now?" she teased, licking her luscious lips. Her bun had long come undone and once again, her hair fell in a cascade all around her. She looked like a goddess. And it was time I worshiped her.

I flipped my body over and took her with me.

"Caleb," she laughed as she found herself under me. Her laughter faded away as I stared deeply into her eyes.

At that moment I wanted to tell her. I wanted to tell her I loved her more than the moon and the stars. More than my own life. But I knew she wasn't ready. It was too soon for her. She hadn't been pining for me for twelve long years. To her, she just met me a couple of weeks ago. I crushed my lips to hers and tried to bury the words into my kiss.

She responded to my urgency and desperation to be completely engulfed in her. I moved my hands down and lifted her legs. I swung them around my shoulders. That elevated her lower body completely off the bed. Her thighs were open to expose her sweet, sweet cunt to me.

With my hand going underneath to hold her in place I plunged my cock into her soaked and pulsing opening. And that was all it took. She exploded into a mind shattering orgasm. Her eyes rolled back into her head, as I fucked her through it all. Plunging my cock into her clenching pussy again and again. My groin slamming into her gorgeous ass. The erotic slap of flesh on flesh filled the room.

"'Caleb!" she screamed, her hands clawing desperately at the sheets.

I didn't think that there was anything I loved more than watching her unravel in this way.

When the raging waves of ecstasy had subsided, I shifted my weight onto my elbows and carried on fucking her. I could smell the scent of our desire in the air.

I wanted now to slowly fuck her out of her mind. I wanted to take her away to a completely different place, to establish an unforgettable moment she would recall over and over again.

I ground my cock into her sex and she whimpered with pleasure as her back arched off the bed. Deliberately and slowly, I tormented her, until her whole body trembled. I watched with pride as her eyes rolled into the back of her head once more.

"Oh God." She violently fisted my hair. I could feel the shuddering of her body as intense pleasure rushed through her in waves. Tears rolled down the corners of her eyes.

"Caleb," she cried and tried to hide her face in my neck, but I stopped her.

"Look at me," I commanded, but she shook her head and she

turned away, her face twisted at the delicious agony tearing through her.

I leaned into her ears and spoke. "Willow, look at me."

Then I slammed back into her.

"I want you to know that I'm here."

I rammed into her again.

"For always. Never hold back when you're in front of me."

Another thrust.

"Let it all go and let it all out. And leave it to me to pick up the pieces."

"Stop," she cried, but she tightened her hold around me.

"I can't take it. It's too much."

I covered her lips with mine and continued making love to her. My lips planted kisses all over her face and then moved to her breasts. I sucked her nipples. I bit them until she cried out. Then I sucked them again.

I felt the tension build and rise dangerously within her, and when she was finally ready to let go again, she exploded with a shout beneath me. I kept moving, soothing the ache, prolonging the orgasm for as long as possible.

"Oh, my God," she sobbed beneath me.

I held tightly onto her as she fell apart. When it was over she looked at me with no defences in her eyes.

"Now do you want to know what my fetish is?" I whispered.

Her pupils almost as large as her irises. "Yes," she mouthed soundlessly. I left her on the bed and went to my suitcase. I took out the four silk ropes and brought them to her. Her eyes widened.

"Yes, Willow, I want to do the exact same thing you wanted to do to me. Tie you up and torment you. But I want to do it for hours."

She lay there quietly while I spread-eagled her and I tied her up to the four posts. My Willow looked beautiful. Then I began. I began to eat her pussy. I have no idea how many orgasms she had. Every time she begged me to stop. She said it was too much. She couldn't endure another climax. She was too sensitive. She called me names. She shouted at me. But I never stopped. For hours I sucked, I licked, I drank from her pussy.

Finally, finally, when dawn was breaking, and her pussy lips were so swollen they protruded out of her, I stopped. Her eyes were wide, her face was flushed, her hair messy from where she had turned her head from side to side. She was all mine.

I untied her and filled her with my seed then.

"Now you know what my fetish is, my sweet Willow."

40

Willow

One week later

Once again, I caught myself staring down at my phone. My thumbs were suspended above the screen, but I couldn't bring myself to place a call or even send a text.

"Flowers are here," Sandra announced.

I dragged my attention back to reality.

"You seriously didn't hear Bradley's van?" she asked, making a baffled face at me as she walked towards the front door, her hands were still sheathed in the gloves she'd been using to work with in the back.

I stared blankly at her, not a single response coming to mind.

"God, you really have it bad for him, don't you?"

I dropped the phone and went out to assist her to bring in the flowers.

Bradley barely met my gaze, and the cold reception from someone I had been friendly with for years made me feel a bit sad, but I no longer felt any guilt. Why should I? To start with I never encouraged him or promised him anything. Hell, I didn't even know he felt that way about me. It was his fault for not having the courage to make any kind of official advance, so we could have put the matter to rest ages ago and he wouldn't have wasted all these years hoping I'd magically realize he was interested in me and return the feelings.

Ignoring his sullen face, I focused on unloading the daylilies that we'd ordered. Bradley had brought a friend along so he joined us in unloading the flowers and fertilizers from the van. Soon enough, the task was completed.

I left Sandra to handle the log with him and returned to my phone. The moment I again pulled up the NASDAQ's site, something I had never dreamed I would ever be doing. I gasped. The market just kept falling. The entire day was worsening! I couldn't hold it in anymore. I dialed his number. When he answered I rushed to speak. "Babe, I'm so sorry for calling right now. I just needed to check in. Any updates on your end?"

"Four clients just ordered us to close them out. Combined they've suffered about $1.5 million in losses."

I went silent. I didn't know what to say to that.

"I'm going to start trading now," he said. "I'm going to close out the positions against me and allow the rest to run."

"Alright," I said. "Alright. I'll leave you to it. Don't be too disheartened, things will be okay."

"Thank you, sweetheart. It'll be fine in the end. Don't let this bother you."

"Okay," I said, and ended the call so that he could get back to work. I realized I was the center of attention.

"What's going on, Mrs. Wolfe?" Sandra asked. "Everything okay?"

I frowned at her. She had taken to calling me Mrs. Wolfe in the last couple of days. "Caleb is just having some issues with the stock market, but all should be well."

"You're married?" Bradley's friend suddenly asked, looking from me to Bradley with confusion. Bradley looked shocked before he quickly returned his attention to his order clipboard.

"I'm not," I replied, and sent a disapproving look to Sandra.

She ignored it. "She basically is," she said. "She and her boyfriend act like they've been married for a hundred years. Since he got here a couple of weeks ago he probably knows more about her than I do, and we've been best friends since high school."

Bradley's friend laughed. "You sound jealous."

"I am! A hundred percent," she replied. "So to taunt her, I call her Mrs. Caleb Wolfe. Maybe one of these days I'll even slip up and say it in front of him."

My head shot up. "I'll kill you if you do!" I threatened, my teeth were bared.

"I know of a Caleb Wolfe from way back. I was in freshman year," Bradley's friend, Henry said. "He was quite infamous. He was convicted of murder and sent to prison. Shocked the hell out of the entire county."

"Whoa," Sandra exclaimed. "What high school was that?"

"Met West in Bitter Creek," he said.

Something struck my chest.

Sandra immediately caught the connection too. "Met West? Willow, isn't that the combination school you attended before you moved here to Folsom?"

"Yeah," I replied, then turned to meet the surprised look in Henry's eyes.

"Neat," he said, with a shrug.

The room had gone eerily quiet. Or maybe it was just in my mind.

"Willow, what if your Caleb is that *Caleb Wolfe?* Wouldn't that be creepy as hell?"

She turned to the guy who had just dropped the bombshell. "Do you have any more details? Do you know who he murdered and why? How old was he at the time?"

"I'm not sure. I didn't pay too much attention, you know. I was just a kid, but I think he might have been fifteen, but don't quote me on that. But I remember it was his age that made the case national headlines. It was the first time a kid had killed a priest."

"A priest? Wow! That is freaking insane," Sandra gasped. "That must have caused quite a buzz. Strange I didn't hear about it. Having said that I had no interest in news at that age. I was so caught up with what was happening in our school even though the most interesting thing that ever happened there was someone getting off with their teacher, or a random hallway fight. A murder takes the cake on high school delinquency."

"Yeah, it was big news."

"Do you know what happened to him?"

Henry shook his head. "He's probably still behind bars."

I had to admit, until he said the boy killed a priest, I was feeling uncomfortable, maybe even starting to think that boy could be Caleb. After all, Caleb Wolfe was such an unusual name, but the moment the guy said he killed a priest, I completely relaxed.

I knew it would never be Caleb. That was just not him. Even when he threw that man across the dance floor, there had been nothing evil in him. He hadn't lost control, or taken pleasure in hurting the man. He just wanted to get him away from me.

Killing wasn't him now, and it wouldn't have been him as a boy.

41

Caleb

I had lost thirty-five million dollars.

In one afternoon, the entire arbitrage had flopped.

I glanced over our trades and calculations and waited. The evening passed with me staring at my computer and by the time midnight came, I got the expected phone call.

"What the hell happened?"

"'You saw it too," I replied. 'The market went against us."

"'That's not enough to cause this kind of loss. Was there an error or something?"

There it was again. The question of the hour. "I'm trying to work it all out."

The man roared into the phone so loudly, that I had to pull it away from my ear. "You're trying to work it all out? You're trying? My clients have lost millions. In one fucking day. And you're telling me you're trying?"

"Tyler, you knew the risk involved with this arbitrage. You've been well aware from the start that you could lose all your profit, and you agreed with me that you were willing to take the risk. Well, your clients have lost exactly the profit they made. No more no less."

"God, damn you. I called you earlier and told you to close me out, but you convinced me to fucking stay, and now this is the result?"

"I'm sorry, Tyler, but your clients should be happy they're walking away without a real loss. It's a blood bath on the markets today ..."

"You know when I contacted Frank in prison, he told me that you were a genius. The absolute best he's ever seen, but after this I'm thinking of taking legal ac—"

"Great. See you in court," I said and cut the call.

I turned away from my computer screen and gazed out of my window. Soon, I wouldn't have this magnificent view any more. But I didn't care. I had done the right thing. And that brought a warm glow of satisfaction in my guts. In time this storm would blow over and I would start again. I knew from experience the truth in that wonderful line:

This too will pass.

I could lose all my money today and it wouldn't bother me one bit. Because I knew how to get it all back again.

But a few minutes after nine the next morning I got a different call, and I realized the storm was going to last longer than I expected. They were more tenacious than I had given them credit for.

"Willow," I said, with a frown. She never called at this time.

She hadn't yet said a word, but I didn't miss the harshness of her breathing. It seemed like she was trying to put herself together before she spoke to me.

My hand tightened around the phone. "Willow, are you alright?"

She took a deep breath. "I know you're having a hard time right now with the market and everything, but I didn't know who else to call. And I definitely can't call my parents."

I rose to my feet. "What's going on?"

"The shop, Caleb," she said and I could hear the pain in her voice. "It's been broken into. Someone came in last night and destroyed the entire place."

My heart slammed against my chest. "Are you at the shop now?" I asked as I grabbed my keys.

"Right in front of the store."

"Go to your van, and lock the door. Don't get out till I get there. I'm on my way."

"Caleb I—"

"Willow! Please listen to me. Go to your vehicle now and keep your head low. I'll be there in twenty minutes."

She finally caught the urgency in my tone. "Alright," she said, and ended the call.

I'd never driven so fast in my life, and in no time, I was at her shop. Even from outside I could see that the entire place was in shambles.

Parking at the opposite side of the street, I got out of my car and instantly spotted her van just a bit further down. She had done as I had said. I hurried towards her, my eyes darting around to catch any unusual movements or people. The moment I knocked on her window, she jumped and I saw the terror in her eyes. She had been so preoccupied with her thoughts that she hadn't even seen me approach. Relief washed over her face, and she rushed to get out of the car. She immediately jumped into my arms and I held her tightly to my body.

"I'm sorry," I said to her. "I'm so sorry."

She thought I was consoling her for the incident at the store, but she didn't know I was apologizing because it was my fault. If not for me this wouldn't have happened to her little florist shop. I could tell that she was trying her very best to hold her tears back, but when she couldn't any longer, I felt the slight tremble of her body as she broke into quiet sobs against my chest. I stroked her back gently and spoke to her calmly.

"It's okay. It's okay. We'll build it all back. Everything will be back to exactly what it was. That much I promise you."

A few minutes later she pulled away and wiped her eyes. Then she forced an incredibly sad smile to her lips, and my heart twisted at the pain that she couldn't hide in those eyes.

"Can you tell me what happened as far as you know?" I asked, holding on to her hand.

She sniffed. "I thought it was a burglary, but why would anyone even try to rob such a small flower shop? I looked around and just as I had suspected there is nothing missing. The till is smashed, but all the money is still on the floor. I don't think it was a burglary at all. I think that the person or people that did this wanted to send a message. But what I can't understand is why they would do this. What sort of message does someone want to send to me, or my parents, that would make them resort to destroying our little shop?"

I had a very good idea of what the message was, and who had sent it, but I couldn't tell her. "Look, I'll help you to rebuild your shop and we'll install surveillance cameras so this never happens again."

She nodded and we headed back to the shop to properly assess the damage.

42
Willow

The police had come and gone, and now it was just us three, Caleb, Sandra and I, left trying to see what we could salvage in the store.

"Maybe it was a burglary," Sandra said. "Maybe whoever it was thought they'd be able to find some cash lying around. But then when they broke in and found nothing, they got pissed and took out their anger on the entire store."

I couldn't respond.

All I could do was step over destroyed plants and flowers, shattered vases, and overturned shelves. They had attacked almost everything they could, and the entire floor was covered in soil and rubble. Even my little office had been destroyed, my desktop shattered, the folders torn open, and my carefully filed receipts strewn all over the floor.

Two years of my blood and sweat, and it had been turned into nothing overnight. And I had taken my parents' money to start this shop. I was waiting for the moment my heart would give out. I could already hardly breathe, each breath felt like I was sending shards of glass through my system. How was I going to tell them? What was I going to do?

"Willow," Sandra called.

"Yeah," I responded gruffly.

"We have a few online orders to fulfil this morning. Should we wait to handle this mess first and then deal with those later?"

I cleared my throat before I spoke again. "'No, let's try to fulfil the orders we have. This mess can't be handled that easily."

"Alright," she replied. The last thing in this world I wanted to do right now was to work, but I couldn't disappoint the customers who had already placed their orders for the day.

"I'll call Bradley to quickly deliver what we need again."

I nodded and then turned towards Caleb. He was standing in the corner, and although it seemed like he was just watching what was going on, I could tell, like me he was racking his brain to decide on what the next course of action would be.

I knew he was having a tough time and the last thing I wanted was to trouble him any further. I walked over and he shifted his gaze from the carnage on the floor to me. He pulled his hands out of the pockets.

"You should go home," I said. "You have your own troubles."

"I've evaluated most of the damage, and I think we can get things somewhat back to normal at the latest in a week. A few days earlier if we're faster."

I frowned. "Babe, we can't handle this mess that quickly. These things cost money. I estimate it will take us a few weeks to recover. I think we'll just start with the windows and doors and then slowly work our—"

"No, I'll pay for it," he said, pulling my hands into his. "Don't worry about the cost. I'll pay for the entire renovation so that you can be up and running by the end of the week."

I was surprised. "Why? Why would you want to pay for it? You're not the one who destroyed the shop."

I pulled my hand away from his, and took a step backwards.

I saw a slight panic flash through his eyes. He ran a hand through his hair, as he briefly looked away in contemplation. Although he still appeared fairly calm, as was his usual demeanor, I could tell he was also quite worried about something else.

"Babe, please go home." I stepped forward and lightly held onto his shirt. "I don't want to feel guilty for keeping you here. I already feel guilty enough for all of this damage."

His voice turned cold, and so were his eyes as they bored into mine. "Why would you feel guilty for this? You're not the one that destroyed the place either."

I tried to alleviate the concerns that I knew he felt for me. "It happened under my management," I replied. "My Dad told me to set up an alarm system, but I didn't think it was necessary. I figured no one would be interested in a tiny florist and I preferred to keep the cash just in case I ran into trouble. I can't help feeling inept."

"It's not your fault," he said. "It's mine."

The conviction in his tone took me aback. "What do you mean? How is this your fault?"

"Willow." He sighed deeply. "I need to tell you something."

I stilled, my eyes on his. In all the time I had known him, I had never seen him this serious before. There was nothing casual about his stance or gaze, and most definitely not his tone.

"Let's go out to the back," I said, and I went with him.

43

Caleb

We didn't need to sit down. I went over what I wanted to say in my head, and wished with all my heart that I didn't have to say a word, but things had changed and were potentially about to get worse. I couldn't keep her in the dark anymore.

I was the one whom had exposed her by coming into her life, and since I had no intention of leaving I was going to make damn sure that she was protected.

I tried my best to make my words as concise and as clear as possible. "Willow, I think the attack on your store has something to do with those people who want me to make their Ponzi scheme for them."

She blinked, hard. "What?"

"They know that you're in my life, so they must have done this to get some sort of response out of me to fix it."

Right now, there was nothing I hated more than the look on

her face. It was of fear and worry. The fact that I was the one to cause it made me sick to my stomach. To my surprise however, she suddenly smiled, and taking a step forward, placed a hand on my chest. The warmth that began to spread into every cell of my body at the simple contact, stunned me.

"Are you sure about this?" she asked. "Or are you just saying this so that I'll let you take on the responsibility of these renovations?"

"Willow, I wouldn't say this to you if I didn't have to. Trust me, the last thing I ever want is for you to worry or to make you unhappy. But, as I told you, the men I am dealing with ... are not the very best of people, and a huge sum of money is at stake here. They will not stop at anything to bring me to heel. I guess this is one way they're trying to light a fire under my ass."

"Why now?"

I sighed again.

"It's a long story and I don't want to get you involved. The less you know the better it is for you, but basically, my losses yesterday made them nervous. They are lashing out at me."

"Oh, my God! What will you do?"

I grinned. "Are you worrying about me?"

"Of course."

"I'm a master of the numbers. I'll survive."

She frowned. "Caleb, you didn't lose that money deliberately, did you? Just so you won't have to make their Ponzi scheme."

I put my finger to my lips and my eyes widened. Then I said, "Of course not. That would be illegal."

She moved her hand to my cheek to comfort me, and I felt even more guilty and undeserving of her.

"I'll fix this, Willow. I promise, I'll fix all the damage. Just give me a few days and you won't even know there was any damage. Let me take care of all the renovations for you. I'll bring you the labor and materials that you need right now, and they'll begin immediately. Just tell them whatever you want done, and include as many upgrades as you would like."

"Okay," she whispered.

"Secondly, I'm going to put a security team on you."

Her lips parted to refuse me, but I put my finger against her lips. "Please. For my peace of mind. You won't even see them, I promise you that, but I need their eyes on you just in the meantime."

She sighed, and leaned her forehead against my chest, "Fine. I understand, but only temporarily, right?"

"Absolutely."

She lifted her head to gaze into my eyes. "I'm worried," she said. "About you. If they can do this to frighten me it means they can do the same or worse to you."

"If they wanted to hurt me they would have done it already;

they're just doing this to force me to speed things up. Don't worry about it at all."

"Alright," she said and even though she was scowling, lifted to the tips of her toes to press a kiss to my cheeks.

After our agreement, it felt as though a huge weight had been lifted off my shoulders. We walked back into the store, and saw that one more person was now present. It was the idiot who had purposely dropped a plant on my feet during my previous visit, the one who was secretly in love with her. I had checked him out to confirm he was sane, his jealous attitude was the only loose screw he was dealing with, and he was all clear. I ignored him and turned to Willow. I put a hand on her arm.

"I'm leaving now," I said. "Keep me in the loop and send me updates as often as you can."

She nodded and folded her arms as if she was cold. Usually, she kissed and embraced me before my departure. She was either distracted and disturbed by the break in, or it was out of consideration for the idiot who was still watching us with a sullen, hostile expression.

"Willow," Sandra called.

Willow gave me one last look filled with concern, and moved from my side towards Sandra, who was trying to salvage some plants from the floor.

I started to head towards the door, but the idiot approached me. He stopped right in front of my face and I carefully reined in my temper. Willow didn't need me to add to her misery. As long as she considered him her friend, I would remain polite if it fucking killed me.

He stared me in the eye, then leaned in and said, "You murdered someone, didn't you?"

His voice was a mere whisper, but it struck like a sucker punch to the gut.

I didn't respond and his smile became smug.

"I can't fucking believe it," he said. "Your eyes are a dead give-away, mean and dangerous. Henry was right. You're the same Caleb Wolfe. Does Willow know? That the man she's chosen as her boyfriend is a killer?"

It took everything inside of me to hold back my temper, but I did. Oh, I did.

"Bradley, is everything alright?" Sandra called out.

"Yup, everything is peachy." Then he addressed me. "I'm going to give you a week to come clean to Willow, and break up with her quietly. Otherwise I'm going to tell her everything I know about her lover boy convict."

I lost it. I'd never taken well to threats and this one had come at the worst time possible. All I wanted was to mind my own business and make a life with Willow and I couldn't because of all these privileged shits standing in my way, trying to spoil it for me all over again. He was the last fucking straw. I grabbed a fistful of the limp coward's shirt and dragged him with me towards the bathroom. I was so pumped on adrenaline he was as heavy as a blow-up doll.

"Hey!" he shouted, his feet trailing along behind him and panic edging his voice. 'Hey!"

'Caleb!" I heard Willow yell outside the red fog in my head, but I couldn't change my direction. Not now. Someone had to pay for my pain. I threw him into the bathroom, kicked the door shut behind me, and locked it.

Then I turned to him, and the useless turd began to crawl backwards. His eyes glittered like a terrified rat. I grabbed him once more, and slammed him hard against the tiled wall.

I couldn't speak, my heart was burning with that much frustration and anger.

"What are you going to do?" he cried out, his shaky voice betraying just how much terror he felt.

I heard Willow's voice outside. As if from far away.

I shut my eyes and forced him to the ground. I tried to rein in my temper. I really tried. It didn't work.

"A-Are you going to kill me too?"

I lifted my gaze to his. Veins were bulging down his temple, and his entire face had turned dark red. He was just a few inches shorter than me, so no doubt the seemingly effortless way I'd handled him must have come as quite a shock.

"If you are so sure I've killed someone," I said through gritted teeth. "Then why do you keep pissing me off? Do you want to be next?"

"I do it because of Willow!" he spurted with trembling lips.

I smiled at him. "You act like you know everything, but you know absolutely nothing."

"I'm not scared of you," he told me, his eyes bulging with fear. "I'm going to tell her what you've done. Exactly who you are."

He truly never learned. I gave him a dead-eyed stare. "After you're done, make sure you dig a hole to bury yourself in. What's more Willow will still be mine and you'll be gone. Forever."

"Are you threatening me?" he blubbered through trembling lips.

"Nope," I said and took a step towards him. Immediately he froze with fear. I picked him up and he began to squeal. It was going to ruin the tiles, but I was paying for the renovation anyway so I swung him like a bat into the adjacent wall and let him go. He began to melt to the floor. At that point, I had to let it go. A) I had made my point and B) Willow was pounding on the door hard enough to break it.

"Caleb! Caleb!" she shouted desperately.

I felt even more furious at what this bastard had made me do in front of Willow. I kicked him once and turned around to leave, but again the shit stopped me with his words. "You don't deserve her," he mumbled. "How could an animal like you even think of being with a girl like Willow?"

Those words nearly pushed me over the edge. Again. But I clenched my fists and crouched down next to him. His body was twisted and lying in a strange angle, no doubt he was in too much pain to rise.

"And you think you do?"

He didn't have the guts to respond.

I stared into his eyes. "I might not be worthy of her but I deserve her, more than anyone else in this entire universe. I gave up everything for her, and I'll continue to do it over and over and over again. What about you? Can you do the same? Will you do the same?"

"Yes, I can and I will," he said.

His answer maddened me. He was a liar. I knew without a doubt he wouldn't go to prison for years and years for her, let alone what I was about to do for her. I drew my fist out, and when it landed brutally on the side of his face, blood and spit spurted out of his mouth and stained my knuckles. His scream of pain reverberated around us and beyond. Then he passed out.

"Caleb!" I heard Willow scream, and I rose to my feet.

When I pulled the door open, both girls retreated from me. Their gazes went to the blood on my fist. I waited for the split second it took for Willow's gaze to return to mine.

She was shocked.

I didn't say a word. My blood was still boiling. What was there to say in front of Sandra anyway? Let them go care for the blubbering coward behind me. With one last look at her, I left the shop.

44
Willow

I couldn't believe what had just happened.

I stared down at Bradley as Sandra tried to revive him. I honestly didn't know what to feel.

At the confirmation that he was still breathing, relief washed through me but not much else. Emergency services soon arrived and he was taken away with them straight to a hospital. When they left, Sandra turned to me with a glare on her face. I couldn't remember the last time that she had been so furious at me.

"Willow," she said. "Caleb crossed the line."

I knew that he had been wrong, but I couldn't accept the condemnation so easily.

"As did Bradley, the second time for that matter."

"He was confronting him!" she said. "He was trying to protect you."

Her words confused me. "What the hell are you talking about?"

She took a deep breath, and I knew whatever was coming was something major. "Willow, he made me promise not to tell this to you, at least not yet. At least until he was able to get Caleb to come clean and tell you the truth."

It felt like I was going to have to sit down for this, but there was no chair anywhere. I felt fragile, as if I could break. I didn't want to hear it, but my voice, soft and scared floated out of my mouth. "What truth?"

"Bradley called me last night with information he had found. I dismissed it, I thought that he was just acting dumb and letting his jealousy take over his brain, but after today and this ... wreckage, I don't know what to think anymore. And the way Caleb reacted to Bradley? Was it just because Bradley provoked him, or was it because Bradley threatened to tell you the truth himself if he didn't?"

Blood rushed to my head, and I felt quite faint. All my dreams and hopes were tied up with Caleb. He was the only man for me. I'd already decided that. I fought back the desire to tell Sandra to fuck off and mind her own business. Both her and stupid Bradley. Why did anybody have to interfere? I didn't go around telling other people how to live their lives. "Tell me what?" I asked harshly.

"I'm so sorry, Willow, but Bradley thinks, and now even I agree with him, that Caleb is the same boy Henry was talking about yesterday. The murderer that was sent to prison. Bradley said he was going to investigate more before he approached you, but he must have freaked out after today and confronted Caleb about it."

I gazed at her in shock. "What?"

She moved towards me, her tone gentle. "I know you're in love with him, Willow, but there are now two things pointing towards the fact that Bradley might be right."

She tried to touch me, but I flinched and glared at her as I took several steps backwards.

"Willow," she said, "you might be in over your head, and neither Bradley nor I can be silent anymore. Please speak to Caleb directly. Let's give him the benefit of the doubt. Please ask him about this and see what he says. It could all be some major misunderstanding, but you still have to ask, and quickly, before you fall even more deeply in love with him."

"You want me to ask Caleb if he's a convicted murderer?"

"It's either that or you wait for a little while longer while we investigate this properly to find out the whole truth. But even with the bit of suspicion we have, I don't think I want him anywhere near you. Even if you can't ask him outright about the conviction then why don't you ask him about this break in? Ask if this is in any way related to him."

My heart was contracting because I already knew the answer to that question. "And what would that prove?"

"It proves, Willow," she explained in a patient voice, as if she was talking to a child, "that he runs in dangerous circles. Anyone who can so easily attack someone else like this is not ordinary. I need you to approach this as logically as possible. Three months ago he was just a stranger to you and you were fine. Don't fight to hold onto him now without even making the effort to find out if these allegations are true. Maybe he's not the only one for you, you know."

I couldn't help it. My body jerked away in response to the very idea.

"I promise you that hearts do mend even if it feels like they never will. After he is out of your life, you'll be fine again."

"I don't want to talk about any of this anymore," I said, and walked out of the store. In a strangely calm state of mind, I walked down to the cafe around the block. I ordered a pot of tea, something I never do, and sat down at a table by the window. Then I took out my phone and began making notes, breaking down all the renovations and repairs that we would need to quickly put the shop back in order.

Half-an-hour passed by before I was done. I had not drunk the tea and it was cold. I looked at the cakes behind the glass counter. They made good blueberry pies and usually, I would have ordered one. Now the thought made me feel slightly queasy. I looked down at my notes. Now I needed to hand this list to Caleb just as we had agreed, so that he could begin to mobilize the resources that we needed.

I looked out of the window. A man was walking past with his child. She was licking a lollipop. My hand trembled. For some inexplicable reason, I felt angry with the man. I didn't even know him. It was simply because he let the innocent child eat the lollipop. I turned away. There was something very wrong with me.

The words Sandra said came into my head. Caleb was a murderer. He had been in prison. And I was supposed to leave him because of that.

She had to be joking.

45

Caleb

I had lost my cool in Willow's shop and there would be consequences. The shock on Willow's face told me that, but at the moment I had a more pressing problem to handle. First, I made a call and arranged for security for Willow and her parents. Then I got my secretary to hire a team of workmen to start that morning.

Then I called Finnegan. "You smashed her shop?"

His laugh was curt. "Shouldn't you be thanking me that I didn't touch her?" My blood ran cold at the thought, but this was no time for losing my shit again.

"I told you I was working on it," I said as calmly as I could.

"Well, we heard you were busy losing a lot of money yesterday and we wondered if you were trying to be clever."

"You think I lost money to be clever? To start with I don't

control the stock market and most of my own fortune was wiped out."

"If you get careless, that's your fucking problem. We just wanted to let you know that we don't care if you lose other people's money or even your own. We still want our product."

"So you went out of your way and made things personal?" I growled.

He laughed again, it was a cynical laugh. "Frank told me how murderous you could be. How brutal you could be to protect yourself. But Wolfe, that was prison. This is the real world, and out here, you can't so easily defeat your enemies because not all of them line up next to you at the canteen. I left the woman alone because I just wanted to send a little message that we know just how important she is to you. You have a week to bring me results."

He ended the call, and it took every ounce of strength inside to calm myself down to the state where I didn't want to find him and smash his head in.

Then I was back at my office sitting at my desk. As I hoped, Finnegan hadn't guessed what I was up to. He thought I'd deliberately incurred those losses to make them nervous about my ability. True, I had deliberately allowed those losses to happen, but I had a deeper plan. And now, I had another week to watch my plans unfold, but I knew if I really needed the time I could stretch even that week out.

I had tried my best to think of and to cover every eventuality. My life still felt like it was hanging from a thread in a storm.

I wished I hadn't lost my cool with that sniveling bastard. It was almost certainly going to come back to bite me in the ass. I knew the coward would tell her what he knew, and I would have to handle that issue when I was just not yet ready for it.

When a call came in right then, and I saw Willow's name flash on the screen, I stared at the phone on my desk as if it was a snake. What was our conversation going to entail?

I picked up the phone. "Willow," I called softly.

"Hey," she said abruptly.

Immediately, I noted the difference in her tone. It was guarded and tense and I knew immediately that she had heard what Bradley knew. I hated to hear her voice sound so strange and distant. "Willow," I began.

But she cut me off. "I'm done taking account of the repairs and possible renovations that we need. I'll email the full report to you now."

I knew, like me, she didn't want to deal with Bradley's accusation right now. "Okay," I said quietly.

"The men that you sent to help us clear out the damage have been at it all morning. Thank you."

"No problem," I said.

"Right. Caleb?"

"Yeah."

"Take care of yourself, okay?" Her voice broke then, and she quickly cut the call.

"Fuck," I swore. I stood up and paced the room. I felt so angry, frustrated and damn helpless. I wanted to go to her and comfort her, tell her I loved her, I'd always loved her. Tell her what we had done together. What we had promised each other. Tell her about that night. How we stood in front of the burning house and made a blood promise to each other, but that would be selfish. Yes, I would make her finally understand, but would the price be too high.

No. I would bear the pain. I had broad shoulders. Step by step I would win her back. First I needed to take care of Finnegan and his lot. As long as she was safe, I knew she couldn't resist that thing between us.

I was putting the finishing touches on a letter to my clients who had lost big yesterday, when my phone vibrated. It was a call from one of the bodyguards I had put on Willow.

"Thought I should let you know, Mr. Wolfe, looks like she has a tail on her," he said. "We're still in the shop and there's a dark sedan parked down the street, opposite the launderette. It's been there for the past four hours. Looks like there's a man in it."

"Keep an eye on him," I said, shooting from my chair. "I'll be right there."

In no time, I'd jumped in my car and was heading to Willow's shop. Night had fallen, so it was quite easy for me to arrive unnoticed. I parked some distance away, took my gun out of the glove compartment, and got out of the car.

He never saw me coming.

He had gotten lax in his surveillance from inside the car so by the time he looked up from his phone and noticed my approach, I was already at the passenger's door of his car.

His window was rolled down and he was now staring down the barrel of my gun, which was pointed at his forehead. Horror flashed across his face. When I saw that it was the same guy who I had caught trailing me the last time, I shook my head.

"You again?" I muttered.

"I don't know what you're talking about, man. I'm just about to go into the launderette."

"If you move even an inch, I will blow your head off right now," I warned, as I got into the car.

"Listen, I don't want no trouble."

"Shut up and give me your phone," I commanded, and with my gun pointed at his head, he didn't dare refuse. He threw it at me and I began to scroll through his previous calls as I spoke with him.

"Who hired you?" I asked. I realized then that I should have done this from the very first time I met him. I had been too careless, but not anymore.

He shifted nervously. "I don't know, man."

I looked up from his phone. "How have they been keeping in touch with you then?"

"The number's untraceable. All I get are instructions."

"What about your payment?"

He looked around him. "It's dropped in random locations, and I'm told to go pick it up."

"What were you told to do here?"

He tapped a cigarette out of its box. "Do you mind if I smoke?"

"Yes," I said curtly.

He put the cigarette back and looked at me sullenly. "I was told to just keep an eye on the girl."

"What about me? There are no eyes on me?"

"I don't know nothing about that. I just do what I'm told," he said.

"Take me to where you live," I ordered.

His face fell. "Look man. This is just a job to me. I have no idea what all of this is about. All I have is receipts, but even those are just records of dates and times."

"Where are the receipts?"

"Home," he admitted reluctantly.

In a way, I felt sorry for him. He was so wrong for the job. I'd met guys like him inside. Their lives were never their own. They were always somebody's bitch. I'd learned a long time ago, there was no place for pity in my life. Pitying someone could mean you ended up dead.

I lowered my gun, cocked it and pressed it to his ribs.

Dejection filled his face, but he had no other choice than to do as he was told. He drove me to his house. He tried to engage me in conversation, to get me to feel sorry for him, but I told him to shut up. Twenty minutes later we arrived at a modest house just outside town.

"Get out of the car," I instructed.

He hesitated. "My kids are in there, man. And my wife. Please don't do this."

The audacity of human beings truly astounded me. They protected their own at all costs, but the harm they caused to others was inconsequential. I felt absolutely no sympathy for him.

"You're going to take me inside, and you're going to give me all the information I need on every member of your family. The schools your kids attend, where your wife works and all of your social security numbers. You should thank your good luck that I'm not blasting your head off right now."

He did as he was told but just before we got into the house, he stopped me and pleaded. "Please put the gun down. My kids are in there. I'll get you everything you need. Just keep the gun out of sight, okay?"

I pushed him in, but the moment I got in and saw his three kids playing in the living room I put the gun away.

He got me all the information I needed and I gave him my instructions.

"I'm going to give you forty-eight hours. Figure out who's behind your commission, and bring his name to me. Otherwise, your family's going to be gone. And don't even try to run because I will chase you all to the ends of the earth."

46
Willow

True to Caleb's predictions, repairs weren't taking even half as long as I'd expected them to.

It was under a week and the men had not only made significant progress, but they had turned the place that I had more or less cobbled together with Sandra and one handyman into an upmarket boutique florist.

Jake, the foreman, had insisted on repainting the walls using the most expensive paints, replacing even the windows that were not broken so they would all be the same flawless design. He broke the tiled floor that had been in place when I came to the shop and gave me a sparkling granite surface. Even the ceiling was fitted with new cornices and painted a soft gray to match the rest of the color scheme. Then, the counters were all ripped out and gorgeous new rounded counters made of glass and marble arrived. I watched in amazement as they were expertly fitted in by a team of men. Just one look at them told me they must have cost the earth.

At that point I had protested, but Jake was having none of it. "Look, Ma'am,' he said. "I've been hired to do an awesome job, and I'm going to do it to the best of my ability within the budget I've been given. If you are not happy with any part of my work, just let me know and I'll rip it out and redo it."

I backed off then. I wanted to ask what the budget was, but I bit my tongue and let it go. It certainly seemed as if the budget was in the hundreds of thousands.

Although, to be honest, my mind wasn't on it. I cared less about the windows, tiles, even the shop, than I cared about what was happening to Caleb.

He kept in touch twice a day, like clockwork, but he never visited or invited me over to his place. I worried about him constantly, but I knew I had to give him space and time. His troubles were worse than mine. Until he got those monsters off his back I had no business making life harder for him. I threw myself into work and waited for his twice daily calls. They were always brief and I always clutched the phone so hard my fingers ached. And every time I wished he would ask me to go over to him, but he never did.

When the call was over I would put the phone down and miss him terribly. Until this morning, when I could bear it no more and decided to surprise him with dinner.

"Have you asked him?"

The question came out of nowhere. I quickly slipped my

phone back into my pocket and returned to wiping down the vases. My response was tinged with frost. "Asked him what?"

"Willow, you can't avoid this forever," Sandra said.

"I want to focus on what's important and that's getting the shop renovated."

She didn't listen. "You're suspicious too. That's why he hasn't come around, isn't it?"

I glared at her.

She turned to look out outside. "Well, well, what do you know, Bradley's here."

At the racket of his rusty engine outside the shop, my heart sank. He was the last person I wanted to see, but I didn't want it to seem like I was avoiding him either, so I continued on with my work of wiping down the dusty vases.

"Did you order something from him?" Sandra asked.

I shook my head. "No, did you?"

She shook her head.

I sent a dark gaze towards the door. It was that look that he encountered when he walked through and it immediately stopped him in his tracks. One side of his face was still bruised from the punches that Caleb had landed on him, but I felt absolutely no sympathy for him. He diverted his gaze towards Sandra who was much happier to see him.

"Hey, how are you?" she said, while I pretended to be very busy with my vases.

"I'm alright," he said to Sandra, then he came over to me. "Willow, can we talk?"

Suddenly, I felt angry with him. He had ruined my dream. "About what?"

He sighed. "I know you're mad at me, but how I acted that day was not without reason."

I stopped then and turned to him. "Bradley, I get that we have known each other for years, but I just can't understand where you get off just butting into my life without permission."

He was so taken aback by my tone that his eyebrows shot up. Even Sandra was shocked.

"Willow."

"I don't want to talk to you," I said, slapping the rag I'd been using down. "And you owe Caleb an apology."

I began to walk away, but his words stopped me. "Did you already know the truth, but pretended to yourself? Is this why you're so angry? That I brought it to light?"

"What?"

"You already knew that he was the one that killed your uncle and set his house on fire, didn't you?"

I felt the breath knocked out of me. "What?"

"Bradley!" Sandra yelled and instantly went over to him. She stood in front of him and muttered something to him.

I didn't need to hear what she was saying to know that she was scolding him for opening his mouth. What on earth was going on? I ran to him and pushed Sandra out of the way. "What the hell did you just say?"

There was a tinge of fear on his face, but also defiance. He was glad he had said it. He was glad he had ruined my dream.

The world around me spun. I felt as if I was going to faint. I looked at Sandra. I felt wild, desperate. I needed help. I was spiraling out of control.

"He killed my uncle? And set his church on fire? What the fuck are you both talking about?" My voice was trembling and my eyes filling with tears.

Oh the frustration of being unable to remember anything. I constantly felt like I was a breath away from being hit with a brick about something detrimental to my identity as a human being, and this was one of those times. Unless they were joking with me or wrong in which case I would never forgive either of them.

"Sandra," I turned to her and she came over to lightly hold my hand.

I snatched my hand out of her grasp and stepped away from her. "What the hell is he talking about?"

Bradley looked shocked as his gaze moved from Sandra to me and back to her. "She really doesn't know?"

"Know what?" I yelled.

Sandra's voice became sheepish. "Willow," she said. "Your

uncle's death wasn't caused by a simple fire. He was killed in the church and the murderer set the place on fire to cover his tracks."

Tears burned my eyes. "The *murderer*?' I turned to Bradley. "And you're saying that *murderer* is Caleb? Are you both out of your minds?"

Bradley was undaunted. "I couldn't bring it up with you the last time because I wasn't sure yet. All I knew was that there was the possibility that he was the same Caleb Wolfe who Henry had been talking about, so I showed Henry his picture that night and he swore that he was the same person. I confronted Caleb about it, and well, you know what happened. I told him that he had a week to tell you the truth and he attacked me like a wild animal. I couldn't even face you then because I didn't know enough, but after finding out even more this week I've realized just how dangerous he is."

All the strength had drained out of my body.

I was exhausted, mentally and emotionally. Were they playing with me, or was life playing with me? Why was this happening to me?

"Who told you all of this?" I whispered.

"I searched up his record, and there was some news written about it at the time. Although his picture wasn't shown to protect him since he was a minor at the time, it was absolutely clear that he must have been the person."

My knees gave out and I screamed for Sandra. I felt so lost. Sandra ran towards me, but I didn't allow her to touch me. I didn't want anyone to come close to me. It felt as though once again, everything had been reset and I knew absolutely nothing.

I'd never felt so defeated. "Show me what you have," I snarled.

With a sympathetic look on his face, Bradley pulled his phone out of his pocket.

47

Caleb

https://www.youtube.com/watch?v=QvYSckKSL5g

Willow was coming over.

At first, I'd been surprised by her sudden call, but what concerned me even more was the coldness in her tone. She sounded like a stranger. An emotionless robot. My mind went to that bastard, and I wondered if he had finally poured his poison into her ear.

Waiting for her to arrive was *the* most excruciating time of my life. The last time I had been half as nervous about anything was the week after I'd been arrested, and the Sheriff told me that Willow had lost her memory. When I realized Willow had forgotten me. Twelve years later, I was experiencing it all over again at the possibility that Willow was going to forsake me again.

The very thought was enough to devastate me.

But I promised myself that even if she had learned of what I'd done, I would never tell her why I'd done it, because my love for her was greater than my love for myself. I promised myself that she would never find out what her uncle had done to her from me. I would guard her from that knowledge with my life. For as long as I lived. I would rather be in prison for the rest of my life than remind her she was abused and raped by her own uncle for a whole year.

And that was what scared me the most.

Because if she had found out then, was she coming to ask me the reason I had done it? But I would never be able to tell her. I watched her suffer once, and I'd be damned to hell if I had to watch her suffer twice from the same pain.

I met her at the elevator and she wasn't expecting that because she froze the moment she saw me. Then she forced a smile to her lips, and stepped out. I didn't smile back. I couldn't. I felt as if my heart was breaking inside me.

I watched her fiddle with the strap of her purse. She couldn't meet my eyes. Without running into my arms for a hug or kiss as was her habit, she continued on her way towards my office.

We arrived in my office, and she quickly moved towards the window.

"How have you been?" she asked in a quiet voice.

"Okay," I murmured.

"That's good," she said woodenly.

"Will you take a seat?" I asked.

She shook her head.

I knew I needed to sit down for this, so I headed over to my chair and lowered myself into it, and met her gaze. With every breath I took, I could feel her slipping away. Further and further. And there was not a damn thing I could do about it. It seemed as if this would be one of the last times I would ever see her in my life. After this she would become a stranger. She was almost one already.

A smile trembled onto her lips, but I could see the tears that had welled up in her eyes. Then she began to speak.

"I just had a talk with my parents and they told me that—"

She paused a few seconds to get herself together. "They confirmed that the man who killed my uncle was named Caleb Daniel Wolfe. Bradley says ... Bradley says that you're the same person. I can't believe I'm asking you this, but ..."

She turned away as the tears rolled down her face.

I wanted to go to her. To apologize for how cruel the world was because it wouldn't even let me show my real self to her, or allow me to keep the promise I had made to her to protect her forever. Well, I would keep that promise even though the cost of keeping the truth from her would cost me the privilege of being her man, her husband, her lover, her best-friend, the father of her children, her rock through everything life threw at her.

That, I had to live with. That, I would live with, even if it killed me.

"Are you—" she began but couldn't continue.

I did nothing. I just stared at her. I drank in the sight of her. Memorized every aspect of her. Her hair, her eyes, her lips, her eyebrows, the curve of her cheek, her throat, her body, that she had covered in a drab shirt and the baggy jeans she used when she was planting.

A few seconds later she summoned up courage. "Are you the one? The same Caleb Wolfe?"

Before I could open my mouth to speak she spoke again, her voice trembling.

"Don't lie to me. You told me that you would never lie to me."

"I won't," I replied and turned my face away. "I'm sorry, Willow."

"So ... you're saying—" Her voice had become shrill with disbelief. Even though they had told her and even though it all made sense she had come here praying it was not true.

"They're right. I killed your uncle and set his house on fire."

As I had expected she didn't run from the room screaming. She stood her ground, straightened her spine, and met my gaze head on and asked the one question I could never answer.

"Why?"

I clenched my jaw. I could do this. I could do this for her.

"Why did you kill him?" she repeated, her voice rising hysterically.

I continued staring expressionless at her.

"That's it. You're not going to answer me?" she demanded incredulously.

I shook my head slowly. I wasn't going to tell her the truth, but I wasn't going to make up some lie either.

She took a step forward. "Did he do something to you or did you kill him for fun?"

I shook my head again.

"You bastard," she screamed. "Why? Why did you come here? Was all of this just some sort of sick joke to you? Are you like one of those serial killers that go to the funerals of their victim? Did you come here to gloat?"

"I never meant to hurt you, Willow. Never," I whispered.

"Then what were you trying to do, by fucking the niece of the man you killed? And you cannot tell me that it was all a coincidence because you knew who I was from the very beginning, didn't you? You came to the shop and you approached me. Why? Did you want to mock him all over again?"

"No," I said harshly.

She drew a sudden breath. "That watch. That's my watch, isn't it?"

I blinked at her.

"Answer me, damn you."

I nodded.

"Did you steal it?"

I couldn't take any of this any longer. Anymore, and I would crumble right there at her accusation ... at the coldness in her gaze, at the pain that had engulfed her heart.

"Willow, please leave. There's no need to take this any further. You know the truth now."

"And if I don't leave, are you going to kill me too?"

That hurt, more than she would ever know. I took a deep breath and released it slowly. I felt as if I was committing hara-kiri on myself. The pain was incredible. Without looking at her, I said. "Yeah. I just might. When I get angry I ... lose control of myself. You should leave."

I didn't need to look at her to tell that she was shocked at my admission.

"Is that why you killed him?" she asked. "Because you lost your temper?"

"Yes." And that was the truth. I killed that animal in an uncontrollable rage. After I had killed him I kicked his dead body to a pulp. And if I had to do it all over again, I would. "Now leave. I don't want to turn on you too."

Her final words came out in breathless, difficult bursts. "I can't believe ... I actually fell in love with you."

Then she ran out of my life.

48

Willow

https://www.youtube.com/watch?v=y2zeudxXjuU

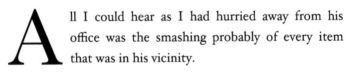

All I could hear as I had hurried away from his office was the smashing probably of every item that was in his vicinity.

I was a complete mess. My face was soaked with tears, my heart felt like it had been ripped to shreds. I felt lost and alone and afraid. I was not afraid of him, I was afraid of myself. Even though he had just admitted he was a killer, and he had killed my uncle, I still wanted him. I wanted to run to him and punch his mouth and tell him to take it back and lie to me instead.

I ran to the elevator and got on it just as I heard his roar. I turned towards the sound then. I wanted to go to him. I wanted him to love me back the way I loved him. He was my heart. I couldn't imagine my life without him. I hit my own chest in despair.

Don't. Don't go to him, Willow.

With tears streaming down my cheeks, I pounded on the elevator button. When the doors opened, I rushed inside and clenched my hands until the doors shut. I closed my eyes and kept myself held tightly in check until I reached the ground floor. As soon as the doors parted wide enough to let me through, I dashed out.

There was no one about and I ran across the empty lobby towards my van. I slammed the door and drove home in a daze. When I arrived home my parents were sitting in the living room. My father was watching TV and my mother was knitting. She looked up with a smile, but when she saw me her face changed. She jumped up and took a step towards me. "What is it?" she asked, her eyes filled with concern.

I couldn't talk. I just held my hand up to indicate that my mother shouldn't follow me, and hurried up to my room. There I locked my door and buried myself underneath the covers. I was so heartbroken I wanted to go to sleep and not wake up.

But I couldn't leave my parents and neither did I want them to find out how destroyed I was. I also couldn't bear for them to think anything bad about Caleb. I knew he had done wrong, I knew he was a murderer, but he was my murderer and I still cared how others perceived him. I wanted my parents to remember him as the man I had originally presented to them. In spite of everything I was hopelessly in love with Caleb. Deep down I still couldn't understand or even believe how I could have been so wrong about him.

My phone rang, and for a second I thought it was him. I shoved aside the covers and grabbed my phone. It was Sandra. I didn't want to speak to her, but I was worried my mother would call her and ask what was going on so I took the call.

"Don't tell my parents any of this business with Caleb," I said.

"Of course not. Err, have you spoken to Caleb yet?"

"I have."

"And what did he say?" she prompted.

My heart constricted with misery. I formed words in my mouth, but no sound came out. What had happened in his office still seemed like a nightmare that I couldn't wait to wake up from.

"It doesn't matter," I said. "From now on, I don't want to talk about him anymore."

"What?"

"Look, Sandra. I'm really grateful to you for looking out for me, but I really can't talk about him to you or anyone. Not yet. Maybe one day, huh?"

"Okay."

"I'll see you at the shop tomorrow."

"See you tomorrow. Willow?"

"Yeah."

"I'm really sorry it worked out this way."

"It's okay. I guess it was not meant to be."

Willow

https://www.youtube.com/watch?v=G4yRUO5IR8o

By the middle of the following week, my new normal became an empty gaze and a blank face. I had completely lost my appetite and I found it hard to sleep at night. Sandra did her best to cheer me up, she made jokes, and she never referred to Caleb. I was grateful to her for that.

Around my parents I forced myself to maintain my usual, somewhat light-hearted self, but every time my mom slipped up and asked about him it cut like a knife.

Bradley continued with his deliveries but he didn't dare face me any longer. He knew I was hurting and he didn't dare bring up the reason why. Perhaps he was just biding his time until I recovered enough for him to speak normally to me.

For my part I couldn't even imagine the day when I would become normal again, when I would stop thinking of Caleb. Day and night an insidious voice whispered, 'people change. He was just a kid. Everybody deserves a second chance." Or I would find myself wishing he would come looking for me. That he would come to me and tell me he loved me. He would ask for my forgiveness and we could be together. Then I would catch myself for being so pathetic. He had lied to me. Worse, how could I even want to be with a murderer? Especially a man who had killed my only living relative and burnt down his house.

The pain in my heart was a physical thing. I lay in bed and stared into the dark night and cursed him for coming into my life. For the first time in my life, I wished darkly that I would once again lose my memory. That all the time we had spent together was somehow erased because it haunted me like a never-ending nightmare. His laugh ... the tenderness I'd seen in his eyes ... the way he had taken care of me as though I was precious beyond belief.

It was all a lie.

And that was what haunted me the most. How could the same person that had killed my uncle because he had lost his temper, return to my life and treat me the way he did? It didn't make any sense.

I lashed out in frustration, and only at the scream that broke the silence did I realize that I had knocked over a ceramic vase. I turned to see Sandra with her hand on her chest in shock. I moved my gaze to the shattered pieces of the vase on the floor. I just stared at the broken shards dumbly. The image before me seemed to eerily and perfectly mirrored the state I was in.

It was almost a relief that something could show perfectly just how I felt inside. I picked up my phone then and dialed his number.

I had let him go too easily.

He had come into my life and broke me into pieces, and he had to find a way to put me back together. The fucking bastard.

"Willow, don't!" Sandra said.

I didn't listen to her. I put the phone to my ear and she came over to try to snatch it away but I exploded at her. "Don't you dare touch me!" I stormed away and headed to the bathroom. I shut the door behind me and when I looked in the mirror I could barely recognize myself. My eyes were hollow and bloodshot and my complexion was deathly pale and sickly.

I couldn't even remember the last time I had eaten, or slept for that matter.

His number rang out. After multiple tries I gave up. Part of me wanted to collapse in tears on the floor, but I didn't. I had to be strong. I smacked my cheeks to force some color to my face ... wiped the tears from my eyes, and returned to work. I walked into the shop and saw a woman talking to Sandra. She was tall and middle-aged, with a wavy bob of brown hair, and kind brown eyes. As soon as I arrived at the door, she turned towards me.

"Willow," she called.

My eyes darted between her and Sandra in surprise. I had never seen her before in my life.

"I'm Marie Spencer," she answered. "Caleb's lawyer."

Sandra's tone turned hostile. "What do you want?"

I waited for the woman to answer her question. She didn't beat around the bush. "I need you," she said, "to reach Caleb."

My heart dropped into my stomach at her words. "What?"

"He's disappeared from the office since Wednesday night and has cut off contact with everyone." Her gaze on me was accusatory, as if that was my fault.

"And what does that have to do with me?" I asked aggressively. I was the hurt party not him. He was the one that lied to me. He was the one who betrayed my trust in him. I was the one who fell in love with him.

"It has everything to do with you," she said, and I could hear the impatience in her voice. "Everything has something to do with you."

I frowned. "What does that mean?"

"His office is in disarray. His company has been blacklisted and an application has already been made to strip him off his brokerage license. He's lost everything. All the money he's earned in the last twelve years is gone. He will even have to sell his home to pay off his debts. You need to make him understand that there are people depending on him. That it's not all over. That he's young and he can start again. You need to bring him back."

I lost it and screamed at her, the tears I held back earlier poured out of my eyes. "What the hell does that have to do with me? Don't you know what he did? Don't you know who he is?"

She was completely unfazed by my outburst. "I know exactly what he did. And if you knew too, you wouldn't abandon him. He gave up everything for you back when he was fifteen and he's doing it all over again now. He loves you more than I ever thought it was possible for a human being to love another. Now that he's falling apart I'm not going to sit back and watch. You have to go put him back together."

I stared at her in shock. I could hardly believe what she was saying. She must have misunderstood the situation.

"Excuse me, but have you lost your mind?" Sandra blew up next to me. "He killed her uncle."

"To save her," Marie said calmly.

I froze. "What?"

She turned to me. "I'm bound by attorney-client privilege so I can't say anymore, and moreover Caleb would kill me if I said another word to you. But I'm not going to go easy on you until you put him back together. He does not deserve to be destroyed twice on account of the same woman."

I was shaking. "He killed my uncle to save me?" I repeated incredulously.

"Exactly. You were in trouble back then and he put himself on the line for you. Threw his youth away and rotted in prison for you. You're not going to find out the exact details from me so you better go to him, put him back together and get him to tell you the goddamn truth."

With that she turned around, and stormed out of the shop.

50
Willow

https://www.youtube.com/watch?v=kOYcbod5Jow
-lost but won-

"I don't believe her," Sandra said.

I couldn't tell what expression was on my face but from the way I was feeling, it wasn't one I wanted anyone to see. I lowered myself to the floor and began mindlessly picking up the pieces of the vase I had shattered earlier.

"Willow, do you believe her?"

I gritted my teeth. "Why would she lie?"

"Because they're sick in the head? The both of them."

I gave her a sharp look and she immediately took a step back. I rose to my feet with the shards I had gathered and threw them in the trash can. The truth was I wanted to fly to him, but I felt as if I had been hit by a truck and I needed a bit of time to process everything in my head. I turned to Sandra. "I'm not ready to make any decisions either way or even talk about this rationally. Let's leave it for now and get on with the orders, okay."

"Okay," she agreed.

I managed to keep my cool for the remainder of the day until I closed the shop and walked to the van. I sat in my van and I knew exactly what I must do if I wanted to remain sane. I pulled out my phone and called his number but got the same response. It rang out. I felt a slight pinch of worry. What if Marie was right? The part of me that was afraid to hope immediately pushed the thought away.

I searched for Bradley's number. Having to contact him or even speak to him brought a feeling of unease to my belly, but I knew I had to. I dialed and waited. He picked up on the second ring.

"I was wondering if I'd ever hear from you again," he said, and I noticed that his voice was different, his words were slurred. He was either half-asleep or he'd been drinking.

I didn't care.

"I want to know everything," I said. "About what you found out about Caleb, how and where. Could you please send me all the links?"

For a couple of seconds there was silence from his end. Then he spoke, his voice sour. "Of course. The one time you contact me and it's of course about him."

I didn't have time for his tantrum, but I didn't want him to hang up on me either. Right now he was my starting point.

"Bradley—" I began.

But he cut me off. "Come over," he said. "And I'll tell you everything that you need to know."

He ended the call and I was left staring at a silent phone. I was about to call him back to refuse when a text message arrived. It was his address. I didn't hesitate. I started the van and drove to his house.

Bradley's place was one of the old, smaller Southwest houses on the outskirts of Folsom. My thoughts kept drifting off to Caleb and I missed the directions from my navigation system a couple of times. When I finally found it, the light drizzle from earlier had turned into a full-blown downpour.

I didn't have an umbrella with me, so I decided to run for his door and pound heavily on it. He must have been watching out for me because he answered before I could even start knocking. He ushered me in with a loose smile.

I could tell instantly that he was intoxicated. He grasped the doorknob tightly to keep himself stable, and his eyes ... were glazed and oddly haunted.

"You're finally here," he said with a light slur. He shut the door behind him, and then turned to face me with a sly smile on his face. "And you're wet."

"Bradley," I said with a frown. "Tell me everything you know."

All the amusement disappeared from his face and he stared hard at me. "Why? Are you planning on forgiving him?"

I wanted to tell him that it was none of his business, but since it was clear he wasn't fully sober the best thing for me to do would be to get the information I needed from him as peacefully as possible and be on my way as quickly as possible.

"Bradley, you came to me with unsolicited information about my boyfriend. Now I'm asking you for the details. Is that wrong? You were the one who told me to come over."

The blank expression on his face was slowly replaced by an embarrassed smile. "You're right. I'm being an idiot. You're my guest. I'll get you a towel."

"No need, I just—"

"You want to be sitting down for what I have to say," he interrupted. "The living room is through there. Have a seat and I'll go get you that towel."

He began to walk away and all I could do was head further into the dimly lit house. I was glad to see it was clean and neat. He wasn't a slob. I didn't want to be here longer than was necessary. I took a seat on an armchair and hugged myself. I felt wet and cold and wished he would speed things up.

He returned with a towel and handed it over to me. I accepted it, but for some weird reason I was loathe to let it touch my skin. Since he was watching, I lightly patted it down my wet arms before putting it aside.

"Bradley, it's getting late. My parents are going to get worried," I pointed out, even though I had called them and told them I was going to see Caleb so they were probably not even expecting me to come home for the night.

He plopped himself on the sofa opposite me. "What do you want to know?"

I swallowed the irritation. "Apart from what you said at the store what else is there? Where exactly did you get the information from? I checked online and there's hardly any references."

"Of course, there's very little information about his crime. He was a minor then."

"You said what you had to tell me was serious enough for me to sit down."

"I did," he said. Then he tried to get to his feet, but fell back twice before he could eventually rise. I watched him lurch towards a mini refrigerator. Holding on to the top of it, he pulled it open, and he grabbed a bottle of liquor from it. He poured himself another drink and I rose. It was clear to me then that coming here was a total waste of time.

"What I don't understand is why you need to know all this shit. Surely, you don't still want him."

I slung the strap of my bag over my shoulder. "What?"

He looked at me incredulously, contemptuously. "You're

thinking of going back to him, aren't you? I can see the look in your eyes."

I gave him a hard look, and began to move towards the door. "Thanks for your help, Bradley."

He suddenly smashed the glass on the floor and I froze from the shock. Realizing that he was about to lose control, I ran for the door. Just as I pulled it open however it was slammed back shut. I couldn't believe he could move so fast. He seemed to be so drunk.

"Bradley!"

He was crowding me, his hand over my head and his body much too close to mine. I could smell the liquor fumes on his breath, and see the anger burning in his gaze, but what shocked me was how sober he seemed to be. Had he been pretending to be drunk to get me off my guard?

"Bradley, let me go," I ordered.

"What is it about him?" he asked. "Is it because he's rich? Come to think of it, haven't you wondered where he got all that money from since he's been in prison since he was fifteen years old?"

With my hands against his chest, I tried to push him away, but he couldn't be budged.

"Answer me," he snarled.

"Let me go," I screamed, but he grabbed my forearms and shook me so hard my teeth rattled. "Fucking answer me! Is it because he's rich? Because I'm not too bad looking, am I?"

He tried to kiss me then. His lips almost connected with mine but I sharply turned my head away.

I was panting and my heart was pounding so hard

He laughed bitterly. "I don't deserve even a kiss? After all these years of putting you first? Bradley, can you come in an hour? Bradley, do you mind dropping my flowers off first? Bradley, it's Saturday, but can you make a fucking delivery anyway? You've been treating me like a servant."

"What are you talking about? I never asked you to do any of those things. You dealt with Sandra."

"Yeah, but it was your shop. I was doing it for you," he insisted.

"Bradley, I didn't even know she was asking you for all those favors."

He looked at me angrily. "You know what? Fuck you. I wanted to do them for you. And this is what I get."

"I don't believe this."

"What is it about me that you loathe so much?" he asked.

I opened my mouth to answer and he grabbed my chin and crushed his lips to mine. Nausea immediately began to roil in the pit of my stomach. I summoned all of my strength to push him away, but no matter how hard I tried, he wouldn't budge.

With tears in my eyes, I bit down hard on his lips, and with a shout he jumped away from me. I tasted the blood in my mouth as I collapsed to the floor. I couldn't believe this was happening. The instinct for self-preservation kicked in. My mind became crystal clear and strength flowed into my limbs. I realized the window of escape I'd been given. I jumped to my feet and jerked the door open.

But it wouldn't open.

He had locked it. I tried to turn the key desperately and just as it was beginning to catch and turn, I felt his presence behind me.

"You bitch!" he roared.

Then I felt his steely grasp lock around my neck. He pulled me away from the door and I screamed. I was thrown to the floor, and my head hit the floor hard. And then the weirdest thing happened. The ceiling of Bradley's house disappeared and instead I saw a different ceiling. It was blue with little stars on it. It terrified the hell out of me. I blinked and then Bradley's ceiling appeared again.

Suddenly, there was a sharp agony in my head as though I'd been struck by a hammer. I couldn't even open my eyes. The pain was that brutal. I was sure he had hit me, but when I swung my hand out in defense, my hand connected with nothing. I felt his hands close around my ankles, and ...

Memories began to flash across my mind. Horrible, horrible things. Unbearable. Horrendous. Sins of the flesh. I heard the sinner's laughter, but I couldn't see the face. I didn't want to see. I opened my eyes to try to put an end to the torment but it was of no use. The memories there even when my eyes were open. My white cotton panties were lying on the floor. My skinny little legs were open. And the sinner was forcing himself into me. "You like this," he was saying. A maddened scream erupted from my throat.

Bradley began to drag me across the floor.

I felt like I was screaming at the top of my lungs, but whether that was my actual reaction, or from the memory that was replaying, I had no clue. I was out of strength and life, and the only name I could think of was Caleb's.

I screamed out his name and it felt like an echo. Was that what I was doing now or was it once again a memory? I could hear too many voices around me ... maybe it was the sinner, or Bradley's. I couldn't tell.

"Caleb," I screamed again, and his name shattered the wall that held my memories at bay. The final domino fell, his face came rushing towards me.

I saw him then ... my uncle. The smug smile ... the lustful glaze. The wall that was erected in my mind had fallen. I killed him. I killed him and Caleb took the blame. I was the murderer. I went into shock, no longer even cognizant of what was happening around me. I stopped breathing. I couldn't breathe. My chest heaved, but I couldn't draw any air into my lungs. My lungs burned with the lack of oxygen. I was dying.

Then I felt the sharp sting across my cheek.

Bradley had struck me, and the pain forced air into my lungs again. For a while he did nothing and all I could hear was my harsh wheezing.

I shot up and scuttled backwards. My gaze was beginning to clear, my face was soaked, as Bradley came back into focus.

"What the fuck is wrong with you?" he asked.

He was poised over me. I looked down to see his cock out, already red and hard. My own underwear had been pulled down and bunched around my thighs. He was about to rape me. The rage I felt inside me could not be described. I'd just discovered I once killed a man for this. I looked at him with hate. I saw the shock in his eyes as he watched the transformation inside me. We were by his mini fridge on the floor, and on top of it was the bottle he had used.

I grabbed it and with vindictive strength, slammed it into the side of his head. It didn't explode into shards of glass as it did in movies. Instead it made a dull thud and it made his skin split. Blood poured down. With a cry of pain he fell, his hands grabbing his head.

I didn't waste any time.

I staggered to my feet, and attempted to run, but the underwear still bunched around my thighs sent me falling back down to the floor. The fall sucked the life out of me, and for a few seconds all I could do was lie face down in complete helplessness. Then my eyes opened, and my hand connected with my purse.

The memory of Caleb bursting into the parish house after I called him. I saw it all as vividly as the day it happened. I showed him my uncle's body. He was so livid, so insanely angry, he lost it. He kicked my uncle's dead body repeatedly until I had to scream for him to stop.

When he finally did. I felt no fear as I told him I knew I was going to prison and asked him if he would wait for me, but he wouldn't hear of it. He told me he would go to prison because he should have been the one to kill my uncle. It was his privilege. He asked me for my watch. I took it off and gave it to him. Then he set the house on fire. We stood outside and we made our promises. We made them in blood. My heart felt as if it was breaking in a million pieces when I thought of the sacrifice Caleb had made for me.

"Caleb," I heard myself call. I found the strength to try and rise. I pulled my panties up, then looked at Bradley. He was curled up and moaning with pain. I pulled myself up, grabbed my purse and staggered out of his house.

The moment I got to my van, I locked the door and drove away. In the dark of the night, there was only one place I wanted to go to.

Oh, Caleb, Caleb, why didn't you tell me the truth?

This was what Maria had meant when she'd said he'd given up everything for me. I slammed my palms against the steering wheel as tears stung my eyes. He had gone to prison trying to protect me, and damn I had forgotten it all. Trapped behind a wall that had only now collapsed. As I drove ... more and more memories came crashing back. The first day I met him, the countless laughs we shared, the love, God, the love ...

How could he bear it? What he must have been going

through all this time. To see me, to hold me, and not tell me. What a man. What a saint.

I couldn't stop the tears continuing to fall. Everything made sense now. My hatred for lollipops. My uncle called his cock a lollipop. "Suck the lollipop," he used to say to me. Ugh. And the feeling that I had lost someone important. The sensation I was waiting for someone.

My legs felt too weak to carry my body, but I forced myself not to collapse before I arrived at his home. He had given me his key, which I attached to my key ring. I got out of the car, and staggered to his door.

"Caleb," I screamed, but my voice sounded muffled and puny. I struggled to find the key and when it seemed all I managed to do was slot in the wrong ones, I began to pound desperately on the door.

"Caleb" I cried, unable to gain control of myself. I had never felt so raw, so exposed ... so broken. Then the lock turned. I had found the right key. I pushed open the door and entered the deadly quiet house.

"Caleb!" I croaked. Then I collapsed to the ground, no longer able to hold myself up. I thought I saw a pair of feet and legs running towards me, and I reached out for them, but I only grasped empty air. "Caleb, where are you? Where are you, my love?" I whispered.

And that was the last thing I remembered.

51

Caleb

https://www.youtube.com/watch?v=r8qpTLɪwxGQ

T he thudding sound woke me up from the drunken stupor I'd been wallowing in. For the amount I'd consumed it should have been damn near impossible to wake me up, but my years in prison had ingrained the need to sleep lightly. Especially, when I first arrived. I was fresh meat then, barely a man and there were too many people who wanted me to be their bitch.

My head was pounding like it had a fucking pneumatic drill inside it. I remembered attempting to drag myself off to bed, but I must have collapsed halfway through and just fallen asleep on the floor.

I lifted my head and listened to the sound, but it had gone quiet. I would have put it down to my imagination and just gone back to sleep on the floor, but something felt wrong. My chest felt tight. I felt the same way that night when Willow called me. My heart instantly slammed against my chest, and I struggled to my feet. Bare chested I ran towards the front door. It was Willow. There was no doubt in my mind about that. It was Willow.

Willow had come to me.

I got to the corridor and froze. In darkness I saw the open door and the still body lying just inside the entrance

"Willow!" I shouted and ran towards her. I skidded to the floor next to her and quickly began to check her breathing. She was still breathing and that was a tremendous relief.

"Willow!" I called.

I quickly checked her body for any injuries before I tried to move her. There seemed to be none that was obvious, but why was she unconscious. I decided not to move her.

I got my phone and called 911. Then I gently pulled her head onto my lap and waited.

My eyes stung with tears to see her like this. I rocked her gently in my arms. What had happened to her? If someone was responsible for hurting her I swore to God, I was going to make them pay.

The ambulance arrived and they put her on a gurney. I pulled on a shirt and shoes and told them I was going with them. They saw the state I was in and decided not to argue.

While she was admitted and examined, I found a vending machine and got myself a coffee. My head was killing me and

I felt strange and brittle. I leaned against a wall and drank the bitter coffee. It was vile. I let my head touch the wall behind me and closed my eyes. Jesus. What a mess.

"It's horrible, isn't it?"

I opened my eyes and saw a woman standing next to me. She was painfully thin and her eyes were red.

"I'm here because my boyfriend overdosed. What happened to your girl?"

"I don't know what happened to her."

"Oh, I thought she overdosed too."

"No, she doesn't take drugs."

"Lucky her. And she's got you. I wish I had someone like you. Someone who cares like you. All he cares about is getting high." Her voice ended on a sob.

"I'm sorry," I said.

"Yeah, it's a shit life. I've got no money. Can you spare some change for the coffee machine?"

I fished out some notes from my wallet and gave them to her.

"Yeah, like I said. She's one lucky gal." Then she went away without getting herself a coffee. I guessed that I just bought her, her next high. I threw away the coffee cup and went to wait for the doctor to be done with Willow.

Eventually, he came out.

"She is not severely hurt apart from some light bruises."

I could tell that he was watching me carefully, wondering if I had lied about finding her in that condition and if I was the one responsible for her injuries, especially given my disheveled and half-crazed state.

"If she doesn't have any injuries then why did she collapse?"

"Emotional distresses."

My heart stopped. "What?"

"The only diagnosis that I can arrive at right now, is that she most likely experienced a very distressing emotional episode. It's left her completely drained. I can't know anymore until she wakes up and explains it to us herself, so the best we can do now is to monitor her until then. You can go and be with her if you want."

I nodded and went to her room and pulled the chair closer to her bedside. After brushing her hair away from her face, I lowered my head on the bed and watched her as she rested.

52

Willow

https://www.youtube.com/watch?v=9EHAo6rEuas

I could sense a hand holding mine.

It was warm and gentle. I felt weak and drained, but I opened my eyes and saw the full head of hair next to me. He was asleep. I watched him and the memories began to slowly trickle back. I tried my best to hold it all in, but it wasn't long before I was sobbing quietly. No wonder my young mind had decided to block them away.

Here he was. Protecting me. Caring for me. Just as he had always done. Putting me first.

I felt it then, the powerful bond we had shared twelve years ago. Two hurt and lonely kids, finding peace, comfort and even joy in the other.

As I looked at his silky hair my heart felt like it might burst.

Just then I felt him stiffen, and my heart slammed into my chest. He raised his face and looked into my eyes. God, I couldn't hold back the emotion. All these years ... All these years.

I felt his hand on my face, wiping away the tears.

"Why are you crying?" he asked.

His calm, deep voice sent ripples of emotions through me. Joy ... pain ... love ... guilt. The sacrifice he had made for me filled me with sorrow.

He was my angel. I didn't know how to express the gratitude I felt for him. But before all else I needed to be in his arms. Somehow, I lifted myself off the bed and slipped my arms around him. A small groan sounded from his lips. He probably didn't know I had remembered everything.

He held me tightly to him until I was ready.

"Take me home," I told him.

"Just as soon as the doctor says you can go," he said gently into my ear.

A little while later, we were in a taxi. He was giving the driver the directions to my parents' house, when I laid my hand on his and said, "Not there. Your house. Your house can be my home, right?"

He couldn't speak, but his Adam's apple bobbed. Then he nodded and quickly turned his face away so that I wouldn't see how deeply affected he was. I gave the driver his address and snuggled up against him.

He looked so incredibly unkempt, which was such a stark difference from the Caleb I had become familiar with. He had allowed his beard to grow out, and his eyes were sunken. Maria had been right. He truly had given up on everything and gone home to mourn. It hurt me all over again.

"I remember everything now," I whispered.

He turned to look at me. The pain in his face ripped through my insides.

"You ... you remember?"

"Everything."

Tears of joy filled his eyes. "How? When?"

I didn't want to tell him about Bradley because I didn't need to hurt him more, but I didn't want to lie either. I held his hand and spoke quietly, and by the time I was done, he had gone as still as a stone. That scared me more than anything.

"Caleb, forget about him. He got nowhere. I hurt him more than he hurt me. He'll never be able to face me again."

His hand shook with fury and he spoke through gritted teeth. "How dare he? Take advantage of your vulnerability. The fucking bastard."

"I'm so sorry." My voice broke. "I don't know why I keep getting caught up in these situations."

He cradled the side of my face. "It's not your fault if men are assholes."

"I'm so very sorry, Caleb, you had to go to prison for all those years. Even though you wanted to take the blame to save me. The truth is If I had not lost my memory, I would have told them everything. They would never have sent me to prison. It was not fair. You suffered way too much for me." I thought of all the hardship and torment he must have suffered in a prison with dangerous people for twelve long years on my account. And yet he had come back to me without a trace of bitterness.

"You should have told me," I said. "From the moment you came back. How could you bear all of it alone?"

"Your life had moved on. You'd gotten yourself a little business and I was proud of you, Willow. I didn't want you to remember what that beast did to you."

I shut my eyes against the flash of images in my mind, and fought the urge to throw up. I looked away from him and tried to bring myself under control.

"How could I make you remember that? I was glad that you had forgotten, and I hoped that you'd never have to remember."

"I love you, Caleb. I love you so much."

"I love you more," he said simply.

I leaned my head on his shoulder, and wrapped my hands around his arm as we rode home.

When we got out of the taxi he turned to me.

"Do you want something to eat?" he asked as we got into the house.

"I'm not hungry," I said. "What about you?"

"I just need a shower."

"So do I," I whispered.

I followed him to his bedroom ... *our bedroom*. The room was a complete mess. Over the last several days, it seems he had retreated into it and drank himself to oblivion. All around, were empty whiskey bottles and take-out food cartons. He began to pick up a bottle, but the motion must have made his head ache because he winced and straightened.

"I'll help you," I said and walked over, but he stopped me.

"No, there's too much to do," he said. "I'll get someone to come clean it up in the morning. Let's use the guest bedroom for tonight."

"Alright," I agreed with a smile.

He took me to one of the other bedrooms. I stood at the doorway watching him. Suddenly, I remembered what Marie had said.

"Marie came to the shop. She told me you've lost everything, even your license. She said you will even have to sell this house to pay for all your losses. Is it true?"

He stopped in his tracks, then turned to look at me. "Yes, it's true."

QUOTE

"When Death smiles at you, all you can do is smile back.

They are barbarians, all who cannot understand true love."

- Anonymous.

53

Caleb

Two days earlier

https://www.youtube.com/watch?
v=0BirzjRF4aE&list=RD0BirzjRF4aE&start_radio=1

One of the Don Carlo Bambino's goons held the door open and I walked into his study. I stood at the entrance of the dark wood paneled room and waited. It was very quiet in the room even though there were three people in it. Two men in dark suits, whose sole purpose was probably nothing other than intimidation, were standing behind the Don, and the Don himself.

The Don was sitting behind a big mahogany desk with a green leather surface. There was nothing on the desk except an elaborate Christie's lamp, an intricately carved golden box, and a black gun. Where I stood I could see he had a flabby white face and pitiless, dead eyes. He was what one would call a thoroughly ugly man. He kinda reminded me of Hitchcock. His corpulent body was dressed in a charcoal black silk shirt and a beautifully cut white suit. He looked like a poisonous frog in it.

He leaned back in his chair and waved his hand towards the gold box.

Immediately, one of the men who had been standing behind him rushed to open it, take out a cigar, cut and light it. His head was slightly lowered as if he was in the presence of greatness. He held the cigar out for the Don as if it was an offering. Foul cigar smoke drifted towards me. Through the curls of smoke his dead eyes watched me.

"I like that you didn't presume to come forward." His voice was surprisingly smooth and cultured. Like a radio personality's. "Come in and sit down," he invited.

I walked to one of the two chairs on the other side of him and sat down.

"Can I get you something to drink?" he offered, as he took another puff.

"Whiskey, neat," I said.

He waved his hand again, and the same man who had rushed to prepare his cigar poured me a drink. He watched me take a sip. He didn't have one himself.

"Good?" he asked.

I shrugged. "I'm not a connoisseur."

He smiled, and it made him look even more dangerous. "No, they don't serve whiskey in prison, do they? Not even to the smart boys."

I didn't smile back. "No, they don't."

"You went to a lot of trouble to find me. What do you want?"

"I want to say I'm sorry. I fucked up and put your project in jeopardy."

He blew smoke in my direction. "Jeopardy? How so?"

"I made a miscalculation and lost a lot of my own and my clients' money. I believe I have already been reported for mismanagement and there is a good chance my license will be revoked, and I will no longer be able to continue with my work on your project."

"Hmmm ... I spoke to Frank yesterday. He couldn't believe you could make a rookie mistake like that. He didn't understand why you didn't sell when you had the opportunity. Why didn't you?"

"I believed the market would rebound. I realize now I was too naïve, too optimistic, too inexperienced."

He waved his hand to indicate he wasn't interested in my excuses. "How do you intend to make it better?"

"I have a few million parked in a different jurisdiction. I would be happy to transfer it to you."

He nodded. "How many million?"

"Three, give or take a few thousand."

He nodded. "Yes, that would be acceptable. What about your house?"

"That will be sold to pay off my debts."

He shook his head. "I want it."

Of course, he was not happy with emptying out my bank account. Blood was not enough for him. He wanted a beating heart. "Right. I'll work something out."

"Good. What about the girl's shop?"

I clenched my hands, but I kept my face expressionless. "She doesn't own the property."

"Yes, I know. I wondered what it would take to infuriate you. Now I know. You can go. My men will tell you where to transfer everything."

"Not so fast. You can have everything I own, but I want something back."

He smiled. It never reached those snake eyes. "I never negotiate. I tell you what I want and you give it to me."

"No, that is not how this is going down."

"You know, I was exactly like you when I was young. Brash. Arrogant." He reached out and stroked his gun as if it was a cat. Then he took it in his hand, stood and walked laboriously around the table towards me. He put the gun at my temple. "Tell me, how is this going to go down, then?"

I could feel a muscle ticking in my jaw, but I stared straight ahead. "I walk out of here and we never meet again, you never send your men to ask me to do anything for you again. You forget me or my woman even exist."

He cocked the gun and the room went deadly silent. "And why should I do that when it is clear you can be very useful to me in the future?"

The cold metal on my temple had no effect on me. I felt no fear. My hands were steady and my heartbeat was normal. I knew he would be wasting a bullet if he shot me now. No money, no house. I looked at the painting behind his desk. It depicted the scene of a battlefield. Could have been Italian or French. I was not an expert on paintings, but the old antique frame suggested it was a very important painting. I didn't turn my head.

"Because," I said softly. "You have stuff on me from many years ago, but I have dates and times and names that very interestingly connect to some unsolved murders." I started to mention some names and dates. The pressure of the gun didn't ease, but I felt that instinctive jerk in his body. "I have no intention of ever doing anything with that information. It is being stored very carefully by solicitors in New York and Boston. If anything happens to me or my family, and that especially includes my girl and her family, then they will be released to the FBI and all national papers. All I want is to live my life in peace. You have all my money, you'll have my house. All I ask is to be left alone to live a small life. A life that doesn't include crime. I have no Intention of ever seeing the inside of a prison again."

He lifted the muzzle away from my neck and took a step back. "Well for that part, Wolfe, I can't blame you, we try to stay outta there too, kinda bad for business. Where did you come by your information?"

"That is for me to know and for you never to find out."

He walked around the table. "You remind me of myself when I was young."

I couldn't imagine how, but I said nothing.

"That is exactly how I would have played it."

"It isn't," I said softly.

He laughed. "You are right."

Then it was suddenly over. He had played his hand and I had dealt him mine.

Don Carlo Bambino jerked his head and the unblinking robot behind him immediately went to open the door. I stood and walked out.

The night sky was full of stars, and though I'd never been religious I couldn't help think that maybe the stars were an omen. You know like when the shepherds were guided by the stars in the sky.

Well, maybe they were there tonight for me.

54

Caleb

https://www.youtube.com/watch?v=luwAMFcc2f8

"It's history repeating itself again, isn't it? All your wealth is all gone because of me. Without me in the picture you'd have done it differently, wouldn't you?" she murmured after I told her everything that had happened.

I walked up to her and stood in front of her. "You think I care about what I lost? I don't have *anything* if I don't have you, Willow. Yes, I would have done it a different way. Might not have given it all up on a plate to that snake if you weren't in the picture, but I couldn't live with creating something that would hurt ordinary people, Willow. I got tricked once into creating such a scheme when I was young and foolish, and I won't allow anyone to use me like that again."

She looked at me with enormous eyes and I reached and touched the soft curve of her cheek.

"The choice to deliberately make those risky bets and lose everything was easy for me. Then it was even easier for me to be rude to my clients so they would be so furious they would report me. I needed the authorities to revoke my license for sheer incompetence. Without my license, I was useless to them. Not even worth the price of a bullet. But I also knew it would not end there. It never does when these bloodsuckers have something on you. The only way I would be left alone by the Don was to turn the tables on him."

"What you did, Caleb, was incredibly dangerous. What will you do now?" she whispered.

"Ah, there is one other card I didn't reveal to the Don. I have a secret stash, but we won't dip into that yet. We'll save it for our kids' college fund. Now we'll play the part of paupers for a little while. We'll live in a rented apartment, you'll have your shop, I'll get a job, maybe we'll have a baby or two. In a few years, when the coast is clear, I'll work my magic with numbers again and we'll buy something even better than this house."

She touched my face. "You were always good at planning long term."

"Always."

She began to take her clothes off. Slowly. I stood back so I could watch her in all her glory.

This was my Willow. "Everything I wished and hoped for the last twelve years has just come true, and I feel as if I'm in a dream. I still can't truly believe you're mine."

"I'm yours, Caleb. I'm yours even when my mind had forgotten you. I couldn't go with any other man because I was always waiting for you."

I watched that intoxicatingly, excruciatingly slow striptease, until she was dressed in nothing more than her underwear. Her full breasts were completely exposed to me. It was not the first time I was seeing them, there was now a new meaning to everything.

I no longer felt like the stranger who was forever unable to convey the depth of his love for her. Finally, she understood how much I cherished her. More than I would have ever been able to explain.

Suddenly, she stopped. Some part of her must be still too vulnerable. Her eyes lowered as her hands went over her breasts to shield them from my hungry eyes.

I moved forward and lifted her hands away. Then I licked her nipples. They were hard as pebbles. "I love you, Willow."

Slowly, I pulled her panties down her legs. They pooled around her feet. Then I picked her up in my arms and carried her to the shower. I put her down on the ground and switched on the shower and waited for it to become the right temperature.

She moved and began to undress me. Her fingers fumbling, hasty. When we were both naked, I scooped her up and carried her into the cascade.

I felt its warm blast run down my skin like a massage. I didn't move, and remained still so that the water could soothe the tension and aches that had accumulated in our muscles from the last twelve years. Slowly, magically, it chased away my splitting headache. I now had every reason in the world to relax. She stirred in my arms.

Heat whipped up like a storm inside my chest. I needed to taste her. Not, taste, eat a full meal. I was ravenous. I put her down on the ground.

I held her face in my hands as our tongues danced wildly against the other's, coaxing, stroking, teasing, and sucking.

It was a long while before we came up for air. She staggered slightly and I punctuated the kiss with a soft nip on her bottom lip. She melted even further against me.

"I love you," she cried and threw her arms around my neck. "Caleb, I fucking love you with all my heart. I know that I'll never be able to fathom even a fraction of the pain you've had to endure over the last twelve years, but I swear to you ... I'll spend the rest of my life making it up to you. I swear it."

"You can start by letting me taste you again," I said.

She widened her legs and I ate her out. It was like being in heaven. When she came I held her tight. When I rose she clung to me. She buried her face in my neck and whispered, "I'm going to protect you. From now on, I'm going to be the one protecting you. No one will dare hurt you on my watch. I swear it. I fucking swear it."

It was endearing. Truly it was. The thought of little Willow protecting me. I tried not to smile as I pulled her away so that I could see her face, I wrapped my arms around her waist and asked her the question that I knew would embarrass her.

"Did I hear you say the rest of your life?" I asked. "Did you just propose to me?" I thought she would immediately try to correct her words, but instead she held me even more tightly to her.

"I don't need to propose ... you're mine. You've always been mine and mine only."

"You're stealing all my lines," I groaned. This level of joy had to be unreal. Every nerve in my body was so tight with excitement and love I felt as if I would explode. I just crushed her soft wet body against mine.

"My darling, I'm not going to short change you. You're going to get everything the other girls get. You'll have an official proposal and you'll have a big white wedding. Everybody who knows you will be there and you will be the belle of the ball. Afterwards, you'll be whisked off to a dream honeymoon," I said. For some reason, I got carried away with my own words and found myself going down on one knee.

She laughed. Water poured off her. She looked so beautiful I wanted to weep.

"Are you going to propose without a ring?" she asked.

Shit! I jumped to my feet. "I'll be right back."

"No need," she grabbed my wrist. "There are things I want to do to you first."

"It'll only take a—"

"Later," she breathed softly. "We have forever, remember?"

"Abso-fucking-lutely, we have forever." I lifted her up, and spun her around as water cascaded on us. She squealed and screamed for me to put her down.

"You've made all my dreams come true," I said. "Do you realize that?"

She leaned down to kiss me. "And you've done even more than that for me."

I let her slide down my body, as my eyes bored into hers. "I still want to make an official request. You need a good story to tell when you're asked about it."

Her smile made my heartbeat go even wilder. "What do you have in mind?"

Once again, I dropped down to one knee. "Willow Rayne, will you marry me?"

"Yes, I will marry you, Caleb Daniel Wolfe."

My smile widened. "You remember my middle name?"

"I've remembered a lot of things."

I placed a kiss on her belly. She giggled. Then I began to trace the kisses down, and her hands went to my head. "Caleb," she called, "not again." But it was too late. My lips were already over her soaked sex. A gasp tore out of her lips.

"Caleb," she breathed, and twisted above me.

"Let's give you a proposal story that you won't ever get tired of telling."

'Caleb!" she squealed, and I dug my tongue into her sweet, sweet pussy.

By the time I was done with her, the pads of her fingers were like prunes and she had screamed *yes* a hundred times.

EPILOGUE 1

Willow

One Month Later

We had just moved into our modest apartment and I was standing on a chair rearranging the topmost shelf in Caleb's closet when I felt the box. I knew without being told it was private. It contained secrets. I stopped and considered whether to take a look at it, or to just continue with my chores. But that morning I found out I was pregnant and I knew I didn't find the box by accident. I was meant to find it today.

It was a simple cardboard box.

I brought it down and sitting on the chair, I opened the lid.

Inside were photographs and photocopies of documents. As I began to sift through them my jaw dropped. For a little while I stared out of the window. My love for Caleb grew every day.

Stronger and stronger. Every night, I got onto my knees before bed and thanked God. My lot was bountiful, indescribably beautiful.

I know it was supposed to be a horrible thing, us becoming poor, and moving into this small apartment, but I loved it. Of course, I would love the big house that Caleb promised to build for us, but for now I adored being so cozy here. Just him and me holed up in our own little world. It was sheer heaven. Soon it would be autumn and I could already see Caleb and me curled up on the couch as snug as two bunnies in a hammock as the days became shorter and shorter.

As I looked around the small bedroom, I heard the door close. I knew without him calling out to me it was him. He was back. The apartment always felt empty until he came into it. His energy reached out and touched me.

I smiled as I imagined him throwing his keys into the little ceramic dish my mother gave us and heading into the living room. I didn't want him to come looking for me so I quickly headed over to my purse and retrieved the test result. Burying it among the pile of photos and documents inside the box, I went to the kitchen. The television was on in our little living room, but from the smell of spices and the clang of ceramic, I knew he wasn't in the living room.

I stood at the doorway of the kitchen. Mr. Wolfe was looking delicious in a dark T-shirt and jeans.

"You're back," I said, placing the box on the island counter.

He turned around, his raven hair, slightly tousled by the wind and falling to the side of his face. A slight stubble dusted his jaw. I loved the clean-cut version of him, but I really loved this rugged version. Maybe because of the way it felt on the inside of my thighs.

"Yeah. We ran out of ham," he replied, looking at the box.

It was precisely at that moment when I noticed the brown bag of baguettes by the corner. I gasped softly, and completely forgetting my mission, I dove for the bag. I broke a piece off the freshly baked treat and put it into my mouth.

"Hmm," I moaned, closing my eyes. "This is just what I needed."

"You're just trying to get me all hot and bothered, aren't you?"

I opened my eyes and saw him watching me hungrily.

"And you're just trying to distract me from the scandalous contents of this box, aren't you?"

He smiled.

"I can't believe it," I said. "I can't believe *you*. You stalked me during the years you were in prison!"

"No," he corrected calmly. "I kept my eyes on you. I needed to know you were okay at all times."

"Isn't that what all stalkers say?" I tossed another piece of bread into my mouth, and opened the box. "I mean, look at all these pictures. Me at a play in high school, me waiting for the bus, me in a wet T-shirt for God's sake ... me at the grocery store with Mom. Hmm ... I was frowning so much here, I wonder why."

I peered closely at the picture, spotted the soda cup in my hand, and remembered why.

"Ah! Mom refused to get me the Reese's puffs cereal I wanted. She said we already had enough cereal in the house. Ooh, and here's one of Sandra! God, she was so young, and her hair has streaks of pink. Even I can't remember that."

I heard his low laugh, and raised my head to see him laughing at me.

"Caleb! This is unhealthy. No wonder you knew exactly where to find me the moment you got out."

He took the corn chowder he was making off the burner, and brought it to the counter along with a coaster. After setting it down, he took a spoonful of the creamy liquid, blew on it to cool it down, and tasted it. When he noticed my look of disappointment, he chuckled.

"Here." He lifted another spoonful out of the pan, blew on it, then fed it to me.

I licked my lips at the delicious taste, and savored the creamy corn flavor. "I love your corn chowder." The way he was watching me made my core begin to tighten with desire.

He leaned towards me, forgetting the hot pot. It burned him.

"Oww," he complained.

I couldn't hold back my amusement.

"My pain is funny to you?" he asked, pushing the pot out of the way. He rounded the counter, and I immediately ran to get away from him, but I might as well not have bothered in that cramped space. He caught me easily and by the waist. In no time I was plopped down on the counter, with him between my legs.

I leaned up and kissed him, the lingering taste of the chowder mixing erotically with the aphrodisiac that he was. Already, I was out of breath. When he pulled away from me I could see that his eyes too were glazed with burning passion.

There was nothing I wanted more than to be fucked senseless by him on that counter, but there was something else I had to reveal to him first. I took a moment to think about how I was going to do that as he started working on the clasp of my bra. Only one way came to mind.

I reached out to grab the box, but he wouldn't let me out of his arms.

He lifted up my white T-shirt and buried his head underneath it. My bra came lose. Damn him. His mouth closed around my nipple and I lost myself.

"We're not done," I managed to rasp out.

He sucked hard on the engorged peaks, and it instantly made me wet. My toes curled at the sensation, but I didn't want this moment to pass. Before I completely lost my senses, I reached desperately for the box which almost displaced his greedy mouth.

The battle that ensued as our different intentions fought for domination made me laugh.

Finally, the box's contents spilled out and the countless photos of me dropped out. "Hey? I missed this. How the hell did you get this?" I said, picking up a photo of my prom night.

"I hung this photo above my bunk for a very, very long time," he said with feeling.

I could tell. It was creased and lightly stained and folded through. I put on a stern face. "Are these stains ... cum?"

"They sure are, ma'am," he joked.

"Oh, you are bad," I said shaking my head, but my heart started to hurt. Every time I thought of him in prison and the terrible experiences he'd had to endure, I always felt sad and guilty. The great irony was the world thought he was a sinner, but truth was he was a saint. A true saint.

Suddenly, he spotted the test result I'd slipped in. "What the hell is that?"

I feigned surprise. "Yeah, what the hell is that?"

Impatiently, he pulled the plastic out of my hand ... and tossed it away. Then he swept the photos and the box out of the way, some even fell to the floor.

"Caleb!"

He slanted his head and overwhelmed me with a kiss. It was hard and fast. I knew him well enough to tell nothing was going to break through his urgency. My news would have to wait.

I let go and wrapped my legs around him. My shirt came off and so did my underwear. I was quickly splayed out on top of the kitchen counter and I reveled in it.

Caleb went down on me. It was his magical show that somehow seemed to get better and better as time passed. Every time he made me lose my mind with his mouth, I was left incoherent, spent and absolutely certain that it was the best head he'd ever given to me, but then the next time happened and I was left even more stunned. In the time we'd been together, he'd gotten to know my body even more and he used every bit of that knowledge to his advantage.

In less than a minute, he had me squirming and writhing. "Oh!" I gasped as I drove my hips into his expert mouth, chasing my release like a crazed woman.

When I eventually exploded into his mouth, it was with a scream.

Before I could even recover he set his cock free. With his hands underneath my thighs he jerked me roughly to the edge, settled the head of his cock at my entrance, and plunged into me.

Jesus!

"Ahhhhh." It was beyond satisfying to have him so tightly sheathed inside me. When he wasn't inside of me, I felt the emptiness and the ache of his absence. I threw my head back and cupped my breasts in my hands. I massaged the heavy tender mounds.

Of course, that caught his attention.

He pushed my hands aside and began to mold my breasts, teasing and pinching the hardened nipples at just the right intervals. The brief shot of pain spurred my desire on even more. When he began to move out of me I quickly lifted my hips to meet his thrusts.

With my hands on the counter I hoisted my body up and channeled all of my strength into the swinging of my hips.

He slammed viciously into me, the smacking sound of flesh against flesh quickening every sensory nerve in my body.

"Put your arms around my neck," he rasped out, and I set myself down so that I could do as he'd said. He lifted me off the counter, and flipped me over so my whole pussy and ass were on display.

"Hold on to that edge," he ordered.

I almost exploded from the excitement.

Then he began driving into me with the intensity of a drill.

The position was perfect, and sent him so deeply into me that it was almost painful. He didn't stop until an almighty orgasm tore through me. It was like a bomb went off in my core.

Everything spun. He turned me around and pressed my back against the refrigerator, and pounded into me with the ferocity of an animal to milk out his own orgasm. Every muscle in his body was clenched.

His roar resounded around our home, and I felt the hot spurt of his semen inside of me.

I cradled his head as his hard, strong body jerked against mine.

"Willow," he cried out, over and over again.

I could do little more than bask in the euphoria of our union. It took quite a while for things to subside, and by the time he peeled me away from the refrigerator I was too drowsy to even open my eyes.

"Sofa," I breathed. "I can't stand or sit."

"We're going to the bedroom," he said with a laugh.

I didn't have any complaints. Bed sounded about right. The moment he put me down we crawled under the covers, and clung to each other as we both drifted away into a light nap. There was little else that I loved more than these weekend mornings in bed with Caleb.

We were both usually too busy during the weekday mornings to enjoy each other like we got to do at night, but these weekend fuck sessions always made me feel like I was being reborn to the world of pure pleasure.

My announcement that I hadn't been able to make yet came to mind just before I fell asleep, but I pushed it away for later on.

I was awoken a few hours later by soft but insistent taps. "Willow, Willow, Willow."

When I opened my eyes, I saw Caleb staring down at me. There was so much love in his eyes.

"I have something to tell you," I whispered.

"You want more sex?" he asked cheekily.

"I always want that, but it's something else. Something very important."

He frowned. "Yeah. What?"

"You know that plastic thing you swept off the table."

"Yeah, the pen?"

"That's not a pen"

He looked at me curiously. "What was it, then?"

"It's a pregnancy test."

He looked at me in astonishment, shock and wonder. "Yeah?"

I made little nods and looked encouragingly at him.

He swallowed, as if he dared not say it. "You're pregnant?" he finally blurted out.

I nodded.

"Oh, my God," he breathed. "Are you sure?"

"Yeah, I did the test twice."

He pulled away, and gently held my face in his hands. "Why didn't you tell me earlier?"

"Well, I tried to."

"Wow! I can't wait to have a whole bunch of little Willows running around."

"Hey, I want a few Calebs too, you know. When you're old and I'm old, and I break my hip, I'll need a couple of strong, strapping lads to carry me around."

"That's my job," he said possessively. "I'll always carry you, Willow."

I smiled softly at him. That there was the truth. He would always carry me.

His face suddenly filled with horror. "Oh God! You're pregnant and you let me do that to you in the kitchen? My God, I was rough with you."

"Um," I was amused by his alarm. "Don't you dare treat me differently because of this baby. At least until I start really showing."

He kissed me. "I won't."

"I'm serious." I pulled my lips from his.

"So am I. Don't worry, I'll still fuck you as hard as you want, but with caution, of course."

"Are you worried the baby will bite your dick?"

"You do know you're crazy, right," he said, throwing his arms around me.

We both fell back onto the bed amidst laughter and boundless joy. We deserved it. After everything we'd been through.

EPILOGUE 2

Willow

Two Months Later
https://www.youtube.com/watch?v=NBE-uBgtINg
-now we are free-

Anna, my hair stylist was busy adding the finishing touches to my hair, and a handful of our friends and relatives were grouped in clusters doing their makeup and hair.

"Er ... how did Caleb propose to you again?" Sandra asked cheekily. Ever since I told her what happened that night of the fire and exactly what Caleb had done for me, she had hugged me tightly and promised she would love Caleb almost as much as I did.

"Shut up!" I muttered as my eyes darted towards my mother.

"Didn't he propose to you at home?" my mom asked. She turned innocently to Sandra. "Sandra, don't you know how he proposed?"

"Oh, I know," she said, her eyes agape with mischief. "I'm just wondering if you know, Mrs. Rayne?"

My mom lightly tapped my arm, looked from me to her, then back to me. "What is she talking about?"

"Ignore her," I said, and gave my mischievous friend a fake glare.

Sandra just laughed. One of the bridesmaids in the corner taking selfies called and she went to see what they wanted.

"You look beautiful," my mom said.

"You really think so?"

"I'm know I'm biased, but I've never seen a more beautiful bride than you."

"Awww ... thanks, Mom."

"How are you feeling?" she asked.

"A bit nervous."

She rested her hand on my bare shoulder. "Everything is going to be great."

"I know," I said. "I'm just worried I'm going to trip and fall or do something else embarrassing."

"I trust you." She nodded. "And I am more than happy to trust Caleb with you too." Mom always had a soft spot for Caleb, but once she found out what he had done for me, she became his greatest ally. I once joked she was more loyal to him than me.

"Thanks, mom."

Her eyes filled with tears. "Now, I'm just being silly."

I pulled her into a hug. "I love you, Mom."

She gave me a kiss then, and walked away.

"All done," Anna said, picking up a big round mirror that she held behind me.

I looked at the mirror to assess the swirly chignon adorned with pink dainty roses she had created for me. My makeup had been applied flawlessly, and my eyes were sparkling with anxiety and excitement.

"Wow," I said. "You guys did an amazing job."

"We had amazing material to work with," she replied. "I cannot wait till your groom sees you."

"Neither can I," I muttered under my breath and jumped to my feet.

It was finally time to put on my dress. My mom and Sandra returned.

Sandra helped to slip the dress up over my hips and chest and zipped me up. Then Anna fitted the little crown veil on my head, and I turned around to look in the mirror.

"Oh, my God," Sandra gasped. "You look incredible."

My mother's eyes were filled with tears and she began to carefully dab at the corners so as not to ruin her makeup.

I stared at myself and almost didn't recognize myself. I was still not showing and the exquisitely beautiful dress fit beautifully. Mom and I found it in a boutique by accident. The moment we saw it, we both knew it was the one. It was simple and yet utterly and completely perfect. It had a gorgeous train that made me look tall and elegant. All the things I wasn't.

It had taken almost thirteen years but finally, I was ready for Caleb to tell the whole world I was his. And I couldn't wait.

A little while later, my father hooked my arm around his, and the processional hymn began. At the end of the beautifully lit aisle was the love of my life.

Caleb Daniel Wolfe.

He stood in a dove-gray suit, tall and broad, as he waited for my arrival at the altar.

He didn't have a best man, but he did have Maria, who wore a tuxedo next to him. She was a lot shorter than him, and she appeared to be bouncing up and down with excitement. I smiled when I saw her pat his shoulder encouragingly, and playfully offer her handkerchief to him.

Then he was turning. Turning to look at me. He smiled slowly at me. After all these years we were finally going to be joined in the eyes of God.

My hand shook and my father turned to look at me. "You all right?" he whispered.

I was so emotional, so full of gratitude, I could not speak, I could not think. I could not even nod. I could barely put one foot in front of the other. My father understood and he held my hand tightly. "It's gonna be fine," he said. I pressed my lips together to keep from crying. By the time I arrived in front of him, my eyes were full of tears.

Caleb took my hand and gently guided me up to the altar with him.

Sandra excitedly arranged my train, and I peered through my veil at Caleb. He looked so incredibly handsome. My head filled with memories of him. From the first day at the new school when he had walked up to me.

"I'm Caleb," the tall boy had said.

"I'm Willow," I replied.

He smiled and that was it for me.

I thought of the time we had eaten ice cream under a tree in the storm.

"It's dangerous to sit under a tree during a storm," he had said.

"Then hold me," I answered.

We had made our life promises to each other, and I thought of that night we had mixed our blood and made our promises. For all intents and purposes that would always be my wedding day. I had promised myself wholeheartedly to him, body and mind. Today would be to iterate it before our friends and family, but it was just a formality.

We got married twelve years ago. I forgot for a while, but he never did and my body never did.

"Are we still alive?" I whispered to him. "Did I die in Bradley apartment, and you at the Don's house?"

He smiled slowly. "I don't know, but it sure feels like I'm in heaven."

I stared deep into his angelic eyes. "I won't tell, if you won't."

He shook his head. "Not me. Nobody needs to tell them. They wouldn't understand. All they need to know is we got our HEA. And we did, didn't we, my little Willow."

"Yes, we did. We finally got our happily ever after."

The priest had barely concluded reciting the vows when I blurted out, yes.

I thought Caleb might laugh or chuckle at my eagerness, but he didn't.

He ruined the order of the ceremony by pulling me in an extremely passionate kiss. When it was over I was breathless. Our friends and my family were cheering.

The priest had a sense of humor. He said, "I pronounce you man and wife. You may now kiss the bride *again*."

Caleb didn't disappoint. He lived up to his name and pounced on me like a hungry Wolfe. And yes, we lived happily ever after.

Everybody here does.

The End

COMING NEXT...

BODYGUARD BEAST

SAMPLE CHAPTER 1

Angelo

(Unedited)

My hands and feet were bound with plastic ties as I swam through the blue water, alone and totally at peace with myself. I made countless laps up and down the pool. There was ten minutes left before I finished my full hour when I sensed movement above the water. It was way past midnight, and much too late for any member of the family to be wandering about. Unless it was security.

Nevertheless, it was an annoying interruption to my drown-proofing training.

I maneuvered myself to the bottom of the pool. Bouncing on the toes of my tied feet, I headed up to the surface and I broke water. The indoor pool space was dark, illuminated only by the distant lamps of the compound that came through the floor length windows. I saw a girl I'd never seen

before making her way towards the lounge chairs. I couldn't
see her face because she was holding her phone in front of
her face, but it could only be one person, the boss's daughter,
just returned from her education overseas.

Her ears were plugged with air-pods and she hadn't turned on
the lights upon her entrance, so I deduced that like me, she
wanted to be alone. I accepted the fact my time in the pool
was over and started to swim towards the other end of the
pool when she screamed.

The scream was followed by the sound of water splashing.

Through my goggles, I watched her flailing underwater. She
was actually trying to catch her phone, but it evaded her
grasp and sank to the bottom. She was obviously not a good
swimmer because she immediately struggled up to the surface
and started clinging to the edge of the pool.

"Hey you!" she yelled. "Can you help me please?"

My first thought was to ignore her. I had no time for spoilt
little girls, but she was the boss's daughter, and I sure as hell
didn't need that kind of trouble. I swam towards her and
stopped a wary meter away.

I'd heard the rumors that she was a looker, but it was a shock
to see how insanely beautiful she was. Seeing was indeed
believing. The lights in the floor of the pool turned her eyes a
green that was almost unreal. Like a doll's eyes. They were set
wide apart and fringed with long, wet lashes. I wondered how
she would look while she was climaxing, then caught myself
mid-thought.

What the fuck is wrong with you?

Yes, she was heartbreakingly beautiful, but I wasn't into shallow, selfie-taking, narcissistic, manipulative Cleopatra types who needed a bunch of servants just to get dressed. And even if I was, lusting after the boss's daughter was a bad, bad idea. It usually meant ending up in an unmarked grave in a field somewhere. Nope. Not for me. I turned away from her.

"My phone," she gasped. "Please help me retrieve it or it's going to be ruined."

I paused. This was the deepest part of the pool and it would be quite a feat to get my face to touch the bottom. To soothe my sour mood, I accepted her request as part of my training for the night, and dived back into the water. With my teeth, I gripped the phone, and swam back towards the surface. With a swing of my head, I flung the device out of the pool.

Sucking in a lungful of air, I began to head towards the steps. On the edge was a knife. Retrieving it with my teeth, I dropped it into the water, and dived down after it. A few seconds later, the ties around my wrists and ankles had been cut off, and I was free. I pulled myself out of the pool and began to head towards the changing rooms.

"Hey!" she called out, and I could hear the irritation in the Princess's voice. "Aren't you going to help me?"

I didn't bother turning around. She would eventually get herself out of the pool. She was the boss's daughter, after all.

SAMPLE CHAPTER 2

Sienna

How rude! How unbelievably rude?

I could hardly believe what that man just did. First, he held my phone between his teeth as if he was some kind of animal, then he flung it out of the water straight onto the tiled floor. If it hadn't been damaged by the water, that would definitely have done it. Even more unbelievable, was the way he callously abandoned me when all I was asking for was a bit of help getting out of the deep end of the pool.

I watched him walk towards thela changing rooms, water sluicing down his impeccably broad shoulders down the gleaming slabs of muscles in his back. And down the skin-tight briefs that left almost nothing to the imagination. The cheeks of his butt were firm and round. More water ran down those perfectly muscular, thick thighs as he took long and sure strides. As I watched in a daze of shock, he lifted one powerful hand and raked his fingers through his raven hair.

He looked like a big, wet Greek God, but he had to be one of my father's guards. They frequently used this indoor pool for their training sessions. The outdoor one was designated for leisure and entertainment and used solely by the family, but I hadn't felt like battling mosquitoes, and had headed here. As a result I'd clearly interrupted his training session, almost given myself a heart attack, and doubtless destroyed my phone.

He had been so quiet as he had swam through the water that I hadn't seen him when I entered and when he had come into my peripheral vision I had mistaken him for a corpse floating on the surface. The shock made me slip off the edge and fall in the water.

It was a sheer miracle I hadn't broken several teeth.

In fact, I had bloodied my elbows and they stung as I clung on to the edge of the pool and made my way back to the shallow end. I could swim, but I'd always avoided these deeper parts. For some inexplicable reason I had an irrational fear of deep water. When I was at the shallow end I could swim like a fish, but I felt an irrational terror overwhelm me when my feet couldn't touch the bottom.

Maybe I was dropped into deep water and suffered trauma when I was too young to remember, or maybe it was a memory from a past life, but the fear was real. Hanging on the edge of the pool I threaded water and pulled myself along until I got to the shallow end. As soon as I knew my feet were only about two feet from the bottom, I let go and swam to the steps, and pulled myself out of the water.

I sat on cool tiles and realized that even my air-pods were

lost. And it was all his fault. If he had not startled me. If he had not treated me as if he was pure and I was some infectious disease. Who the did he think he was anyway? Asshole. Hell, I could have had a panic attack and died in the water.

Brushing my hair out of my face, I jumped to my feet and began to march towards the men's changing room. Without knocking I barged in.

"Hey!" I called out. "Hey!"

There was no response.

I stopped to listen and heard water running, so I immediately headed towards it and found him in a stall.

I pounded noisily on the door. "Hey!"

I was fuming, my chest nearly about to explode with anger. "How could you just leave me there? I could have died."

The arrogant brute didn't respond.

'There's something called basic human decency, you know. Like helping someone when they're in need, especially when you're the cause of their almost death in the first freaking place." I kicked at the door to the stall.

The cascade of water ceased, and I froze. No doubt he was expecting me to run off, but I stood my ground and waited, ready to give him a piece of my mind the moment he came out.

True enough, the door to the stall was pushed open and he appeared.

"You owe me an apology—" I began but the next words, whatever I had planned to say, were snatched out of my head.

He was naked.

I was a civilized person and I had assumed, wrongly it would seem that he would emerge with a towel wrapped around his waist, instead he had deliberately appeared naked before me.

I pulled my jaw off the floor and shot my shocked gaze up to his face. Wow, without the goggles he carried the blue-green Caribbean ocean in his eyes. He was looking at me with an irritated expression as if I was a nuisance he could do without.

He took a step towards me and I instinctively, took a few steps backwards. It gave him the space he needed to turn left and walk away from me. It took few seconds before I recovered enough to get my brain working again. A feat given what I'd just seen.

The man, was hung like a damn horse!

I'd followed the tanned muscles of his torso, partitioned into perfectly, proportionate slabs and still glistening with the steam from his shower, and down there, shadowed with a dusting of dark hair across the top of his groin was cock. Half-raised as if in arousal, but it was probably just the stimulation from the shower. Not that I would know much about that.

Either way, the slightly paler shaft had been beyond impressive. It made me shiver to think of how it would look... and feel, when it was fully erect.

He hadn't seemed even a little bit concerned that he was exposing himself to a complete stranger, and I knew then what his problem was; he was completely shameless. If he thought he could embarrass me into not speaking my mind because he had flashed me he had another think coming. I marched after him.

I found him seated on one of the benches in the locker room, and thankfully he was already covered in dark briefs. The arrogant stud didn't even turn around to acknowledge my presence.

"You're one of the bodyguards, aren't you?"

He remained silent as he rose to his feet, and began to rummage through his locker.

I went on. "If you are, then you must know who I am. Why didn't you help me?"

Silence.

I didn't want to be that insufferable bitch no one liked, but I had already pursued the matter this far, and my pride needed a response.

"I can report this," I threatened. "And there's no way it's not going to get you in trouble."

He slammed the locker door shut, and I couldn't help but jump.

"Sure," he finally spoke. "Report that you couldn't do something as basic as to get yourself out of the pool. Such incompetency would no doubt make your father proud."

I was astounded. Robbed of speech all I could do was stare as he began to dress himself. First came his jeans, and then he carelessly pulled a dark tee over his head. He grabbed his bag and began to head out.

I recovered then, and jumped in front of him.

He stopped at the sudden ambush, a slight frown tugging at his brows.

Hell, up this close, he was really handsome with an aristocratic Roman nose, sensuous lips and those eyes. Those wonderful eyes. It made me wonder why I hadn't seen him around. I even started to doubt he was one of the bodyguards that resided in the compound. I couldn't imagine one of my father's employees being so rude to his daughter. But if he wasn't a bodyguard, who the hell was he?

"Apologize," I said. "And then I'll let this go."

"Why do I owe you an apology?"

"You should have helped me."

He shrugged those powerful shoulders. "I'm not obligated to do anything without your father's instruction. And I did retrieve your phone."

"Which you broke!" I accused. "You flung it on the tiles."

"I don't have time for this," he said impatiently. "Get out of my way!"

"No, I'm not moving until you apologize."

"Then you're going to be here a very long time," he drawled.

"What's your name?" I demanded, getting exasperated. "Because I'm not going to let this go."

He took a step towards me.

It took everything I had not to take a backward step. I folded my arms defiantly across my chest, suddenly aware then that I was half-naked before him, and that the movements had brought my breasts together to create a not-inconsiderable cleavage. But his eyes didn't stray. Not one bit. He was totally uninterested in my charms.

"Angelo Barone," he replied. "That's my name. Off you go, little brat. Go and do your worst."

I was actually too shocked to respond.

He stepped around me and walked away.

Speechlessly, I turned to watch him leave.

What an asshole!!!!

Preorder the book at Amazon
Bodyguard Beast

ABOUT THE AUTHOR

Thank you so much for reading my book. Might you be
thinking of leaving a review? :-)
Please do it here:

Saint & Sinner

Please click on this link to receive news of my latest releases
and great giveaways.
http://bit.ly/1oe9WdE

and remember
I **LOVE** hearing from readers so by all means come and say
hello here:

facebook.com/georgia.lecarre

ALSO BY GEORGIA LE CARRE

His Frozen Heart

The Man In The Mirror

A Kiss Stolen

Can't Let Her Go

Highest Bidder

Saving Della Ray

Nice Day For A White Wedding

With This Ring

With This Secret